Cutter looked ove

approaching.

Keep him talking, Cutter thought. Maybe there was still a way out of this.

"Who are you?"

"Who am I?"

The warforged was silent for a moment, and when it spoke again it was in a soft whisper that caused the hair on the back of Cutter's neck to rise.

"I am the unnamed. I am the fear of darkness. I am the night stalker. I am the will of the Shadow, and I do his bidding."

Cutter swallowed. *The Shadow?*

"Enough of this," said the warforged. "It is time for you to embrace the darkness."

"Embrace your own darkness."

Cutter swung . . .

the inquisitives

Bound by Iron
by Edward Bolme

Night of the Long Shadows
by Paul Crilley

Legacy of Wolves
by Marsheila Rockwell
(June 2007)

The Darkwood Mask
by Jeff LaSala
Forthcoming...

the inquisitives

Night of the Long Shadows

Paul Crilley

NIGHT OF THE LONG SHADOWS

The Inquisitives · Book 2

Published by Wizards of the Coast, Inc. EBERRON, WIZARDS OF THE COAST, and their respective logos are trademarks of Wizards of the Coast, Inc., in the U.S.A. and other countries.

Printed in the U.S.A.

Cover art by Michael Komarck
First Printing: May 2007

9 8 7 6 5 4 3 2 1

ISBN: 978-0-7869-4270-1
620-95936740-001-EN

U.S., CANADA,
ASIA, PACIFIC, & LATIN AMERICA
Wizards of the Coast, Inc.
P.O. Box 707
Renton, WA 98057-0707
+1-800-324-6496

EUROPEAN HEADQUARTERS
Hasbro UK Ltd
Caswell Way
Newport, Gwent NP9 0YH
GREAT BRITAIN
Save this address for your records.

Visit our web site at www.wizards.com

Dedication

To my parents, for always making sure I had plenty of books to read when I was growing up.

To Caroline, for always being there. If it wasn't for you I wouldn't be where I am today, writing the dedication in my very first book. Thank you.

And to Isabella. If your life is filled with a fraction of the wonder I feel every time I look at you, you'll have a happy life indeed.

Table of Contents

Prologue

The first night of Long Shadows

Zor, the 26th day of Vult, 998

Torin heard the noise again, a loud banging as if someone was pounding on the walls.

He frowned and looked up. The shelves of Morgrave University library receded from the tiny pool of light his everbright lantern created, melting into the shadows of deep night. He listened, but all he could hear was the rain pouring down outside the huge window behind him. He looked over his shoulder. The panes of lead-lined glass revealed only the darkness of Sharn. The panels glimmered slightly as runnels of rainwater caught the light of a distant skycoach.

He was alone. Or at least, he thought he was. Who else would be here at this time of night? *He* shouldn't even be here, but Wren had told him to do a bit of research for a case he was thinking of taking on. A bit of research. That was a joke. He'd been here half the night already and he still hadn't found the information Wren wanted.

But that was typical of the way things worked. Torin did all the leg work while Wren threw one of his lavish parties.

There. There it was again. A muffled thud. But louder this time. And it hadn't come from inside the library, but from outside, in the university commons.

Torin swiveled around and carefully slid off the high stool, landing on the wooden floor with a slight thud. He gave a small sigh. Why didn't they supply chairs for people his size, anyway? It wasn't as if dwarves were a rarity in academia.

He padded silently to the stairs, leaning over the banister and looking down. The stairwell descended into blackness. He couldn't see any lights or anything else that would reveal that someone was inside. So where had the noise come from?

Then he heard a loud crash, like something smashing through a wall, from the floor below him. Torin hurried down the stairs and paused on the landing. It led into a corridor where some of the professors had their living quarters.

Maybe it wasn't any of his business . . .

He heard a cry of pain. No, something was going on. Torin ran down the passage to the door through which the noises were coming. He tried the handle and the door swung open into a brightly lit room.

Torin took a small step inside.

And froze, his eyes widening in shock at the scene before him.

A huge man, over six feet tall, with two strangely curved blades held in each hand, stood over a horribly mutilated body. The man was covered in blood and breathing heavily, staring down at the victim.

A gasp escaped Torin's lips and the intruder swung around to face him. The man's hair was so short that he looked almost bald. Strange tattoos worked their way up his arms and around his neck, partially concealed beneath the blood and gore.

Torin fumbled in his jacket for his knife. The hilt snagged in the lining. He tugged at it, desperate to free it before—

He looked up. Too late. The man was running straight for him. Torin stumbled backward, managing to free the knife. The man lashed out, smacking the dwarf in the face and sending him crashing into the door frame. Torin quickly climbed to his feet, his blade held defensively before him, but the man was running up the stairs.

Torin sprinted after him, grabbing the banister and hauling himself up the steps in pursuit. When he reached the library, he stopped, sucking in great gulps of air, and peered up the stairwell. The man was already at the top floor. There was no way the dwarf could catch him.

Torin winced, feeling a stitch coming on. Host, but he was unfit. It was all that expensive food Wren insisted on eating. How was he supposed to resist it?

He turned and walked slowly back down the stairs. He'd have to find someone and tell them what had happened.

At least the murderer shouldn't be too hard to find. A six-and-a-half foot tall maniac with a dragon tattoo on his arms?

Even the Sharn Watch should be able to handle that.

Chapter One

The first night of Long Shadows

Zor, the 26th day of Vult, 998

E*arlier that night.*

Cutter's brother used to say there were two ways you could live.

One, you fought against everything, spent every moment of your life wanting to be somewhere else, regretting you hadn't done better, made more money, married that girl you knew when you were younger. You fought yourself with every breath and blamed everyone else for the mess you were in.

Or two, you accepted your lot no matter what the deal, and you lived your life in each and every moment, not waiting for the future or looking back over the past.

You lived *now.*

His brother had lived according to number two. He died in the War, but he left behind a legacy of good deeds and good advice.

Cutter hated him for it. He could almost feel his brother's

ghost hovering over his shoulder, shaking his head at the choices Cutter made, at where those choices had led him.

Here. Staring out a grubby window in the back room of a seedy Lower Menthis tavern.

Rain thundered from the night sky. It streamed down the cracked glass of the window and trickled inside, soaking into the damp wood beneath his fingers. Everbright lanterns were spaced widely along the street, covered in an oily grime even the rain couldn't wash away. The light they cast was sickly and jaundiced, and so faint that all they did was create thick pools of lurking shadow for the cutpurses to hide in.

It always rained here. Even if the sky was clear up above, the runoff from the upper wards—sluice water, condensation, sweat, and slops—all blended into a muggy mixture that trickled down the mile high buildings and fell over the lower wards in a fine, misty drizzle that made the skin feel oily. You couldn't shake that feeling—as if you were coated in a constant sheen of grease and dirt.

Or maybe that was just the company he kept.

Cutter heard his name spoken behind him. He frowned and turned from the window.

Nothing had changed. Elian was still tied to the chair, his arms bound tightly behind him. He was breathing raggedly, his thin face covered with blood. Cutter could tell he was trying not to look at the pointed ear lying in a small puddle of blood by his feet.

Tiel had done that. He always got carried away with the violence.

Cutter shifted his gaze and looked at the halfling. Tiel crouched on the warped floorboards, his hands dangling between his legs as he stared unblinkingly at his captive. He'd been holding that position for half a bell, his wiry muscles supporting him without even a tremble of complaint.

He put Cutter in mind of a desert snake, watching its prey as it waited for the best moment to strike.

"The thing is," said Tiel in his reasonable voice, "it's not just me you're letting down. When you don't pay me what you owe, I can't pay my people what I owe, and they tend to get upset. Isn't that right, Cutter?"

"That's right."

Elian looked at Cutter. Cutter stared back, unblinking. Cutter was a big guy—over six-three, with a thick neck and dark hair so short it was barely stubble. A dragon tattoo crawled up his arms and around his neck, seeming to writhe whenever he tensed his muscles. He *knew* he looked scary. That was why he did what he did. He was good at it.

Cutter could see the fear in the elf's eyes, the fear that he was going to die. That was how Tiel liked to work. Take everything away from them, then give something back. Gratitude alone usually made them cough up what they owed. But Cutter still had to work them over a bit. Just so they didn't try it again.

"And Cutter here"—Tiel paused and slapped the elf's foot—"look at me when I'm talking to you."

The elf jerked his head back to look at the halfling.

"That's better. As I was saying, Cutter needs his money." Tiel leaned forward conspiratorially. "See, his woman's a courtesan, and Cutter likes to give her money so she doesn't have to work so much." He rocked back on his haunches again. "Me, I could never be with someone who gets paid for sex, but that's just me. I have my pride."

This time Cutter didn't meet the elf's gaze. He looked away, uninterested in the conversation. He'd heard it all before. It used to annoy him, the way Tiel put him down, talking about him like he wasn't there. But not anymore.

Bren, Tiel's bodyguard, had approached him one of the first times Tiel talked like that, when Cutter was leaning against the bar trying to stop himself from shoving a knife into Tiel's stomach.

"You respect him?" Bren had asked.

Cutter hadn't moved. "What?"

"I said, do you respect him?"

Cutter turned his head to look at him. "Who? Tiel?"

Bren grinned and nodded. "Yeah, Tiel. Is he someone who's opinion matters to you?"

Cutter thought for a moment. "Not in the slightest."

"Then why do you act like what he says makes a difference? You don't respect him. He knows that. So he takes shots at you. He wants to see how far he can push you. See, he knows he's got me to watch over him."

"And you're good at what you do?"

"The best. So stop letting him get to you. You're ugly enough without me having to rearrange your face."

Just then, Bren was leaning in the shadows against the far wall, clenching and unclenching his new adamantine arm. He was about the same height as Cutter, with long, black hair, but his build was slimmer. That didn't mean he was weak. Cutter had once seen him drop a half-orc with one well-placed punch. No. He definitely wasn't weak. His strength was simply . . . more focused.

Cutter knew he was listening, even though it looked like he wasn't. Cutter still didn't know Bren's story. Just that he'd been kicked out of his Dragonmarked House and ended up here. With all the rest of the rejects and outcasts.

"So what should I do?" asked Tiel. "What would *you* do?"

Elian licked his lips, trying to work up some moisture. "Uh . . . I'd—I'd let you go."

"*Would* you now? You hear that, boys? He'd let me go. How nice of you."

"B-but with a warning."

"With a *warning*. Well, why didn't you say so? That seem fair to you, Bren?"

Bren glanced up. "Not really."

"Well, it sounds fair to me. My friend, today is your lucky day."

Elian's face brightened with tentative hope. "You're letting me go?"

Tiel smiled. "No. I'm not. Cutter? Do your job."

Tiel got up and stretched, then backed away. He didn't like getting blood on his clothes. Cutter sauntered forward, letting the fear build. There was an art to being a bruiser. It wasn't just about beating a guy until he passed out. At least, not to Cutter. The aim was to scare him, to make sure he was healthy enough and willing enough to pay up next time.

The way Cutter did this, he caused head wounds. They bled a lot, scared the mark. A couple of punches to the face to add some real pain, and the guy was usually begging to pay Tiel.

Cutter didn't bother untying the elf. He picked up the chair by the arms and threw it against the wall. The elf cried out as his head slammed against the uneven plaster. He fell to the floor, the chair breaking apart beneath him. Cutter hung back a second, letting the elf feel his head for the wound, his hand coming away covered in blood. Then Cutter picked him up by his shirt. Two sharp jabs. One to the nose. Another to the jaw. Blood flowing now from the scalp wound, dripping from his eyebrows, blood from the nose sliding warmly down the back of his throat. He knew exactly what the elf was feeling.

"That was by way of introduction," said Cutter. "Now, here's how it goes. You tell me where Boromar can get his money, and you get to keep your teeth. You don't talk, we keep doing this until you do." Cutter pulled the elf closer. He could smell the sweat and fear on him. "And believe me, they always talk. It's just a matter of how long they can hold out."

Elian looked at Cutter in confusion. "Boromar?" he mumbled. "He's not a Boromar."

Cutter stared at the elf, not really believing what he had just heard. Could someone *actually* be that stupid?

"What did he say?" demanded Tiel.

"I'd keep your mouth shut if I were you," said Cutter in a low voice.

"But he's not. I know Saidan Boromar. You hear that?" He pushed himself away from Cutter and looked at Tiel. "I know Saidan. He doesn't have any sons." Elian staggered, then steadied himself against the wall.

Cutter wondered if maybe he'd hit the elf too hard, because he certainly wasn't thinking straight. Nobody said that to Tiel. What the truth of the matter was, Cutter didn't know. All Bren had told him was that Tiel claimed to be the son of Saidan Boromar, head of one of the biggest crime families in Sharn. But Boromar had never acknowledged Tiel as blood, a fact that Tiel couldn't accept. Bren said the halfling was trying to work his way up the chain in the hope that his father would name him heir.

Cutter didn't think that would ever happen. He didn't think Tiel really thought so either, which was probably why he went shifter on anyone who was stupid enough to say anything about it.

He glanced at Tiel. The halfling just stood there, staring at Elian. He didn't look angry. Maybe he wasn't going to—

Then he lunged forward and punched Elian hard in the stomach. Tiel was strong for a halfling. Cutter had seen him beat a man almost as big as Cutter until he was unconscious. Elian was no match.

The elf flew back against the wall and Tiel charged after him, throwing punches to his chest and stomach. When the elf sagged to his knees, Tiel focused on his head, raining blow after blow on him until his face looked like it had been dipped in a bucket of red paint. Cutter glanced at Bren, eyebrows raised. Tiel's bodyguard nodded slightly and walked forward.

"Tiel," he said.

The halfling ignored him. Elian collapsed to the floor. Tiel traded his punches for kicks. Elian groaned every time a boot connected.

"Tiel, we need him alive," said Bren. "He needs to tell us where the money is."

Tiel stopped his attack, breathing heavily. He looked at Bren, then down at the elf. He wiped his brow with his forearm and squatted in front of the moaning figure. He grabbed Elian's face, pulling him up so he had no choice but to look Tiel in the eyes. "Who is my father?" he asked.

Elian mumbled something unintelligible.

Tiel shook the elf. "Who is my father?" he shouted.

"Sa . . . Saidan Boromar," mumbled Elian.

"And don't you forget it."

Tiel pushed the elf back to the floor and stood. He looked at the blood that spattered his shirt and trousers.

"Now look what you've done," he said. "My clothes are ruined."

Some time later, Cutter walked through the streets of Dragoneyes, the hood of his oiled cloak pulled low over his forehead. The rain drummed a steady tattoo on the leather, almost drowning out the sounds of the night life around him.

And there was plenty of that, thought Cutter, holding the edge of his hood and looking around. The three days of Long Shadows were upon the city. It was only the first night of the festival and already things were getting more dangerous than usual.

It was said that when the Sovereign Lord Aureon brought magic into the world, he created a creature of darkness that stole his shadow to use as its vessel. The Shadow fed on death and despair, granting power to those who pursued dark magic. The monsters of Droaam, even those that had relocated to Sharn, bowed down before this dark god. As did anyone who followed the black paths of magic.

And the festival of Long Shadows was the one time during the year when the Shadow's influence waxed strong enough that his worshipers dared to leave their hidden sanctuaries to take advantage of their god's expanded influence.

And take advantage they did.

Cutter slowed as two orcs emerged from an alley ahead of him and lumbered across the street. Humans and dwarves scattered out of their path, staring after them in fear. Orcs were common enough in the city, but during Long Shadows they seemed to lose their thin veneer of civilization and regress to the primitive creatures they were before leaving Droaam. It was a dangerous time for the people of Sharn. No one knew what the orcs were going to do next.

A group of goblins emerged from a building, laughing and shouting at the top of their lungs. They passed some kind of vessel between them, something that pumped out thick, greasy smoke whenever they put it to their lips.

Cutter turned off the street. He didn't have time to get

caught up in anything tonight. Tiel wanted his money back at the tavern as soon as Cutter could get his hands on it. He was surprised Elian had been able to remember where it was after all their persuasion.

He stepped aboard a lift at the northern edge of Dragoneyes, the once silvery disc turned black and tarnished, its waist-high railing green with mold. Nobody bothered cleaning the lifts in the lower wards. It was a battle that couldn't be won.

The lift rose quickly through the rain. Cutter watched as Lower Menthis expanded below him, the bright, chaotic lights of Firelight clashing with the ordered lines of everbright lanterns that marked the residential districts of Center Bridge and Forgelight Towers.

He looked to the west of Center Bridge, where the district of Downstairs lay. Rowen would be there, probably getting ready for her appointment. Cutter gripped the railing and squinted through the rain, almost as if he could see her if he willed it hard enough. They'd had another fight before he left earlier that night. About the same thing they always fought over—money. Or rather, getting enough money for them to get away from Sharn, to start somewhere fresh.

The lift rose through a circular hole and came to a jerky halt level with the street of Middle Menthis. Cutter disembarked and walked until he found Fountain Boulevard. Then he searched for the house with the petrified worgs standing guard. Cutter stood and examined them. They looked fake to him, crudely carved creatures that resembled massive wolves. He wondered how much the elf had paid for them.

Cutter took a quartz crystal from his pocket and held it over the lock on the gate. The elf had given it to him, saying Cutter needed it to disarm the magical traps he'd placed throughout the grounds. The lock clicked quietly and the gates swung inward.

Cutter waited a moment, surveying the garden and the gravel path that led to the three-story house. What if the elf had lied about the stone disarming the traps? Nothing moved, but that didn't mean anything.

Only one way to find out. Cutter stepped into the garden and walked up the path to the front door. The house lay in darkness, which made sense since the owner had been tied up in a back room of a tavern since the early afternoon.

Cutter opened the door and stepped into the hall. Cold fire lamps flared to life, revealing a corridor carpeted with imported Sarlonan rugs, some of the most expensive hand-woven carpets in the marketplace. Someone had told Cutter that each rug was woven by three generations of women, the youngest generation learning the craft from her elders as they worked side by side. Each rug took as long as five years to produce.

Paintings of famous battles adorned the walls. Cutter glanced at them. Elian was obviously an enthusiast for the War. Cutter bet he wasn't involved in any of the fighting.

The elf said the gold was hidden beneath a floorboard in his study on the second floor. Cutter checked the rooms on the ground level just to make sure no surprises were lurking unseen, then climbed the wide staircase. The study was at the far end of the corridor, through a set of ornately carved double doors. Cutter pushed them open.

A huge darkwood desk dominated the room beyond. It sat in the middle of a deep red and green carpet, the colors forming a picture of a grassland plain on fire. Cutter shook his head in bemusement. How rich was this guy? Or rather, how rich had he *been?* His luck must have turned sour if he was borrowing money from Tiel. A single everbright lantern stood on the desk, its stand designed to look like a dragon clutching the sun. A hemisphere of metal surrounded the globe, so that the light could be turned in different directions.

The elf had explained that the loose floorboard was underneath the desk chair. Cutter rounded the desk and crouched.

Then he paused at what his new line of sight revealed.

A hobgoblin sat on a chair in the opposite corner of the room. The huge creature watched him calmly, its features cast in shadow by the position of the lamp's shutter. Cutter slowly stood and turned the metal cup so it directed the light away from his eyes and up at the ceiling, until he could see the hobgoblin clearly. Its skin was a dull green, its eyes and protruding teeth a sickly yellow.

"Evening," said Cutter.

The hobgoblin leaned forward, the wooden chair creaking beneath his weight. "I'm glad you didn't say 'good evening,' because I'm afraid it isn't going to be so good for you."

"Is that right?"

"I'm afraid so."

Cutter dropped his arms to his sides and shrugged. His cloak dropped to the floor. He rested his hands on the carved pommels of his curved Khutai knives.

"Am I going to need these?"

"More than likely."

"What if I said I'm here because your boss told me how to get in? That he owes money to certain people and I'm here to collect?"

"I'd say I never said he was my boss."

This made Cutter pause. "Ah. He owes you money as well?"

"A substantial amount."

"Then we have a problem." Cutter drew his knives and reversed them so they lay flush against the underside of his forearms, the points just reaching his elbows.

"Are those Khutai knives?" asked the hobgoblin curiously.

"They are."

"May I ask how you came by them?"

"I traveled with a clan of Valenar elves for some years."

The hobgoblin's eye ridges rose in surprise. "They accepted you?"

"After a while."

"And they presented you with the knives?"

"They did."

"I'm impressed."

Cutter inclined his head in acknowledgment.

"Yes, you seem like quite an interesting human. I would have liked to talk some more. Unfortunately—"

Cutter saw the hobgoblin's eyes flicker, no more than that.

Cutter dropped to the floor and spun, flicking the blades out and slashing through the air as he did so. He saw a pair of massive legs before him, covered in thick leather armor, and the blades bit through and sliced gouges into the flesh. His attacker roared in pain.

Cutter went with his momentum and rolled to the side. He bumped against the wall and rose into a crouch, the knives held defensively before him.

It was another hobgoblin. He clutched at his thighs, blood seeping between his huge fingers. He looked at Cutter and snarled. Then his hand went to the mace hanging from his belt.

Cutter didn't wait. He pushed himself away from the wall and ran straight at the hobgoblin. He knew he had to end this quickly. He'd never be able to slay two of them on his own. He held one arm low and raised the other high.

The creature saw him coming and used both hands to grab the arm aiming for his throat. Cutter thrust hard with the low knife and felt it hit the leather cuirass. He felt an instant of resistance, then the point pushed through and penetrated skin.

Cutter angled the blade upward and pushed with all his strength. The hobgoblin screamed. It released one hand and scrabbled for Cutter's throat. Cutter tried to duck out of reach, but the hobgoblin managed to get a grip. Cutter pushed the knife up as hard as he could. Another bellow of rage and pain, but the hobgoblin kept hold of his throat.

Cutter braced his feet and screamed, pushing forward with all of his strength. The knife went deeper and higher, as far as it could go. Cutter prayed it was long enough to reach the heart.

The hobgoblin's grip tightened painfully. Then it coughed and a bubble of blood burst from its mouth, spraying Cutter's face. The hobgoblin paused, looking at the blood in confusion. Then the creature sagged to the floor. Cutter pulled out his knife and turned—

Just in time to see a club arcing through the air toward him. He hunched down and spun away, taking the brunt of the blow on his shoulder. The force punched him to the floor. Cutter flopped onto his back and saw the club coming down for another strike. He rolled and pushed himself to his feet, darting behind the desk. He angled the light to shine in the hobgoblin's eyes. The creature raised a hand to shield the glare. Cutter took the opportunity. He leaped over the desk and ran past his assailant. He lashed out with his knife as he went, felt it connect with flesh. But he didn't stop. He bounded down the stairs and out the front door, then ran until he reached a street with passing people. Only then did he slow down enough to regain his breath.

He looked around at the people going about their business. A skycoach drifted past with a well-dressed woman seated inside. She stared at Cutter as she went, turning in her seat to watch him until the coach turned a corner.

Cutter shook his head ruefully. That could have gone better.

The Tufted Feather was one of the more upscale brothels in Menthis, despite its location in the lower district of Downstairs. It competed favorably with the more infamous Savia's, the well-known "companion house" in the Firelight District, that was run by Savia Potellas. A low-key rivalry simmered between the two brothels, in no small way the result of a deep-seated jealousy the Madame of the Feather, an aging halfling called Mela, harbored for Savia and her position as the Lower Menthis representative on the Sharn city council.

Tiel and the Boromar clan owned the Tufted Feather. Cutter had a room there, and it was his job to make sure none of the clients got out of hand. He didn't have to step in often. Mela was a formidable presence, despite her size. She referred to herself as the *lath* of the Feather, a halfling term Cutter understood to mean leader. She looked after her girls, and they in turn accorded her the respect she demanded.

Even Cutter was wary of angering her.

The main floor of the Feather was a vast open space filled with couches and tables. Dim lanterns lent a relaxed mood. A bar took up the back wall of the room, and to the right, a wooden staircase led to the upper floors.

Cutter cast a quick glance around the common room, but everything was calm. A slow night, by the looks of it. Only four customers waited, sitting at tables while they impatiently sipped their drinks. Cutter approached the bar. Dyce was doing Cutter's duty tonight, seeing as he'd been otherwise occupied with Tiel. The dwarf nodded at him. The floor behind the bar was elevated so Dyce could move around without having to look up at anyone.

"All quiet?" asked Cutter.

Dyce nodded.

Cutter glanced around. "Is Rowen here?"

"Nah. She left about two hours ago. Said she was heading to the university."

"Thanks, Dyce." Cutter knocked sharply on the bar and climbed the stairs. So she'd gone after all. He'd asked her not to, but they were already fighting, so he didn't think she'd listen. Still, he'd hoped.

He reached the top floor and headed for his room. It didn't have much—a bed, a chair, some books, a trunk for his clothes. He lay down on the bed. It was still messed up from his slumber with Rowen. He could smell her perfume on the pillows, the faint scent of jasmine on a summer day. He sighed and put his arms behind his head. Why did they always seem to fight lately? And always about the same thing . . .

* * *

She'd come to him after her last appointment with the Professor. That was what she called him, like it was a mark of respect or something. So Cutter was already on the defensive, not really willing to listen to what she had to say, to give her a fair hearing.

"He stuck me in this hidden room, like a closet in his wall," she'd said, sitting at her rolltop desk while she wiped the rouge from her face. "I think he thought the door was shut, because he talked as if I wasn't there."

Or he just didn't consider you a threat, thought Cutter, then felt bad about it. He was letting his temper get the better of him again. It wasn't the first time Cutter had let it get in the way, and it certainly wouldn't be the last.

"So what happened?" he asked, sitting on the edge of her bed and trying to ignore the smell of expensive wine on her breath.

"A man came in—I think the Professor called him Salkith."

Cutter sat upright. "Salkith? Are you sure?"

Rowen looked at him in the mirror. "Very sure. Why?"

"I know him. He works for the Boromars. He's a dreamlily courier."

"I knew it!" Rowen spun around in her chair. "The way they were speaking, I knew it was something valuable."

"Wait. Back up here. You knew *what* was valuable?"

"They were talking about handing over some package. Just the way they talked about it, I could tell it was worth a lot. Cutter, this is perfect!"

"What are you talking about?"

"The delivery is next week. I made my next appointment for the same night, said I was busy the rest of the week. Don't you see? I steal the dreamlily and we sell it. We'll make enough money to get out of this place!"

Cutter surged to his feet. "Rowen, get that out of your head. Right now. Do you realize what you're saying? You cross the Boromars, they'll hunt you down. We'll spend the rest of our lives looking over our shoulders."

"We'll run. We'll hide."

"There's nowhere we can go that they wouldn't find us. They won't give up until we're dead. They'll have no choice. If word got out, other people would get ideas. They won't let that happen. It's too risky, Rowen. No, we stick to the plan."

"And what plan is that? You keep working for Tiel beating people up and I keep selling my body? How long do you think we'll last like this, Cutter? You can barely handle it now!"

Cutter couldn't look at her. He stared at the floorboards. "I can handle it."

"No. You can't. Send ten bugbears into a locked room with

you and yes, I'll believe you can handle it. But not this. This is eating you away."

Cutter looked up, straight into her green eyes. "Then give it up."

She turned away. "I'm not getting into this again." She picked up the brush her mother had left her, the one with the pearl handle, and started brushing out her long, copper hair.

"Rowen."

She didn't turn.

"Rowen, promise me you'll forget about this. I'll find another way. I promise. One that isn't so dangerous. Agreed?"

She shrugged.

And Cutter had thought that was the last of it.

Cutter's eyes flicked open. He stared at the ceiling, wondering what time it was. It felt late. He pushed himself up, wincing at the ache in his shoulder blade. The hobgoblin had gotten in a good hit.

He headed to the landing and took the stairs down to the next floor, knocking on Rowen's door. No answer. He searched his pockets until he found his key and turned it in the lock.

He stepped inside. The small yellow everbright lamp on her rolltop was lit. She always left it burning when she was out on a job. Said she liked the familiar glow when she came home.

There was no sign of her. Cutter frowned. Maybe he'd got the time wrong. She was usually back from her appointment with the professor well before midnight. He hurried down to the ground floor. Dyce was packing away his clean glasses for the night. Cutter looked around. No one was in the common room.

"Dyce, has Rowen come back?"

Dyce stopped and scowled. "Now that you mention it, no."

"Host," Cutter swore. "Listen, I'm off to the university to see if I can find her."

"Maybe she just fell asleep or something."

"Yeah. Maybe." Cutter turned and hurried out the door. Gusts of rain slapped him in the face, driving the last vestiges of sleep from his mind.

Both he and Dyce knew Rowen would never fall asleep at a client's place. None of the girls did. It was too dangerous, one of the first things they learned.

So where was she?

Chapter Two

The first night of Long Shadows

Zor, the 26th day of Vult, 998

Cutter stood in the recessed doorway of a tenement building. He breathed through his mouth, trying not to inhale the stale, acidic stench of old vomit. When he first stepped into the shadowed entrance he'd stood on something soft and brittle that crunched and squished beneath his feet. He didn't check to see what it was.

He leaned against the wall and watched the Starfire Dragon across the street. It was the only place he could think of nearby that would still be open at that time of night. It wasn't a theatre, so it didn't close after the last show. It was more of a supper venue with good food and terrible entertainment. But most importantly, the Middle Menthis residents that frequented it were wealthy enough that they would call a skycoach to take them home. All he had to do was wait.

Cutter's patience was soon rewarded. He saw the underside light first, a tiny everbright globe that appeared through the rain as a skycoach slowly descended. The bad weather caused the driver to overshoot his mark, so he turned the coach gracefully, coming to a landing outside the doors to the club. Dim blue lighting from inside the boat-shaped vessel lit the underside of the driver's face.

Cutter darted into the rain. He didn't give the man a chance to see him. He took his cudgel from his belt and slammed it into the back of the driver's neck. The man dropped, smacking his head on the seat as he went. Blood flowed from the wound. Cutter grabbed him under the arms and dragged him from the coach. He propped him against the wall of the Starfire and climbed inside the skycoach. As soon as he did so, the rain stopped falling. He looked up, but the downpour had not slowed. The coach no doubt carried a charm to keep the occupants dry.

He shook the water from his face and took hold of the controls. He closed his eyes and focused his mind, bonding with the elemental that powered the coach. It sensed someone familiar with the craft, and acquiesced to his presence. He hadn't anticipated a problem. There were so many drivers for these skycoaches that they couldn't be bound to any one driver.

Cutter opened his eyes and pulled back on the controls. Just as he was rising into the air, a man and a woman stepped outside, gesturing frantically for him to come back. Cutter ignored them and kept going.

* * *

Driving a skycoach wasn't just a matter of up, down, and forward. Some time ago, Cutter had worked as a coach driver, and it had taken him a month to get the hang of it. It was almost an art to keep the coach from slamming into the undersides of bridges, clipping the jutting cornices and turrets of strangely shaped buildings, and to avoid the unpredictable maneuverings of other skycoaches. Higher up in the skies, drivers had to contend with the Lyrandar airships. They were the worst. They thought they owned the skies, and they were furious that the Sharn council had given contracts for skycoaches to non-Lyrandar companies. If a skycoach got in their way, they'd simply ram it out of the sky.

Cutter took the coach straight up until the curve of a massive tower appeared out of the rain above him. He slowed his ascent and carefully followed the curve as it flared outward and upward. A long strip of glowing white appeared above him. The curve he was following fed into a bridge that connected the tower to another. The white glow came from the underside of the bridge, a safety feature instigated recently by some of the artificers on the council. Cutter wished they'd done it when he was a driver. It certainly made things a lot easier.

He guided the vessel beneath the bridge, then headed forward again. The multicolored lights of other skycoaches materialized out of the night, their illumination haloed and muted by the rain. Everyone was keeping it careful. Too easy for accidents to happen.

He arrived at Dalannan Tower, home of Morgrave University, and drifted upward, the surrounding towers falling gradually away the higher he went, their lights little more than faint twinklings that faded away below him. The air changed. It was still warm, but it was fresher, less oppressive. He lifted his face and took a deep breath, cleansing his mind for what lay ahead.

The coach soared over the top of the tower. He could see a patch of grass below him, and small clumps of trees. He was disoriented for a second, but then realized that it wasn't Dalannan Tower. He must have drifted off course as he rose upward. This was Breland Spire. The parklike area would be the Commons. He'd heard about it before. Sort of a gathering place for students. He leaned over and peered into the rain, searching for a bridge that connected Breland Spire to Dalannan Tower. Once there, he could find a way in.

He landed the skycoach beneath the trees and disconnected the glyph stone that powered it. The blue lights died and the rain trickled through the branches into the coach. He jumped onto the grass and set off across the Commons. He found the bridge and paused beneath the cover of the peaked roof. He shook the water from his clothes and looked around. Shops and stalls, locked up for the night, lined one side of the wide walkway. The other side was a wall that was entirely covered in paper—notices of upcoming events, advertisements, pages of interest from the Breland Ledger.

Cutter hurried along, his heavy boots clumping loudly on the wooden flooring. The bridge opened onto a flagstone pathway lined with delicately pruned bushes. This in turn led up a flight of marble stairs that stopped before a set of vast double doors. The doors let into Lareth Hall, the huge dome that capped Dalannan Tower and Morgrave University.

Cutter tried the handles, but the doors were locked. He stepped back and sized up the strength of the wood. No. There was no way he was breaking these doors down. He slipped behind the jasmine bushes at the side of the entrance and followed the curve of the dome until he reached a set of tall windows. They were made of stained glass, their pictures depicting various scenes from history. Cutter stood beneath a scene showing the three dragons—Syberis, Eberron, and Khyber. The window was divided into sections, each lined with lead framing. At least the whole window wouldn't come down on him.

Cutter slipped on a pair of gloves and lightly tapped the

window. The glass was thick. He pulled out his knife and smacked the window with the pommel. Nothing. He hit it again, and this time a crack appeared in the glass. He tapped it a few more times, not hard enough to send the glass falling away on the other side, but enough to extend the cracks, separating the glass into fragments. He hit one piece hard. It smashed, the shards falling down the other side. He waited, breath held, but could hear no sounds of alarm. Then he pulled the broken splinters out of the frame.

It took a while, but when he finished, the hole in the window was big enough to squeeze through. He poked his head in first. The interior was dim, lit by shuttered, yellow everbright lanterns. No one was about.

Cutter pulled himself up onto the ledge and slid through the gap. His feet touched down on soft carpet. He moved against the wall and looked around.

He stood in an atrium that fed into a wide corridor. Paneled doors opened off both sides of the corridor. Sofas and bookshelves furnished the room. Cutter got the impression it was some sort of gathering area for the university staff.

Against one wall was an old diagram of the college, illustrating the different levels. Cutter stood on the floor that held the administrative and faculty offices. The level below held the vast library. And beneath that were rooms belonging to the staff who lived on the premises. That was where he needed to go.

Cutter headed down the corridor and found the stairs. He peered over the banister to make sure no one was in sight, then padded down to the next level. Light streamed from the library. He paused one turn above and listened. He heard noises below. The soft sigh of pages being turned and the scratching sound of quill on paper. Someone was doing research.

He crouched down, but he could see only the main library

desk. Empty. He crept down the stairs, keeping the banister to his back. As he moved lower, he could see a study desk to the right. Someone was there—a dwarf. And he didn't look too happy. He slammed a book shut. Cutter froze while the dwarf dumped the book onto a pile at his feet and pulled another vast tome from the pile on the desk. He opened it, muttering obscenities about someone who was making him work.

Cutter got moving. He slid around the turn and headed down to the next level. No one challenged him, which was a relief. Now all he had to do was find Rowen's professor. How was he going to do that?

He thought back to everything Rowen had said about her visits to the Professor. Hadn't she said once that she looked out of his windows and saw that some students had defaced the flag on Karrnath Spire?

He walked to the end of the hallway and looked out the window. He stared for a while but it was no use. He couldn't see far enough through the rain. He carefully tried the handle of the door to his left. Locked. So was the one on his right. He made his way slowly up the corridor, checking each door for any clues.

About halfway down the hall, he found a dark stain on the wooden floorboards. He knelt down and touched it. His fingers came away sticky. Blood.

He straightened and tried the door. It was unlocked. Cutter paused, listening for sounds of movement. Nothing. Light spilled through the crack. It was bright, not the kind of light that might be left on while someone slept. He gently pushed the door and peered inside. A neat sitting room lay beyond, lit by delicate lamps. Low couches formed a circle around a sunken fireplace. Rugs were strewn around the floor, so people could sit and soak up the warmth. Cutter looked around the doorframe. A red carpet covered the floor beyond the couches. And doors opened into other parts of the residence.

Cutter slipped inside and closed the door. His eyes searched the area for signs of Rowen, but nothing betrayed her presence. Then again, he wasn't sure these were the right rooms. He swallowed, feeling his stomach tense up. If he wanted to find out if this was the right place, he was looking in the wrong room.

He rested his head briefly against the door and closed his eyes.

Come on, he told himself. You knew the deal going into this relationship. He smiled grimly. Yeah, but he had been arrogant enough to think that he could change her, that she wouldn't want to sleep with other men after she'd been with him. He opened his eyes. How many men had made *that* mistake?

He headed around a couch, aiming for the rooms that opened off the lounge.

And that was when he found the professor. Or what was left of him. He had been ripped apart. Literally. One arm lay half-concealed beneath the couch, the fingers splayed. They had been broken, probably before the arm was ripped off. His stomach was a gaping hole, crimson and purple with exposed organs, the blood congealing into viscous pools. His intestines had been pulled out. His other hand was holding them as if he had fought to keep them inside.

His lower jaw had been torn from his face. It lay next to his right ear, the teeth starkly white against the blood. His tongue hung from the gaping mess that was the lower part of his head. It dangled, swollen and blue.

Rowen. Cutter pushed himself to his feet and threw the first door open. It was a bathroom. Empty. He turned quickly, almost slipping in the blood. He grabbed hold of the doorframe to balance himself and lunged into the next room. This one was the bedroom. He frantically searched the floor, but there was no sign of her body anywhere. He paused and inhaled deeply, relief flooding through his body. He had to think about this. He walked over to the bed. The sheets were a jumbled mess and he could smell Rowen's perfume on the pillows. She'd definitely been here.

So the question was—what happened, and where was she now?

He turned, planning a more detailed search of the room. But instead, he froze. Something wasn't right. He wasn't sure what it was, but he suddenly felt he wasn't alone.

And then the shadows came alive and lunged at him. Something rock hard smacked him in the chest, lifting him into the air and sending him flying backward over the bed. He landed on the edge of the mattress and tumbled to the floor, his chest and ribs flaring with pain. He rolled to his feet, eyes frantically searching for his assailant, but he could see nothing in the dimly lit room. He backed against the wall and pulled out his Khutai knives, holding them in the ready position along his forearms.

He slid along the wall, creeping toward the doorway. Still no sign of his attacker. Cutter glanced to his left, checking the door.

When he turned back, he found himself staring into a pair of glowing white eyes. A black metal face hovered only inches from his own. It tilted to the side, birdlike, studying him for an instant. Then it jerked forward, head-butting him.

Cutter staggered backward into the wall, blood spraying from his nose. He slashed out with the knives, hearing the scrape of metal on metal. He ducked low, barely avoiding a fist that smashed into the wall where his face had been. Plaster showered his head. He stabbed upward with the Khutai, but the blade was turned aside by armor plating. He pushed himself forward, diving headlong across the floor. He scrambled to his feet and pulled the shutter off the everbright lantern near the bed. Yellow light flooded the room.

And Cutter could see what he was facing.

A warforged, but unlike any he had ever seen before. The figure was completely black. Light bounced away from its carapace. Shadows wrapped themselves around its form, almost as if it gathered the darkness as a cloak.

If it had been a human, Cutter would have described it as lithe and sinewy. Its movements were precise, not a motion wasted. He couldn't quite place what it reminded him of.

But when the warforged stepped away from the wall, he realized what it was.

It reminded him of a hunter stalking its prey. This warforged was more animal than anything else.

It loped toward him, and Cutter saw that the face wasn't crafted to look like the usual Cannith-issue faceplate. It was thin, like a fox, sharp and pointed, the mouth pulled into a permanent snarl.

"Where is she?" The voice was quiet, unrushed. It sounded male. "Where is she?"

"Where is who?" asked Cutter. He feinted to the side, but the warforged darted forward and grabbed hold of his neck. It lifted Cutter from the floor and pulled him close. The head tilted again and it sniffed, moving over Cutter's face and neck.

"The girl," it said. "You have her stench all over you. Where is she?"

Rowen. The 'forged was talking about Rowen. Cutter struggled in its grasp. "Why?" he gasped. "What do you want with her?"

"That," said the warforged, "is none of your business."

It stepped forward and rammed Cutter into the wall. His body smashed through the plaster, his head hitting the wooden wall framing.

"I ask again," said the warforged. "Where is she?"

The warforged stepped to the side and jerked Cutter away from the wall. He hit the floor, landing awkwardly on his arm. Groaning, he pushed himself to his feet. He'd managed to hold onto his knives, but they seemed useless against the warforged's plating.

He looked around. The warforged had vanished again.

Cutter realized that the warforged was toying with him, like a predator with harmless prey. Anger coursed through his body and he straightened up. This time he saw the attack coming. He leaned away from the sound of movement and swung his arm in an overhand thrust. He felt the blade connect and sink in, heard a hiss of pain.

Cutter yanked the blade out again.

So the warforged wasn't invincible. It was just a matter of finding the vulnerable parts.

Cutter dropped into a crouch and swung both knives. They connected but didn't penetrate. Sparks flew, then something smashed into Cutter's face. Pain exploded in his cheek. Light flashed before his eyes like lightning strikes stabbing into his head. He was pulled off his feet. He fought, disoriented, but all he could do was scrabble feebly at the metal armor. The warforged pulled him close, then thrust him away again in one smooth, fluid movement. The room flew by, then he was in the light again as he sailed into the lounge.

He landed on his back, his breath exploding from his lungs. He heard a horrible cracking beneath him, then wetness spread along his back. Cutter tried to push himself up but kept slipping every time he did so. What was going on?

Then he realized. He had landed on top of the professor. He felt the bile rise in his throat. He rolled over, momentarily face to face with the shattered visage, then kicked away. He pushed himself to his knees, wincing at the pain shooting through his body. The professor's blood covered him.

The warforged strode out of the bedroom. Cutter shuffled sideways into the sitting area, putting the couch between himself and his assailant. The warforged didn't pause. It walked straight over the professor's body, leaned down and grabbed hold of a couch, and straightened again, sending the heavy piece of furniture crashing into the wall.

Cutter fell back a step. He remembered the sunken fire pit behind him and stepped around it. All he could think about was getting out of this alive. Rowen was in trouble somewhere and he had to find her. He glanced over his shoulder. The door was only a few feet away. If only—

He turned back and shouted in surprise. The warforged was in midair, sailing toward him like a spider gliding along webs.

Cutter dove forward, the warforged passing above him. He tucked his shoulder and rolled straight to his feet, whirling around with his blades held ready.

The construct stood directly in front of him. It grabbed Cutter's neck, lifting him from the floor. Cutter stabbed beneath its arms, but this time there was no give.

"I will ask one last time," it said. "Tell me where she is."

The warforged squeezed. Cutter felt his throat constrict, pushing all the air from his lungs.

"I . . . I don't . . . know."

"A pity."

The fingers tightened even more. Cutter dropped his knives and desperately tried to loosen the grip, but it was impossible. The warforged was too strong. Blackness appeared at the edge of his vision. He squeezed his eyes shut, not wanting his last sight to be that of his murderer. He thought of Rowen, and he prayed that she was somewhere safe, that she hadn't gotten involved in anything stupid. His lungs screamed for air. He felt a lump in his chest, slowly rising, cutting off all feeling as it went. It hit his throat, demanding air, but there was none. It rose higher, into his head, and he felt himself drifting, falling . . .

Cutter hit the floor. A moment later he realized that the fingers were gone from his throat. He opened his mouth and pulled in a screaming gasp, air burning, coursing into his body, driving the blackness away. He rolled onto his back, sucking in great mouthfuls of air, as much as he could get. Cutter opened his eyes and rolled over, wondering what was happening, waiting for the killing blow to fall. He tried to get to his feet but his hand slipped and he collapsed, catching the metallic butcher smell of blood in his nostrils. Cutter stared blearily at the red pool beneath him. He had rolled into the professor's blood again.

Cutter finally pushed himself up. He looked around and saw his Khutai blades lying nearby. He stretched out and grabbed hold of the pommels, dragging them toward him.

He winced and climbed to his feet, looking about the room. There was no sign of the warforged. It had just disappeared. But why?

He heard a gasp of surprise. He turned, still foggy, and saw a dwarf—the dwarf from the library—standing in the doorway, staring at Cutter.

Cutter looked down at his blood-covered body crouched over the corpse of the professor, bloodied knives in his hands.

He looked up at the dwarf. He was reaching into his jerkin for something. Cutter shook his head, knowing there was no point in proclaiming his innocence here. It looked too incriminating.

He staggered toward the door. Whatever the dwarf was

trying to reach was caught inside his clothes. Cutter swung his fist, hitting him in the side of the head. The dwarf fell against the door frame, then collapsed to his knees.

Cutter swept past him and sprinted up the stairs to the rooftop, his breath burning in his lungs and his heart beating erratically in his chest. He crawled back through the window and ran across the bridge.

Only when he was gliding through the air, safe in the sky-coach, did he allow himself a sigh of relief.

Chapter Three

The first night of Long Shadows

Zor, the 26th day of Vult, 998

Abraxis Wren stood on a small hill in Skysedge Park and let his eyes drift down the sweep of neatly-trimmed grass to the crowds milling below him like . . .

What were they like? Sheep? No, not sheep. Like expensively dressed and bejeweled peacocks, strutting about with their feathers in the air—or in this case, positioning themselves in strategic locations so that their jewels caught the light of the gently bobbing lanterns.

He took a sip of his wine and winced, holding it up to check its color. This was supposed to be from Aundair? He didn't think so. He made a mental note to check how much his supplier had pocketed by palming this goblin's piss onto him. How did the idiot think he would get this past a half-elf?

He turned his attention back to the ebb and flow of bodies—

—ants! They were like ants. That was it!

He stared at them, looking for something, anything remotely interesting to catch his eye. There wasn't much. The usual sycophants and boot-lickers, flatterers of women, curriers of favor. He'd already had to fend off three people looking for work, five people wanting an introduction to Celyria ir'Tain—something he couldn't do if he wanted to, as he didn't know her—and three rather intriguing invitations he might follow up on, depending on how the rest of the evening turned out.

He sighed and headed down the slope, aiming for a group of people gathered around a particularly annoying young man he'd had the misfortune of meeting at a gala dinner a couple of months previously.

As he drew closer, Wren could hear the young man's irritating voice as he regaled his audience.

"The thing is, you don't have time for fear. All you do is get on with the job. And even though my superior officer had died in my arms and handed over command of the unit to me, I had to think about it logically."

"What did you do?" asked a vacuous-looking young elf.

His companion, a female elf who was not at all vacuous looking—rather tasty, in fact—rolled her eyes.

"The only thing I could do. I wasn't about to risk any of my men, so when darkness fell, I snuck behind enemy lines and killed the Karrn general myself. Slit his throat."

The elf gasped and put a delicate hand to his mouth. "No!"

"It was war. These things had to be done."

"Tell me," said Wren. "Where did this confrontation take place?"

The young man narrowed his eyes at Wren. "Outside Karrnath."

"Really? Would this be outside Karrnath in the Talenta Plains, or outside Karrnath in the rather unfriendly mountains of the Mror Holds?"

"Uh—"

"Or maybe it was in the Mournland? Yes? No?"

"I . . . I can't remember." The man put a hand to his forehead as if he had a headache. "It's the trauma, you see. It sometimes makes me forget things. But you wouldn't know about that."

"I would, as a matter of fact. And I also know that during the War you were nowhere near the frontline. How did you get in here, anyway? I didn't invite you."

"This is your party?"

"It is."

"I didn't know."

"Obviously."

They stared at each other. Finally, the young man looked away, flushing with embarrassment. "Uh, maybe I'd better go . . ."

Wren waved his hand dismissively. "You're here now," he said. "You may as well stay. Have some wine. It's from Aundair."

"Um, thank you." The young man glanced at the girl, hesitated, then shook his head and wandered off. The girl stared at Wren, eyebrows raised.

"That was rather cruel."

"Was it?" Wren scratched a pointed ear—a gift from his elf father—and frowned. "I didn't notice."

"No, I imagine not. You were too busy staring at me."

"Can you blame me?"

"No, not really." The elf grinned, taking a small sip of wine and staring at Wren over the rim of the crystal glass.

Wren smiled back. Maybe things were looking up after all. He took her by the arm and gently guided her away from the confused elf who had been so impressed by the war stories. "Should we go somewhere a bit less . . . boring?"

"Didn't you say this was your party?"

Wren shrugged. "I'm afraid it hasn't lived up to the hype."

"I see. So, where should we go?"

"Well, my place is not far. We can enjoy the view of the park and enjoy some wine from my cellar."

"You have apartments in Skysedge Park?"

"I do."

"May I ask—what do you do for a living?"

"Oh. Forgive me." Wren bowed low, almost touching the grass with his trailing fingers. "Abraxis Wren. Master inquisitive of House Medani. At your service."

"You're an inquisitive?"

"I am."

"Following philandering husbands and tracking down missing children obviously pays a lot better than I was led to believe."

Wren chuckled. "No, I'm afraid it doesn't. But then, I don't take on those types of cases."

"Is that so? And what types of cases *do* you take on?"

"Ones that interest me. Ones that pose some kind of challenge. I'm easily bored, you see."

"Forgive me for prying, but how can you afford such an extravagant lifestyle?"

"Extravagant?" Wren laughed. "Oh, my dear, you should have seen how my father lived. Now there was an elf who knew how to throw a party. No, my needs are humble. I inherited my apartments and some money when my father drank himself to death. Something my human mother had been warning him about for years. I—"

Wren froze mid sentence and peered over the elf's shoulder. She turned to see what he was looking at.

"What?" she asked.

"Forgive me, my lady. I'm afraid we'll have to postpone

that drink. I smell something interesting."

He handed his glass to the woman and hurried past her. He thought he heard her swearing at him but he couldn't be sure. A shame. She looked like she would have been fun. But better things awaited. He targeted a group of important-looking men clustered around the tall figure of Master Larrien ir'Morgrave, the head of Morgrave University. Judging from the urgent hand gestures and the upset look on Larrien's lean face, something dramatic was afoot.

"Larrien," Wren said, approaching the group. "Enjoying the party?"

Larrien looked up in surprise, his features rearranging into a smile. He smoothed back his fine white hair. "Truth to tell, Wren, it's not up to your usual standards."

Wren looked around wistfully. "I know. I don't know what happened. I think I'll hold the next one in the Cogs, maybe combine it with a hunt. What's the problem?"

"No problem. Why would there be a problem?"

"Larrien, I've played cards against you. I know your stonewalling face. Now, are you going to tell me what's going on, or do I have to find out myself?"

Larrien sighed. "Actually, I could use your help on this one. It appears that a murder has been committed back at the university."

Wren frowned. "A murder? What were they fighting over? A book or something?"

"I have no idea. I've just been told about it myself."

Wren clapped his hands together. "Let's be off, then. Let's see if we can catch ourselves a killer!"

Wren strode briskly down the dark, wood-paneled corridors of the university, Larrien stumbling to keep up with his longer strides. When he saw this, Wren slowed down a fraction.

"What information do we have?" asked Wren.

"Not much. The person who stumbled onto the murder has kept everyone out of the rooms."

"Smart. Who was that?"

"An acquaintance of yours, actually."

"Really?"

"Yes." Larrien's tone took on a slightly accusing note. "Wren, I've asked you before to clear it with me when you need access to the libraries. I won't turn you down."

Wren stopped walking. Larrien forged ahead before realizing he was on his own. He turned back.

"Are you saying Torin discovered the body?" asked Wren.

"Not just discovered the body. He interrupted the murderer."

"Excellent."

Wren started walking again. He rounded a corner and found his dwarf partner lounging against a closed door while four members of the ordained clergy from the Hall of Aureon tried to get him to move. Torin grinned when he saw Wren.

"You know, I was cursing your name all night, making me do research while you were off partying."

Wren waved his hand dismissively. "You didn't miss anything, believe me. The party was a flop."

"That's because I wasn't there."

"No. Because you weren't there, we still had some drink left over and there were no fights." He shooed the clergy away. "Don't you have some praying to do? Go on, move, move."

The clerics spluttered and glared at Wren, but Larrien just sighed and nodded at them to leave.

"What happened to your face?" asked Wren, indicating the

bruise that had spread over Torin's right eye.

"Bastard got a blow in while I was trying to get my knife."

"Makes you look prettier."

"Very funny," said Torin.

"Right. Are you going to move or should we stand out here all night?"

Torin pushed himself up from his lounging position and stepped to the side. "After you, O Great One."

Wren opened the door. "Everyone else stay outside till I've had a look around." Without waiting for a response, he stepped into the room and closed the door behind him.

Wren closed his eyes and breathed in the silence, opening his mind and letting his senses probe. He felt—

Panic. It suffused the air in the room, impregnating the atmosphere with a heavy feeling that settled in the pit of his stomach.

Anger.

Fear.

Pain. So much pain.

Of course, these feelings would hover around any murder scene, but for Wren, they were something more. Torin had once asked if it was a magical talent, but it wasn't. It was pure instinct.

Wren opened his eyes, staring at the exact spot on the carpet where the murdered professor lay. He took in the room, noting the pillows on the floor by the unlit fire. He crouched down and saw the faint shimmer of powdered glass. He looked under the couch close to the door and saw broken shards scattered around. He swept them together gingerly. Crystal. Enough for two glasses.

He walked along the wall, trailing his fingers over the expensive wallpaper. A couch was lying on its side. He looked to the carpet where the indentations of the legs made small holes, then at the deep marks on the walls. Whoever had thrown it was very strong.

Wren avoided looking at the body for the moment and stepped into the washroom. Nothing much in there. He checked the sink and noted bristles stuck to the basin. Someone had shaved recently, someone who, judging by the length of the whiskers, shaved only about once a week. He sniffed, and could smell expensive cologne.

The bedroom was much more interesting. He saw the huge hole in the wall first, where someone had obviously been slammed. A small puddle of blood lay on the floor. Judging by the drip pattern, it was from a hit to the nose, not a knife thrust or slash.

He smelled the pillows and caught a whiff of perfume. He smiled. His suspicions were correct. The professor had been entertaining a lady. Had she seen the attack, then?

He looked under the bed, but all he found was a bottle of wine that must have rolled there during the struggle. Nothing else indicated the presence of a woman in the rooms.

He headed into the lounge. This time, he stopped to study the body. He noted the severed arm and the broken fingers. Interesting. That seemed to indicate someone was trying to get information out of him. Information valuable enough to . . . well, to rip someone apart.

Wren shook his head. The violence of the attack was quite astounding. And the strength needed . . .

"Torin!" he shouted.

The door opened and the dwarf and Larrien appeared. They were joined by someone else, a female dwarf. A cleric acolyte, judging by her robes.

"Who are you?" he demanded.

The dwarf froze, eyes darting between the body on the floor, Wren staring indignantly at her, and Larrien, hoping for some kind of reassurance.

"This is Kayla," said Larrien. "She's my assistant."

"Oh." Wren turned to Torin. "What did the man look like who attacked you? Describe him."

"Big," said Torin. "Over six feet. All muscle. Hair shaved to his scalp. A tattoo of a dragon up his arms and around his neck."

"Strong enough to do all this?"

"Definitely."

"Hmm." Wren took one last glance at the body, then moved to the other side of the lounge and knocked on the walls. "Torin, check that desk over there and see if he kept any kind of diary."

Torin headed to the rolltop desk opposite the door and started rifling through the papers. Wren carried on knocking, getting the same muted thud every time he did so. He reached the section next to where Torin was standing. The rap on the wall became hollow.

"Here we go," he said in satisfaction. He ran his fingers along the wallpaper and down to the floor. It took him some time to find the catch. A tiny switch was set into the floorboards. He pressed it, and a door jutted out with a quiet click.

Wren hooked his finger around the door and stepped inside. It was a tiny room, no bigger than a broom closet. He pulled the door closed, all but a small crack. He peered out through the gap. He was looking directly at the body of the professor.

Wren closed his eyes and inhaled. He smelled the same perfume that was on the pillows. So . . . what had happened? The professor knew his attacker was coming and hid his lady friend in here? Who was she? He needed to know.

He glanced down and saw something glint in the small band

of light that entered through the crack. He bent down and picked up the object.

"Wren," said Torin. The door opened, bathing Wren in light. Torin stood holding a small, leather bound journal.

"What?" Wren stepped into the lounge, closing the door behind him.

"His appointment book. He has an entry written in for today. It just says 'Red.' "

"Interesting. Page back. I think you'll find the appointment repeated?"

Torin thumbed back through the book. "You're right. Every week, actually. For the past three months."

"Hmm." He walked over to Larrien, who hovered by the door, trying not to look at the body. Wren held up the item he had found on the floor. It was a silver necklace, cheaply made. Hanging from the chain was a crystal dragon. "Do you know what this is?"

Larrien squinted at it. "Hold on," he said, and fished a pair of gold-rimmed spectacles from his pocket. He perched them on his nose. "That's better." He took the chain from Wren. "It's a necklace," he said.

"Yes, it is. Well done, Larrien. You should be an inquisitive. Do you know what kind of necklace?"

"I've no idea. It's not really my area of expertise."

"This dragon isn't just any old reptile. It's the Boromar dragon."

He stared expectantly at Larrien.

"Yes?" said the head of the university.

Wren sighed. "These necklaces are given to courtesans in the employ of Boromar. The girls usually sell them, though they don't make much. Was it common practice for professors to have, shall we say, *visitors* to their rooms?"

"No, it was not!"

Wren raised an eyebrow. "Come now, Larrien. Don't lie to me. I'll be very hurt if you do."

"Fine," Larrien snapped. "Yes, it is fairly common for professors to have courtesans visit their rooms."

Wren turned to Torin. "Randy old buggers, eh?"

"You should know. You're about the same age."

"How dare you! Take that back."

"No."

"I demand—"

"Wren," Larrien interrupted.

"What? Oh, of course. Sorry." He pointed at Torin. "We'll talk about this later."

"No, we won't."

"Wren," said Larrien. "What are your theories?"

Wren shot Torin a dark look, then turned his attention back to Larrien. "I never discuss theories while working on a case."

Larrien all but collapsed with relief. "So you'll look into it? Oh, thank Aureon. Does this mean I don't have to involve the Watch?"

"Larrien, you have an all but dismembered body lying in the university. Of course you'll have to call in the Watch."

"But it's all so *sordid*. Do they have to know the details?"

Wren shrugged. "Tell them what you want. Let them do their own investigation. If they can be bothered, that is. Oh, and tell them to call in a cleric. He might be able to communicate with the body and find out some information." He snapped his fingers. "Torin, come."

"Don't speak to me like I'm a dog."

"Apologies. How would you like me to speak to you?"

"Like I'm a person."

"Oh."

Wren grabbed the door and ran into the clerics he had earlier shooed away. He waved his arms in irritation as he pushed his way through them. "Get away from me. Move, move! You're like flies!"

He heard Torin's voice behind him. "And you know what flies are attracted to, don't you?"

Chapter Four

The second day of Long Shadows

Far, the 27th day of Vult, 998

Wren had traveled a lot over the years. He'd spent time in nearly all the Five Nations for one reason or another, usually accompanied by Torin. During that time, he'd come to the conclusion that you could judge the quality of a city by the liveliness of its night life.

And Sharn's night life was the best he had ever found.

He smiled as he walked through the Firelight District of Lower Menthis, nodding genially at faces he recognized, looking around with interest at new inns or taverns that had opened since his last visit. A fortune teller's shop had replaced old Fintal's place. He used to sell the best spiced hot potatoes. And he was open all day and all night. Wren had often wondered how he did it. He'd eventually asked the old dwarf and it turned out he had a twin brother and they worked shifts. Wren had been slightly disappointed at that.

Artificers and illusionists had bent and tweaked magical light into signs of a hundred different shapes and sizes, all of them inviting the lucky customer inside for one form of entertainment or another. It had become something of a competition to those in the trade, to see who could devise the brightest, most outlandish and eye-catching display. Wren had even heard they gave out awards these days.

The familiar noises of the streets washed over him in waves. Not gentle waves, but storm-tossed, violent waves, beautiful yet dangerous, alluring yet life-threatening. It was the cacophony of all things at once: the hoarse cry of stall merchants, the seductive calls of courtesans, the cries of fear or pain as someone became a nightly statistic. It was all here. Every aspect of city life in all its brutality and beauty.

Wren loved it.

"Stop grinning like an idiot," said Torin.

"Come now, Torin. It's a beautiful night. The stars are shining—"

"How would you know? You can't see the stars from here."

"It's stopped raining, at least."

"It'll start up again soon. And anyway, it's misty."

"Torin! Always the pessimist! Look how the mist reflects the lights! Nature and craft, joining together, creating something that couldn't exist one without the other."

Torin shook his head in disgust. "You're so full of it, you know that?"

"Of course I do. And therein lies my charm."

A loud roar erupted from somewhere up ahead, and then three goblins smashed through a glass window and skidded across the road. A second later, a huge minotaur stepped through the opening. It stomped across the street to where the first of the goblins was trying to rise. It pushed the smaller creature back to the ground, then lifted its huge foot and brought it down on the goblin's head with a savage bellow of anger. The minotaur did the same to the other goblins, staring down at them with satisfaction before turning and walking into the mist.

"We shouldn't be down here, anyway," said Torin nervously. "The nights of Long Shadows aren't for normal people."

"Rubbish. It's just a festival like any other."

"Yes, but it's a festival where minotaurs and bugbears creep out of their holes and do nasty things to people like us."

Wren indicated the dead goblins. "How do you know that was anything to do with the Shadow? The goblins could have cheated the minotaur at cards. Or tried to steal from him. This is Lower Menthis, Torin. You don't need a religious festival for the crazies to come out of the woodwork."

"Exactly! Which begs the question—what are we doing here?"

"Visiting a friend," said Wren. "One who may be able to help us." He glanced down at Torin. "What do you think of all this, anyway?"

"Not sure yet," said Torin thoughtfully. "Not enough information. The killer wanted something from the professor. That's a given, judging by his broken fingers."

"You noticed that, did you?"

"Of course I did. This girl you mentioned. Either she was in on it, or she witnessed it. Either way, I think she's the key."

"My thoughts exactly."

They reached the end of the road and turned into a closed-off street. At its end was a huge building with an understated sign glowing above the double doorway. The sign spelled out the owner's name as well as the name of the establishment.

"Savia's?" said Torin. "What are we doing here?"

"I told you—she's a friend who may be able to help."

A hulking bugbear stood by the doors. He stared at them, then evidently decided they posed no threat and opened the door for them. Wren and Torin stepped into a small greeting area, a quiet room with tasteful paintings on the walls and ornately carved furniture situated around small glass tabletops that floated in the air. Violin music wafted from somewhere. Wren made a mental note to ask Savia how she accomplished this. He would love to have music playing throughout his apartments. What a wonderful idea.

A young woman in a low-cut white dress with blue leaves embroidered around the hems approached the two of them, a charming smile playing about her exotic features. Her skin was dark, her hair black as a raven's wings. Wren bowed extravagantly.

"My lady," he said.

"My lord," she replied. She smiled down at Torin. The dwarf blushed furiously. "And what can we at Savia's do for you tonight? Are you interested in gambling? Companionship? A meal, perhaps? We have a new chef from Aundair who is rapidly gaining a name for himself among our more discerning clients."

"Companionship, I think," said Wren.

The woman smiled. "Of course. Male? Female? Elf, dwarf, changeling? Anything you desire we can provide."

"What an extraordinary claim," mused Wren. "Anything, you say?"

"We pride ourselves on it."

"I don't recognize you, my dear. Are you new here?"

"I've been here for two months."

"Host, has it been that long since I visited? How lax of me. Savia will never forgive me."

"Are you an acquaintance of Savia's?"

"I am indeed. We're old friends. Is she available? I'd like to talk to her, if that can be arranged."

The young lady's face took on a sorrowful look. "I'm afraid Savia has retired for the night."

"How disappointing. Is there no way I can convince you to rouse her?"

"I'm afraid not."

"Ah, well. On second thought, I think I'll join the gambling tables. But my friend here—I think perhaps Lia?"

The young woman glanced at Torin, her lips twitching into a small smile. "Of course. If you'd care to take refreshments at the bar, I'll just see if she's available." She smiled again, showing bright white teeth amidst the dusky skin, and turned from them with a swish of her filmy skirt.

"What a remarkable woman," said Wren. "Simply stunning. Wouldn't you say?"

"What are you up to?" asked Torin, ignoring his question.

"Nothing. I just thought you looked tense."

"I am tense. It comes from working with you."

Wren smiled and led them through the door into an open room with tables and chairs for dining and a huge bar that took up two full walls. It was quiet within, but Wren could hear voices and music coming from a doorway to their right. That was where the gambling tables were situated. Many were the times that Wren, unable to sleep, had paid a visit to Savia's and greeted the dawn with fellow players.

Wren turned to Torin. "I'll be in there, waiting for your signal."

Torin frowned. "What signal?"

Wren ignored him and smiled as a willowy elf walked toward them.

"Wren! How are you?"

"Lia! I'm ecstatic now that I've seen you."

"You say that every time you come here."

"And it's always true."

Lia gave Wren a kiss on the cheek. "What brings you here on such a miserable night?"

"I need a favor."

"Sounds intriguing." She glanced at Torin. "Who's your embarrassed friend?"

"This is Torin. A more redoubtable character you will never meet. I want you to be nice to him."

Torin's eyebrows shot up in alarm. "Wren?"

Lia took Torin by the arm. "I'm always nice to my clients."

Torin glared at Wren. "This is why my wife doesn't like you, Wren. You know that, don't you?"

"Of course she likes me. I keep you out of her hair. Now, here's what I want you to do."

* * *

Wren tossed his cards onto the table and tapped his fingers impatiently. How long had they been up there? Over half an hour, surely. Torin wouldn't be—

No, not Torin. He was fanatically faithful to his wife. He wouldn't even consider such a thing. Wren was in awe of people who could make that kind of commitment. To promise yourself to one person for the rest of your life . . .

He couldn't get his head around it. It was like trying to comprehend the number of stars in the sky, or count the grains of sand on a beach. His brain wasn't built for the task.

The dealer swept his cards away and flicked seven more onto the table. This time, she placed the first and fourth cards face up. Interesting. She had been watching Wren's tactics and had adjusted her own mode of play. This could be quite an interesting game.

A high-pitched scream from the rooms above whipped

everybody's eyes upward. Wren watched the players, noting those who took advantage of the distraction to check out their opponents' cards. He yawned and stood up, nodding at the shocked dealer.

"Excuse me."

He left the gambling room and turned to the right. A wide staircase led up to the bedrooms. Another scream echoed through the brothel. A half-dressed man stumbled past Wren, looking over his shoulder in fear. Wren winced. Savia wasn't going to be happy with this. She'd want compensation.

A small crowd had gathered outside one of the bedrooms. The bugbear from the front door was gripping the handle, getting ready to break down the door.

"Wait!" shouted Wren. He hurried over to the room. Courtesans looked at him, fear clear on their faces. Wren felt a twinge of guilt. This was one of the things courtesans feared the most—psychotic customers.

"Wait," he repeated. "Is that Lia's room?"

The bugbear frowned at him. At least Wren thought he was frowning at him. It was hard to tell.

"It is," said one of the girls.

"Then I know who is in there with her. An ugly little dwarf. I saw him come up here. He was *drooling* and muttering to himself."

"I heard that!" shouted a voice from inside the room. "Don't make me angry! I don't want to hurt her, but I will if I have to!"

Wren shouldered his way past the bugbear. "What do you want?" he asked. "Just tell us. We can work something out."

"I want to talk to Savia. Right now."

Wren turned to the closest girl. "You heard him! Fetch Savia. Hurry!"

"But she's sleeping—"

"Are you mad? You have an insane dwarf rapist in there! I think she'd want to know about it."

The girl let out a squeal of fear and ran up the flight of stairs to the next floor. Wren leaned on the door and looked up at the bugbear. The creature looked upset. Probably because his brain was having to do a bit of work.

"Don't worry about it," Wren told him. "Once Savia's here, you can beat him around a bit."

This seemed to cheer the creature a bit. Wren turned his attention to the girls clustered around in various states of undress. "Better be careful, ladies. This kind of weather, you'll catch a chill."

A few moments later, the courtesan appeared at the top of the stairs, followed closely by Savia. Wren watched her appreciatively as she descended the stairs. The woman was tall, her dark hair showing flecks of gray that somehow enhanced her looks. Wren usually liked his women younger than Savia, but there was something about her. She had an air of confidence about her, an aura of intelligence. Not to mention an *incredibly* fine body.

Savia hurried past the girl, pulling a robe around herself. She reached the bottom of the stairs and caught sight of Wren. Her eyes narrowed. Wren could see numerous emotions flashing across her face. First relief, then anger, then a touch of amusement, and finally calculation as she tried to figure out what Wren was up to.

She walked up to them. "You can go, Baras," she said to the bugbear, touching him lightly on the arm.

"I promised him he could beat up Torin a bit."

"Did you now?"

"Just a little bit."

"False alarm," Savia said to the girls. When they looked

doubtful, she raised an eyebrow at Wren. "If you'd be so kind?"

Wren knocked on the door. "You can come out now."

The door swung open to reveal a contrite Torin. Lia sat on the bed behind him, filing her nails. She looked up and smiled.

"I'll deal with you later," said Savia. "I hope you made it worth her while, Wren."

"Of course!" said Wren, offended.

"Good. You can go now, Lia. That goes for all of you. Get back to your rooms."

She waited until the corridor was empty before turning her attention back to Wren. "I suppose you'd better come up to my chambers and tell me what this is all about."

* * *

Despite his best efforts, Wren had never been inside Savia's rooms. For some reason, the woman consistently managed to resist his charms. He looked around the gently-lit sitting area. She definitely had good taste, so she should be drawn to Wren like a Khyber worshiper to a hole in the ground.

Torin stood uncomfortably by the doorway while Wren breezed around the room, picking up small carvings and examining them, bending down to study the porcelain inlay on a small black table. It looked dwarven to him. He came to a stop before a series of stone sculptures depicting a warrior in various poses of prayer. He reached out to touch them, then drew his hand back.

"Are these real?" he asked, seeking out Savia.

"They are."

Wren turned his attention to the carvings. They were Valenar in make. The statues represented the seven deep prayers the elves recited to their ancestors before going into battle. But the statues must have been over five hundred years old. No new ones had been made since the Valenar left Aerenal. They were passed down through the generations and treated with the utmost reverence.

"How did you come by them?" he asked.

"They were a gift. For a favor."

"A *gift!* Host, woman! What did you do for them?"

"None of your business. Now, tell me what's going on."

Wren's gaze lingered on the statues, then he tore himself away and joined Savia on a small couch. On the table in front of them were papers and files, some marked important. Wren realized they must involve the city council.

Savia saw him looking and gathered the papers together. "Focus, Wren. Come now."

"Sorry."

He went on to tell her of the night's events, ending with a description of the assailant and the name they had found in the professor's diary.

"How bizarre," said Savia.

"Does the description strike you as familiar?"

"Well, yes. But that's what I find so strange. The description perfectly matches a man called Cutter. He works for the Boromar clan watching over some of their girls. The establishment isn't far from here, actually. It's called the Tufted Feather. And 'Red' . . . I can only assume that to be Rowen. She's a courtesan, but she and Cutter are an item. The girls think it all terribly romantic."

"Interesting," mused Wren. "Torin, what am I thinking?"

Torin had stepped forward from his place by the door when Savia started talking. He cleared his throat. "You're thinking this Cutter couldn't handle his girl sleeping with other men. That he killed this professor in a jealous rage."

Wren winked at Savia. "Taught him everything he knows," he said. "What do you think? Does it sound feasible?"

Savia shrugged. "I couldn't tell you. I don't know this Cutter fellow. I've only seen him in passing."

Wren stood up. "Come, Torin. I know you wanted to get home to that lively wife of yours, but duty calls." He took Savia's hand and kissed it. "Always a pleasure. Call me if you ever change your mind about dinner. The invitation is always open."

Torin was waiting for him by the door. They exited the rooms and headed into the corridor.

"Does your wife really not like me?" asked Wren.

"Hates you. Do you find that hard to believe?"

"Frankly . . . yes. I think you're lying just to upset me."

Torin sighed. "Believe what you want, Wren. Let's just get this over with."

Chapter Five

The second day of Long Shadows

Far, the 27th day of Vult, 998

Cutter dumped the skycoach a few districts away and returned to the Tufted Feather on foot. He was aching all over from the fight with the warforged, and he was sure the last two fingers on his right hand were broken, or at the very least, dislocated. He couldn't even remember how that had happened.

He slipped through the front door and headed straight for the stairs. The rain had washed much of the blood from him, but he still looked a mess. Luckily, no one paid him any attention.

He checked Rowen's room to make sure she hadn't returned. It looked the same as he had left it. He stood at the foot of her bed and tried to think it through.

She was still out there somewhere. But where? It made sense that she would return here to Cutter. He could protect her.

Unless she thought she was being followed or she feared the warforged would be waiting for her.

So where else could she be? She had no family. Her only brother had been killed last year in a tavern brawl. She had no home. All her friends lived around the district.

Unless she was already—

No. He couldn't think that way. The warforged had asked Cutter where she was, so she must have escaped the professor's rooms. All he had to do was find her and they could sort this whole thing out. In the meantime, he needed to figure out what had happened in the professor's rooms. And Salkith was the key. Cutter needed to track down the courier to find out the part he played in the night's events.

He returned to his room and changed his clothes, slipping on a leather vest beneath a clean shirt. It didn't offer much protection, but it was better than nothing, and he preferred its flexibility to any kind of mail shirt. He located his short-hafted war hammer and attached its loop of leather to his belt. It weighed him down. He preferred the Khutai blades, but the heavy hammer would be more useful against the warforged. One side of it was spiked, and he reckoned he'd do more damage with it than the Valenar knives. Cutter took a small money pouch from the drawer and weighed it in his hands. Tiel hadn't paid him for the last month's work, so he had been dipping into his meager savings. Not much left.

Tiel. He'd be wondering where Cutter was with his money. Regardless, Cutter couldn't spare the time to seek him out and tell him what had happened. He'd have to leave it for the moment. There were more important things to think about.

A knock came at the door, soft and hesitant.

Cutter froze, then looked around his room to make sure he had everything he needed. He unhooked the hammer and crept across the wooden boards to the door. He took a deep breath, then yanked it open.

A woman was standing there. She stifled a scream and stepped backward, staring at Cutter with wide eyes. It was

Renaia, a courtesan from a brothel over in the Firelight District. He lowered the hammer and stepped backward, opening his mouth to apologize.

At the same moment, the window behind him exploded inward, showering the room and Cutter's back with shards of glass.

Cutter spun, slamming the door shut as he did so, and saw the warforged landing on the floor at the foot of his bed. Cutter swung the hammer in an overhand arc. It slammed into the warforged with a dull clang, driving it to its knees. The warforged lashed out with an arm, punching Cutter hard in the stomach. His leather vest absorbed some of the blow, but it still sent him staggering back into the wall, gasping for breath.

The warforged straightened and surveyed the room. It must have followed Cutter, hoping to find Rowen.

Cutter flipped the hammer around and pushed himself away from the wall. The warforged was ignoring him for the moment while it searched for Rowen. Big mistake.

Cutter swung the hammer as hard as he could and felt the spike punch through the metal plating on the warforged's back. The 'forged arched its back with an animal-like cry of agony and jabbed its elbow into Cutter's cheek. His head jerked back. Cutter felt a bloom of red-tinged pain as the skin split and blood flowed.

Cutter staggered backward, blinking to clear the flashes before his eyes. The warforged reached over its shoulder and pulled the hammer free. Blinking, Cutter managed to focus just in time to see the hammer flying end over end toward him. He dropped, and it smashed into the wall, punching a deep hole in the plaster.

The warforged sniffed the air, but when it decided Rowen wasn't hiding anywhere, it turned its attention to Cutter. It held its arms out at its sides. Cutter heard the scrape of metal on metal as two blades slid from the backs of its hands.

"You don't know where she is."

"I . . ." Cutter pushed himself to his feet and grabbed the hammer. "I already told you that."

"Then you are of no use to me."

The warforged advanced on him. Cutter took one look at the blades and grabbed the hammer, thrusting it into his belt. He couldn't be any help to Rowen dead.

So he jumped out the window.

It was a pretty stupid thing to do considering his room was on the top floor of the building, but he didn't have any other choice.

Cutter turned just before he dropped from the window and grabbed hold of the window ledge. He shinnied across and pulled himself up at the next window. The eaves of the roof were about five feet above him. He jumped and caught hold, but the gutter came away in his hand and almost sent him tumbling to the ground. He steadied himself and tried again, this time catching hold of the wooden supports beneath the roof tiles. He looked back and saw the warforged leaning out the window. The construct grabbed hold of the window frame and climbed out.

Cutter cursed the creation of all warforged and pulled himself up onto the roof. He ran carefully along the center peak and leaped across the gap onto the next building.

The three neighboring buildings were all part of the same structure, giving him space to build up speed. But he was rapidly running out of roof. The street on which the Feather was built was nestled between huge towers that soared up on either side. On the lower levels of Sharn, any kind of empty space between tower bases was a much sought after prize.

Cutter glanced over his shoulder and saw the black metal of

the warforged glinting in the light of the surrounding city. That glow was always there, a permanent facet of city life gleaming from windows and everbright lanterns and passing skycoaches. Cutter was thankful for it as he reached the end of the roof, because it enabled him to search for a means of escape.

Not that one presented itself. A wide street opened up below him. The building on the opposite side was over twenty feet away. No way was he making that jump. Cutter cursed himself for not listening to Rowen and buying himself a feather fall charm. She was always saying he would need one.

Cutter pulled out the hammer and turned to face the warforged. It had slowed to a walk and was now only a few arm-lengths in front of Cutter.

"Why are you doing this?" asked Cutter. "What do you want with Rowen?"

"She took something that didn't belong to her," said the warforged.

"I'll find her. She'll give it back."

"It is too late for that." The warforged crossed its arms across its chest, the blades forming a **V** under its chin.

Cutter looked over his shoulder. A skycoach was approaching. Keep him talking, Cutter thought. Maybe there was still a way out of this.

"Who are you?"

"Who am I?" The warforged was silent for a moment, and when it spoke again it was in a soft whisper that caused the hair on the back of Cutter's neck to rise. "I am the unnamed. I am the fear of darkness. I am the night stalker, the killer of children. I am the will of the Shadow, and I do his bidding."

Cutter swallowed. *The Shadow?*

"Enough of this. It is time for you to embrace darkness."

"Embrace your own darkness."

Cutter swung his arm with all his might, the hammer coming around in a wide arc. He released the haft, keeping hold of the leather loop. The iron smashed into the warforged's face, sending it staggering to the side. Without waiting to see what damage he had caused, Cutter turned and leaped into the air, praying that he'd timed this right.

He hadn't. The skycoach was already drifting past. He stretched out with his free hand and managed to grab hold of the stern as he plummeted through the air. His arm jerked in its socket and the coach lurched downward. He gritted his teeth against the pain, then threw his hammer over the side and grabbed hold of the hull with his other hand. He pulled himself up and flopped over the side, landing on his back. Cutter heard the driver shouting something from up front, but couldn't hear what he was saying. Nothing complimentary, that was sure.

He pushed himself up against the side of the coach and stared at two young men who were regarding him from their padded seats with looks of irritation.

"Did you see that?"

"I did. No consideration. None at all. He made me spill my wine. You." One of the men prodded Cutter with his foot–a foot shod in a silk slipper. "How dare you jump into our coach like that. Have you no manners?"

"Of course he doesn't. Look at him. He's a brute."

"Mmm. Quite tasty though, don't you think?"

"I suppose . . . in a *vulgar* kind of way. If that's your thing."

"Oh, definitely. *If* that's your thing."

Cutter sat up. "One more word from either of you and you're over the side."

"What's going on back there?" shouted the driver, trying to see over his shoulder and control the coach at the same time.

Cutter ignored him and got to his knees, looking back at the rooftop.

The warforged was dropping through the air straight for him.

Cutter cursed and rolled backward. He pushed the driver aside and grabbed hold of the controls. He yanked them to his chest, pulling the coach into a steep climb.

He almost made it. The warforged slammed into the side of the coach as it climbed upward. The vehicle shuddered, but Cutter managed to hold it steady. He turned and searched frantically for his hammer. It lay at the feet of the two men. Cutter dived for it, but as soon as he released the controls, the warforged's weight tilted the coach to the side. He rolled with the movement, banging his head against a seat. He saw the driver tumble over the edge of the coach. Cutter hoped he had a feather fall charm on him. His hammer slid along the deck toward his face. His hand shot out to stop it from breaking his nose, and he grabbed hold of the seat to help him to his feet. The warforged was trying to pull itself into the coach, but it had no leverage now that it was listing so far to the side.

The hammer slid along the deck toward Cutter's face. His hand shot out to stop it from breaking his nose, and he grabbed hold of the seat to pull himself to his feet. The warforged was trying to pull itself into the coach, but it had no leverage with the vehicle listing so far to the side.

Cutter looked frantically for a means of escape. An idea came to him, in the form of the huge tower looming large before him. He took the controls and directed the coach upward, trying to keep it at the same angle so the warforged couldn't climb in.

Open balconies revealed rooms and shops in the side of the tower, but that wasn't what he was looking for.

As he rose into the mist, he saw it—a bridge that entered a

wide opening in the tower and tunneled inside.

"You!" he called one of the men. "Yes you, you idiot. If you don't want to die, listen to me carefully. When I jump, grab hold of these controls and hold them tight. Understand?"

"What?" The man looked terrified. "What is that warforged doing?"

Cutter saw glowing white eyes rise over the edge of the coach. Khyber, he swore silently. He had no choice. Now or never.

"Grab the controls!" he shouted. Cutter jumped, kicking the levers forward so the coach dropped nose first into a dive.

The warforged reached out to grab hold of him but was too late. Cutter hit a balcony railing chest first, the breath exploding from his lungs. He couldn't breathe, let alone hold on. His fingers slipped and he fell backward from the railing.

He closed his eyes, waiting for the back-breaking impact, but it didn't come. He forced his eyes open, looking to the side. Nothing was moving. He looked the other way and saw a man with a wand pointed at him. He lowered it and Cutter floated gently to the ground.

Cutter staggered to his feet, looking for signs of the warforged. It was nowhere to be seen. Cutter opened his mouth to thank his rescuer, but only a pained gasp came out. He gave up and simply waved a hand, hurrying along the bridge into the tower.

"Hey!" the man called. "You need to report this to the Watch! I want my reward!"

Cutter ignored him and melted into the safety of the crowds, following the flow of traffic, not knowing or caring where it led him. Just as long as there were people around.

Chapter Six

The second day of Long Shadows

Far, the 27th day of Vult, 998

"Where did she say it was? I wasn't paying attention."

"I noticed. You were too busy watching Savia's backside."

"How dare you! I'll have you know that I value and appreciate Savia as a person."

"Yes. That must have been why you were trying to see inside her dressing gown every time she bent forward."

"You saw that, did you? Can you blame me? She's a fine looking woman. I mean, I know you're married and a loyal husband, blah-blah-blah, but surely that doesn't stop you looking. You can still appreciate the form of a beautiful woman. That doesn't make you unfaithful, does it?"

"Not as such, no."

"Unless you prefer your females to be the same race as yourself? Although I'll admit I never thought that of you."

Torin sighed. "No, Wren. I find females of all races attractive."

Wren continued as if Torin hadn't said anything. "I myself find your wife *incredibly* attractive, and but for the fact that I respect you as a friend, I'd be all over her like a dog in—"

"Here we are!" said Torin loudly, cutting Wren off.

Wren smiled. It was too easy. Really. He looked up at the building across the street. Whereas Savia's was tasteful and discreet, the Tufted Feather declared itself and its intentions with all the enthusiasm of a forty-year-old stripper being ogled by men half her age. Red everbright lanterns adorned the wall above the door in a rather tasteless shape. And in case one was still in doubt as to the kind of business carried out there, a young, half-naked elf was dancing in the window.

"She looks bored," Wren commented.

"Wouldn't you be? Being paid to perform for drunken men?

"Torin, I never knew you felt so strongly. Is it personal? Has one of your family been forced to turn their hand to—how shall I put it? Earning their money from home?"

"Don't be absurd. I simply feel it's degrading and humiliating."

"And what would you have them do?" said Wren. "Beg on the street corners? Die of starvation?"

"Well, no, but—"

Wren pointed upward. "Want to bet that broken window up there belongs to our man?"

Torin looked up at the window. "Why do you say that?"

Wren shrugged. "Just a feeling. People tend not to leave their windows broken for long. Come."

Wren jogged across the street and entered the building. A dwarf stood behind the bar but had his back to them as he poured drinks. Wren moved straight through the common room and up the stairs beyond, Torin trailing close behind.

Wren heard the sounds of fighting as soon as he reached the first landing. They came from one of the floors above. He grabbed a densewood wand from his belt and sprinted the rest of the way to the top floor, but the sounds stopped by the time he arrived.

A woman stood in the corridor, her ear pressed to a door. As soon as she saw Wren, she quickly bent down and picked up something from the floor.

Wren approached cautiously. "What's going on?" he asked the girl.

"I . . . I don't know. I came to see Cutter, but there was a crash—I think the window broke—and he slammed the door in my face. It sounds like fighting."

"Doesn't it just?" Wren turned to Torin. "You owe me for the window."

"We didn't bet!"

"Come, come, Torin. Nobody likes a stingy dwarf. It panders to stereotypes."

Wren held his wand before him and pushed open the door. Silence greeted him. A muggy draft blew through the broken window. Wren stepped inside and glanced around. He replaced his wand. Cutter was gone.

"You can come in now, Torin. The danger has passed."

Wren heard the dwarf swearing under his breath and smiled again. He checked the drawers and the cupboard, but found nothing of interest. The man obviously lived light. There were signs of a scuffle, but no damage besides a hole in the wall. Who was he fighting? And where did they go?

Wren leaned out the broken window, careful not to cut himself on the shards of glass. He turned and looked upward. The roof was close. Cutter could have made his escape that way. Well, he certainly wasn't going to run around on rooftops in the middle of the night. Cutter would be long gone by now, anyway.

Wren ducked back inside. Torin was seated on the bed, and the woman hovered uncertainly in the doorway, eager to be away.

"You can go now, my dear," said Wren.

"Oh. Fine." She turned to leave.

"Just one thing before you leave." The woman paused. "What's in the envelope?"

"Which envelope?"

"The one you picked up from the floor when we arrived."

The woman shook her head. "I don't know what you're talking about."

"Come, come, my dear. Let's not play around. Rowen is in danger, and the more you delay the worse it could be for her."

She looked surprised. "You know Rowen?"

"And Cutter, yes. We're trying to help them. They've angered some very powerful people tonight, and we want to protect them. So why don't you hand over the envelope, and we'll see what the young lady has to say for herself."

The woman still looked doubtful. Wren sighed. Why was it never easy? "What's your name?"

"Renaia."

"Renaia. What a beautiful name." He saw Torin roll his eyes. "Renaia, we know Rowen was involved in something up at the university. Now, whatever it was has put her life in danger. Torin and I—I'm Wren, by the way—we can help her. You wouldn't want to be responsible for something bad happening to your friend, would you?"

Renaia stared at Wren for a long time, biting her lower lip. Wren thought she wasn't going to give it to them, that he'd have to take it by force, but she finally reached into her blouse and pulled out the envelope.

Wren took it from her and ripped it open. Inside was a folded piece of cheap paper. Written on it in a shaky hand was a short message. *Got dreamlily. Hidden at the family crypt. Will meet later.*

Wren handed the letter to Torin. So, the murder had been a

drug deal gone bad. Had Rowen killed the professor? No, that didn't feel right. What, then? Were she and Cutter both in the rooms? Rowen took the drugs, Cutter stayed behind to finish off the professor, deciding to get his revenge on the man who was sleeping with his woman? Possible. But then why the letter? Wouldn't they have made arrangements beforehand? Maybe things didn't go according to plan. Maybe—

Too many maybes. He needed to speak to the girl.

"Renaia, you're not going to like this, but I need you to take me to see Rowen."

"I can't! She made me promise."

"I know, but this is important. I'm sorry to have to say this, but if you don't lead me to her now, I'll take you to the Watch."

"What for? I haven't done anything!"

"You're obstructing my investigation. Renaia, we don't even *want* Rowen. We're after the bigger fish. Rowen's . . . Rowen's just someone who got caught in the middle. I promise you, it's for the best."

Renaia glared at Wren. "Don't have much of a choice, do I?"

"I'm afraid not."

They caught a skycoach to the Gates of Gold district in Lower Dura. The driver dropped them off outside the huge arch, refusing to enter the rundown neighborhood for fear of losing his coach. Wren asked him to wait for them, but the driver just laughed and the skycoach lifted into the air.

Renaia led them through the litter-strewn streets, seemingly at ease in the dilapidated district. Wren kept his wands close at hand, and he saw Torin gripping his sword hilt tightly.

"Is it far?" asked Wren.

"Just a couple of streets," said Renaia.

"Aren't you worried about walking around here at night?" asked Torin.

"No. It might look bad, but it's still a close neighborhood. Slums usually are, you know. We look after our own."

Renaia turned into a wide concourse where ramshackle, sprawling mansions lined the sides of the road. They were practically falling apart, but Wren could see that they had once been opulent.

At the end of the street was another wide boulevard that ran across their path. Instead of following it, Renaia took them straight across the road to a smaller street that led into darkness.

Wren stopped. He didn't like this. Too many places for an ambush here, and he was getting that uneasy feeling.

"Torin?"

"What?"

"Just go on ahead and check that our path's clear."

Torin snorted. "You're funny."

"Fine."

Wren closed his eyes and concentrated, muttering words under his breath. He heard Renaia let out a gasp, and he opened his eyes. A small, smokelike being stood before him, almost indistinguishable from the shadows surrounding them. Tendrils of darkness drifted from its body like long hair in water.

"Be calm, Renaia. It's only my homunculus. Off you go, then," he said to the creature.

It turned and walked into the darkness. Within three steps it was invisible. Wren closed his eyes and watched through the creature's senses. It walked down the street, searching all around for signs of ambush. But nothing stood out as unusual. Wren called it back.

"It seems to be clear," he said, turning to face Torin.

Four goblins stood behind them, waiting patiently to be noticed. They were typical of their kind, squat and ugly, their flat faces making Wren think that whatever god created them had pressed them up against a wall and pushed until all their features flattened out.

"Uh, Torin. Could you take three large steps forward and turn around please?"

Torin did as Wren asked. When he saw the goblins, he cursed and drew his sword. "Where did they come from?"

"I have no idea. And why are they just standing there?" He glanced over his shoulder. "Renaia, please keep well back. Unless you have a weapon?"

Renaia shook her head.

"Fine. Just keep out the way, if you please."

Wren turned from her and muttered some words beneath his breath.

"They don't usually attack like this," whispered Torin. "They usually have a leader or something."

That was worrying Wren. He finished activating the infusion he had cast into his belt and felt a rush of strength surge through his body. And not a moment too soon. The goblins glanced to their left, speaking to each other in their guttural tongue. Wren thought he heard the word *chib,* which he knew to mean "big boss" in their language. He took a wand from his belt and held it ready.

"Torin, you deal with the goblins. I'll deal with whatever else is coming."

Wren instantly regretted his words as an eight-foot-tall creature lumbered around the corner, swinging a mace that was the same size as Torin. A bugbear. Thick, bristly red hair covered its body, and it had lost both ears in some past encounter. It raised a salute with the mace.

Wren didn't hesitate. He pointed his wand and a ball of flame roared into the creature.

The bugbear lifted a shield that looked as if it might have once been someone's front door. The fireball exploded into the wood, blackening it and sending the bugbear staggering backward.

Well, that hadn't done much good. And Wren had only a few more charges in the wand. He knew he shouldn't have left the house without his full arsenal, but he hadn't expected to need any major defenses. He was supposed to be at a party, for Flame's sake!

He could hear Torin shouting at the goblins as he tore into them with his sword. The bugbear looked at its shield, then grinned at Wren, huge sharp teeth jutting crookedly in its mouth. How the creature managed to even speak without lacerating its face was a mystery.

Wren sighed. No other way around it. He would have to get his hands dirty.

He released a charge from his wand, this time aiming for the head of the bugbear. The creature brought up its massive arm to block the blow, but Wren had expected it to do that. As soon as the fireball left the wand, Wren sprinted after it, lowered his shoulder, and slammed into the creature. His enhanced strength knocked the bugbear off its feet with a grunt of surprise, sprawling it on its back. Wren leaped to his feet and fired off the last charge. The fireball hit the creature full in the face. The bugbear screamed as the hair shriveled from its head and its skin bubbled and blistered.

Wren put the wand back in his belt and unhooked one of a pair of specially designed crossbows. He'd constructed them himself and was quite proud of them. That wasn't to say they didn't have flaws. Reducing their size so they fit easily into a single hand put the small weapons under an immense amount of pressure. An unforeseen side effect of this was that once the safety was off, the crossbows had a habit of unleashing the bolt at the slightest bump. Not the most dependable of weapons.

But they were good when their wielder was backed up against a wall.

Wren gagged at the stench of cooked flesh and leveled the crossbow at the bugbear as it writhed on the ground.

"Wren! Behind!"

Wren dropped and turned, loosing the bolt straight into the face of the goblin running at him. The creature's head jerked back and its legs flipped into the air as the force of the blow stopped it in its tracks.

Wren reached into his coat for his second crossbow, but before he could get hold of it, something smacked into his shoulder and sent him spinning through the air. He slammed into a wall and fell to the ground in a crumpled heap, his shoulder numb and useless beneath him.

Struggling to sit up, Wren saw the bugbear on its feet again, flailing with its mace. The beast was blind, the fireball having shriveled its eyes in their sockets. It was striking out blindly. Wren had been clipped by a lucky hit.

Torin was down to the last two goblins, but the bugbear was headed for the sound of their fighting. Wren winced in pain and pushed himself to his feet. He pulled out the other crossbow and staggered over to the creature, pausing to time his attack. The mace flailed through the air in wide arcs, accompanied by screams and sobs of pain from the bugbear. Wren felt a twinge of sympathy for it.

Wren tried to dodge under the swing but the bugbear was moving too fast for him to get close. He stepped back and decided on another route. He waited for the bugbear to turn its back, then jumped up and grabbed it around its huge neck. The creature screamed in anger, but before it could do anything, Wren reached around and loosed the crossbow straight into its mangled eye socket.

The bugbear froze in place. Then it twitched slightly, dropped the mace and shield, and toppled over backward. Wren threw himself to the side before he was crushed beneath the weight. He landed on his injured shoulder and cried out in pain. He kept rolling and pushed himself to his feet just as the creature hit the ground with a clatter of rusted armor.

The noise distracted the last goblin long enough for Torin to swing his sword into its neck, cleaving the creature down to the chest bone. The goblin looked at the wound and opened its mouth as if to say something, but a bubble of black blood welled out and the creature collapsed at the dwarf's feet.

Silence followed, broken only by ragged gasps as they tried to regain their breath. Renaia emerged from the shadows and hurried over.

"Are you hurt?" she asked.

Wren glanced at Torin. "I'm fine. But the dwarf looks like he's taken a few cuts."

"Hah!" said Torin. "Speak for yourself. That arm doesn't look too healthy hanging there like that."

"A mere bruise. Two seconds at a Jorasco healer will do me fine." He winced and rolled his shoulder. It *was* just a bruise, albeit it a very deep and large bruise that would spread down his arm and over his back. He would have to visit a healer, or he'd be stiff for weeks.

"Renaia. Lead the way, if you please. And no more dark streets. I don't have any wands left. Oh, that reminds me." Wren walked over to the bugbear and bent over to examine the creature. He wanted to retrieve his bolt, but it had gone too deep into the skull. He wrinkled his face with distaste. He had no desire to cut it out.

He made do with the bolt from the goblin and reloaded his other crossbow with a spare from his belt. He had only five left. Host, after this he would never leave the house without a full belt of weapons.

They walked away from the scene of the fight. Wren glanced over at Torin. "You're limping! I win."

"What do you mean, you win? You can't move your arm!"

"Yes, but I can run. You can't. Which means I can leave you behind if we get outnumbered. Therefore, I win. Renaia, lead on!"

The house had once been a mansion for a wealthy family, but all that was left was a dilapidated ruin. The windows were boarded up and scrawled over with the sigils and runes of local gangs. The roof sagged dangerously and had a huge hole in the center, almost as if a massive rock had fallen onto it.

Anemic weeds and bristly grass covered the garden. Wren was surprised anything could grow there, cut off as it was from most of the healthy sunlight. The front door was completely missing. Wren stepped through first, his strong night vision giving him an advantage over Renaia.

"Where?" he said softly over his shoulder.

"Straight down the hall. Last room on the left."

Wren led the way down the corridor, stepping around gaping holes in the floor where the boards had been stripped for other uses. No doors concealed any of the rooms. The empty frames hung with broken hinges.

He reached the end of the hall and stepped into the room,

his hands held up to show he was unarmed. Rowen was probably skittish enough without wondering if he carried a weapon.

At first he didn't see her. The room was bare but for a few pieces of dirty sheets. One of the planks had been removed from the window, letting in a small amount of light.

She was seated on the floor, slumped into the corner. At first Wren thought she was looking directly at him, her large eyes wide and staring.

But then he saw the blood, and he realized there was no life left in those eyes. He looked away, bile rising in his throat, but his brain had already registered what he didn't want to see . . . the pool of dark blood surrounding her, the gaping hole in her stomach, the severed fingers, and the angry red line across white skin where her throat had been cut.

Renaia entered behind him. She saw Rowen and screamed, her voice rising hysterically. Wren turned to the door.

"Torin," he said softly. "Take her into the next room."

Torin glanced at the body, his face darkening with anger. He took Renaia by the hand and led her next door. Wren could hear her screams and Torin's soft voice as the dwarf tried to calm her.

Wren leaned forward, his forehead against the wall. He couldn't bring himself to look at the body again. It was one of the few things that got to him—seeing a woman violated like that. He hadn't encountered it often, and he was thankful for that, but when he did, he found it was something he simply couldn't face.

Torin returned to the room. "Are you well?" he asked.

Wren shifted his head to look at the dwarf. "No, Torin, I'm not. Could you . . . ?"

Torin nodded and went to examine the body. "Red hair," he said. "It's definitely her. Fingers cut off. I reckon she was tortured for information."

"The location of the dreamlily," said Wren.

"Possibly." Torin looked thoughtful for a moment. "A cleric could probably find out if she talked."

"She'd have to be a very strong woman not to," said Wren. "But it's a good point. Anything else?"

"Not that I can see. There's a lot of blood. She must have held out a long time."

Wren forced himself to turn around and look at Rowen. People always said that death brought peace to the features, but Rowen didn't look peaceful. She looked angry. "Cover her with that sheet, Torin. We need to speak to Renaia."

He went into the next room and found the courtesan staring at the wall, her tear-streaked face blank and empty. She was shivering.

"Renaia," he said gently. "Renaia, I need you to tell me everything Rowen told you. Everything. No matter how trivial you think it was."

She ignored him.

"If we're to find out who did this, you need to help us."

"Can't," she whispered, still staring into space.

"What?" Wren leaned closer to hear what she was saying.

"Can't. Promised Rowen I wouldn't tell anyone."

"Renaia, that hardly matters now. You may have information that will help—"

"I said I can't!" she screamed, turning to face Wren. "I promised! I said I wouldn't tell."

Wren's patience ran out. He grabbed hold of Renaia and dragged her into the next room. He pushed a surprised Torin aside and pulled the sheet away, revealing Rowen's tortured corpse.

"Do you see that!" Wren shouted, forcing Renaia forward. "Look at her, Renaia! *Look!"* He shook her when she tried to turn her head away. "That was your friend. Someone did that to her. We want to find out who. Now you *will* talk. Otherwise I'll lock you in here with her until you change your mind. *Do you understand?"*

"I promised—"

"No!" thundered Wren. "Wrong answer. I said *do you understand?"*

"Yes! Yes, I understand!" Renaia screamed. "Just take me out of here. Please!" She started sobbing, and Wren helped her to her feet, enfolding her in his arms.

"Shh. I'm sorry, Renaia. I'm so sorry." He led her from the room.

"Out—outside," she said, her voice shuddering. "I can't be in here."

"That's fine."

Wren led her from the house, Torin following close behind. Wren helped her sit on the steps outside the front door and wiped the tears from her face. She took a while to compose herself, Wren and Torin waiting patiently.

"It's my fault," she said.

"No. It's not your fault. Whoever did this—it's *their* fault. No one else's. Now, start at the beginning."

"The beginning. That was . . . earlier tonight. Is that all the time that's passed? It seems like days now."

"The beginning . . ." prompted Wren.

"What? Yes. I ran into her earlier this evening. She was scared, looking for Cutter. She said she needed to hide for a while, and I knew of this place."

"Why did she need to hide?"

"She said she stole something from a client—an old man. I think she called him the professor. She said a man called Salkith came to the rooms to pick up a package. Rowen thought it was dreamlily because Cutter had told her this Salkith was a dreamlily courier for the Boromars. But she said the professor changed his mind and sent Salkith away."

"Where was Rowen during this meeting?"

"In a hidden room—like a closet or something. She . . . she found the package there. When the professor kicked Salkith out, he went to get a drink. She took the drugs and ran."

"Renaia, did she have this package when you ran into her?"

Renaia looked thoughtful, trying to remember. "No, she didn't."

"Interesting." Wren stared out across the garden as he tried to piece together the events.

"Rowen did say she was confused about one thing."

"Oh? What was that?"

"She said she'd overheard the professor planning this, and that she thought the professor was *buying* the dreamlily from Salkith. But when he arrived, it was to *collect* something from the professor."

"I see. Renaia, this is important—did you tell anyone else about Rowen's hiding place?"

"Only our Boromar handler. He looks out for us, watches to make sure we don't get hurt or anything."

Wren stood up. "Thank you, Renaia. We'd better get you back to civilization."

"What? Oh, no, it's all right. I live down here."

Wren frowned and looked around. "Where?"

"At a tavern a few streets over. My brother owns it. That's why I knew about this house."

"Come, then. We'll walk you there."

After seeing Renaia to the tavern, Wren and Torin headed back through the streets, looking for a lift they could use to ascend.

"I think Renaia signed Rowen's death warrant," said Wren after a while. "I think this is most definitely a bad drug deal. Rowen steals Boromar drugs meant for distribution. Renaia accidentally reveals her hiding place, Boromar heavies track her down and torture her into revealing where she's hidden the goods."

"And this Cutter?"

"Mmm. Good point." He thought for a moment. "How about this? They were both in on it. Rowen told Renaia a cleaned-up version of what happened. This Salkith probably did come, and then they killed the professor for the dreamlily."

They walked for a while. "No," Torin said. "That still doesn't feel right."

"I agree. Why would Rowen tell Renaia that Salkith came to pick something up? It's pointless if she's lying. There's no need for it."

"And we know Rowen was hiding in the room. So that part of the story is backed up. It's the professor's death that puzzles me."

"I know what I saw, Wren."

"I know. But this Cutter works for the Boromar Clan, right? What if he was simply told to kill the professor for pulling out of the deal? What if his relationship to Rowen is just a coincidence?"

"You mean he didn't know Rowen would do this?"

"He could have known. But he would have to carry out the deed anyway, to divert suspicion away from her. Host, he might even have enjoyed it. Remember, this professor was sleeping with his girlfriend. What do you think?"

"I think we need to find this Salkith and find out what he has to say."

"I thought you wanted to get home to your bed?"

"Not a chance. This is getting too interesting."

Chapter Seven

The second day of Long Shadows

Far, the 27th day of Vult, 998

The city of Sharn existed in its current form only because it was built on a manifest zone that linked the city to the plane of Syrania. This link strengthened any kind of spell related to levitation and flight, and thus the vast towers within the city were able to soar without risk. If the link between the planes were to fail, most of Sharn's towers would collapse beneath their own weight.

But within this magical zone were anomalies, areas where the magic was slightly distorted, where the influence of Syrania was felt, but in unexpected ways.

The Hanging Gardens was one such place. It occupied the entire top half of a tower in Middle Menthis, and it made the most of its fame by catering to as many needs as possible. It had numerous shops, four restaurants, two theaters, eleven taverns, and four inns. The Hanging Gardens was almost an entire ward in its own right, and entrepreneurs fought (sometimes literally) to get on the waiting list.

What was so special about the Hanging Gardens was that by some strange quirk in the connection between planes, gravity was reversed.

From the perspective of someone entering the base of the tower and glancing up, it was like looking into a mirror. The whole top half of the tower was upside down. The heads of tiny people could be seen as they moved about the pathways and bridges.

Cutter hated it, but he had no choice but to go there if he wanted to get the information he needed. He climbed one of the special ramps designed for access to the Gardens. The ramp started amid normal gravity, but as it climbed around the inside of the tower, it gently curled around on itself until he was walking upside down. He glanced up and saw the Gardens ahead of him, now the right way up. He looked to where he had entered the tower. Everyone seemed to be hanging from the ceiling.

He entered one of four entrance courtyards to the Hanging Gardens. The square was wide and unroofed, as was everything in the Hanging Gardens except private rooms. Pale white marble shot through with blue veins paved the courtyard. Looks like Karrn cheese, Cutter thought. Ivy climbed up the walls all around him, and greenery of all kinds had been planted seemingly at random, giving Cutter the impression that he was standing in some ancient city discovered in Xen'drik.

On the other side of the courtyard was an arched doorway. A decorative trellis carved with the likeness of the Ring of Syberis followed the curve of the opening. The various moons of Eberron, carved from different kinds of precious gemstones, dotted the lattice at regular intervals.

Cutter ducked through and followed the short corridor beyond to a wide thoroughfare crowded with people. This was the main street of the Gardens. Vendors were set up all along the road, selling snacks and clothing, books and drinks. Cutter moved with the flow until he came to a huge tavern on his right. A sign with a picture of a decapitated gargoyle hung from the eaves. He pushed his way out of the throng and slipped through the doors.

A busy night. Cutter used the cover of the crowd to make sure Tiel wasn't seated at his usual booth. He did a lot of his business at the Gargoyle. Cutter was in luck. No sign of the halfling.

Cutter allowed himself a small sigh of relief and headed to the bar. Katain, the halfling owner of the Gardens, spotted him and raised a hand in greeting. He finished serving a shifter, then approached him behind the bar, grabbing a bottle and two glasses as he came.

"Cutter," he said. "What brings you to my humble establishment? Thought you hated the place." Katain poured two shots of the lethal spirits he imported from the Talenta Plains and slid one across to Cutter.

Cutter raised the glass in thanks and tossed it back. He smacked his lips. "I do. But I need information, and you were the only one I could think of."

Katain grinned. "Five years out and you lot still come to me for help."

"Just because you're retired doesn't mean you don't keep your ears to the ground."

"You're right. In fact, I reckon I pick up more information now than I did when I was working for the Boromars. I should have opened this place years ago. To think of all that time standing on street corners in the middle of the night, waiting for contacts to show up. I could have done it all from here."

Cutter shook his head. "You would have been drunk all the time. Too much temptation."

"True. In fact, I'm drunk now." Katain grinned and downed another shot. "So. What do you need?"

"I'm looking for Salkith. He did a job for the Boromars tonight and he hasn't turned up. People are worried."

"Worried about him or worried he's run off with their money?"

Cutter shrugged. "I don't ask questions."

"Wise man." Katain looked thoughtful for a moment. "Salkith. He usually unwinds at a place called Silvermist. It's a dream parlor in Callestan. But if he's there, he might not be much help to you."

"Thanks, Kat."

"No problem." Someone called for his attention. The halfling turned and waved. "I'll leave the bottle here. See you round."

Katain went to attend to his customers. Cutter poured another drink, but this time sipped it slowly.

"Well, well. Always knew I'd find you propping up a bar someday."

Cutter froze, then swallowed the drink and carefully replaced the glass. He took hold of the bottle and turned around on his stool.

He'd often wondered what he'd do if he ever saw Jana again. And now, here she was. She still looked the same—pale skin, black hair down to her lower back. It was even tied in the same tight braid she always wore. But as he stared at her, he noticed there were changes. She looked thinner than before—harder. He remembered how he used to stare into her wide brown eyes and think they were the most beautiful he'd seen, but now they were continually narrowed as if she was suspicious of everything around her.

She still smelled like a miracle, though. Of jasmine in summertime. He realized with a guilty start that it was the same scent he had bought for Rowen. How had he not noticed that before?

He waited a moment to make sure his voice was calm. "Jana. Had a promotion, I see."

"Captain."

"Congratulations. Who's your pet?"

Jana glanced at the man to her right. Cutter reckoned he was in his early thirties.

"This is Corporal Conal. I'm keeping an eye on him."

"Poor man."

Jana cocked her head to the side. "You look older, Blackbird."

"I am."

"No. You look older than your years. Where have you been?"

"Valenar."

"What were you doing there?"

"Being a slave. For four years."

Her eyes widened a fraction. Not much, but enough that he noted.

"And the name's Cutter now," he said.

Jana cocked an eyebrow. "What kind of a name is that?"

"The kind of name I earned. One that I'm proud of."

"What? You're not proud of Blackbird? It suited you so well." She turned to Conal. "He was always after the shiny stuff, you see. Couldn't keep his beak out of trouble."

Cutter took a swig of spirits, watching them both.

"So what are you up to nowadays, Blackbird?"

"None of your business."

Jana stepped forward. "Be nice to me, Blackbird. I can haul you off to jail and no one would even notice."

"Like you did before?"

"*Exactly* like I did before."

Cutter stood. "Well, it's been lovely catching up. We should get together again, have supper or something." He turned to Conal before he left. "Watch your back, corporal. She's a dangerous one."

Silvermist was a dream parlor, a place where people went to experience illusions and shows different from the more run-of-the-mill plays and supper theaters of the upper wards. The changeling Jix even got a write-up in the *Chronicle* for her one-woman opera, a review that gave the parlor a brief dabbling of fame as the upper class, bored with the usual routine, organized coach parties complete with bodyguards and packed suppers (just in case the food wasn't up to standard), to take them down into the dangerous wards of Lower Dura.

This was something that quite upset the Boromar clan, as they secretly owned Silvermist and were using it as an illegal dreamlily den.

Steps had to be taken, and Cutter had been one of the Boromar employees hired to hassle and intimidate the guests until they stopped visiting. It had been his first job for them.

He nodded to the doorman and stepped into a dimly lit dining room. The smells of the night's dinner service lingered in the air. Roasted meat and vegetables. Seafood and lemon. Fried potatoes. His stomach grumbled in response. He ignored it and looked around.

A bright flare of blue and orange light forced him to shield his eyes. An intake of breath sounded throughout the room, sounding like a sigh of wind. He had entered right at the beginning of a show.

The blue and orange light coalesced into a gently spinning ball that hovered in the air over the stage, the separate colors twining and bleeding into each other like paint in water. Then it split into two separate balls that drifted apart until they were hovering close to the walls. They spun faster and faster, their glows growing in strength until one side of the room was bathed in blue, while the other was suffused in orange.

The onlookers' faces were bathed in color. Cutter looked around and saw that the dream parlor had a full house.

The light slowly dimmed. Cutter looked to the front and saw the balls condensing into tiny points of light. After a moment of near darkness, the balls burst open in a silent explosion, flinging globes of multicolored light in all directions. The audience gasped. Some tried to reach up and touch them, but the spheres darted away as if they were alive, drawing appreciative chuckles from the spectators. The balls stopped moving and again shrunk down in size, the light fading until Cutter realized with a small shock of perception that he was actually looking at the night sky, the balls of light now thousands of stars.

Then tiny dragons swooped through the air, banking around tables, swooping in to hover before the delighted faces of the patrons.

Cutter could see Salleon standing on the stage, the gnome's hands extended as he wove the illusion with deft flicks of his fingers, his eyes closed in concentration.

Cutter gave himself a mental shake and pulled himself away from the show, winding his way through the tables to a door in the far wall. The door led to a corridor, with the kitchen and private dining suites on either side. At the end was another door, which Cutter found to be locked.

Cutter knocked and waited. It opened a moment later, and he stared into the face of a half-orc.

Cutter racked his brain, trying to think of his name.

"Uh . . . Dajin, right? How's it going?"

The half-orc said nothing.

"Fine. Listen, I need to speak to Salkith. Instructions from high up."

The half-orc stared at him.

"I know he's here. And so does Tiel. You know who Tiel is?"

Cutter saw the eyes flicker slightly. He took that for a yes.

"Good. Now if you know Tiel, you know he doesn't like to be kept waiting. I have information to deliver. Are you going to let me in?"

Dajin paused for a moment, then stood aside.

"Thanks."

Cutter stepped into a large room. Couches lined the walls, along with glamerweave tapestries depicting cityscape scenes from Gatherhold in the Talenta Plains. Seven doors nestled between the tapestries. "Which one?" he asked.

Dajin gestured at a door to Cutter's left. Cutter opened it and slipped inside the room. The door clicked shut behind him.

The room was tiny. A young dwarf attendant stood beside a bed on which the tanned, wiry form of Salkith was lying. His long, sandy hair was carefully braided and placed on the pillow above his head. The attendant looked at Cutter in surprise, pausing in the movement of lifting a small vial of white liquid to the halfling's mouth.

"What are you doing?" she said. "You can't come in here."

"Wrong. Salkith's needed back at work. How much have you given him?"

The attendant frowned and glanced at the unconscious figure. "He's already had one dose tonight. I was just about to top him off."

"Don't. I need him awake. How long before he comes out of it?"

"It's hard to say."

"Guess."

"About half a bell."

"Thank you. Now, get out and don't disturb us. I may have to hurt you if I thought you overheard something you shouldn't have."

The woman drew herself up in protest. "I resent—"

"Resent all you want. Just tell me if you understand. That way, I won't feel bad killing you if I catch you spying."

The woman paled. "I . . . I understand."

"Well done. Now get out."

The attendant hastily left the room. Cutter waited to see if Dajin would come bursting in, but either she didn't tell the half-orc, or he thought it was best to stay out of it.

The room was empty except for the bed. He checked underneath it and found two drawers built into the frame. They were filled with white sheets, freshly laundered and folded. Cutter pulled one out and used his Khutai blade to cut it into strips, then lifted Salkith's arms above his head. He tied them together with the torn sheet, then ran the strip beneath the bed and did the same with his feet.

Cutter stepped back and surveyed his handiwork. No way he was getting out of that. Cutter pulled the other Khutai blade from its sheath and knelt on the floor, placing the knives to either side of him.

He closed his eyes and waited.

• • • • • • •

It took a little more than half a bell for the halfling to wake. Cutter heard the rustle of the sheets and opened his eyes. He saw Salkith turning his head from side to side as he tried to figure out what was going on.

Cutter picked up his blades and stood. Salkith's eyes widened slightly as he saw Cutter rise up from the floor.

"Who—" Salkith licked dry lips. "Who are you?"

"Here's how it works. You've already wasted my time—"

"I've been *asleep,"* he protested.

"Is that what you call it? Anyway, that's not my problem. I've been waiting here more than half a bell now, and that's all the time I was going to give you. Which means you need to talk very fast to tell me what I want to know."

Salkith strained against the bindings, his corded muscles standing out against his tanned skin. Cutter was glad he'd tied him up. The halfling looked like he could be quite a handful.

"I'll kill you," said Salkith. "And your family. Do you have a wife? A woman? Children? They're dead, you hear me? I'm going to strip their skin and hang it out to dry!"

Cutter stared at him for a moment. "You have no idea what a bad choice of words that was," he said softly. He leaned over the incapacitated halfling. "Listen to me carefully," he whispered. "I'm going to hurt you now. I'm going to keep on hurting you until you tell me what I want to know. If you scream, I'll kill you. I'll slit your throat. If you make any sound above a whimper, any sound that can be heard outside this room, you're dead. Do you believe me? Just nod."

Salkith stared into his eyes. After a long, trembling pause, he nodded.

"Good." Cutter drew the razor-sharp edge of the blade down Salkith's arm. Blood welled from the cut and stained the white sheets. Salkith squirmed and moaned, his eyes never leaving Cutter's.

"That was to show you I'm being serious. Now, what happened tonight at the professor's rooms?"

Salkith's brows drew together at the sudden change in topic. "What . . . happened? I don't understand."

Cutter punched Salkith in the face. Hard. The halfling's head jerked to the side. Droplets of blood sprayed over the white wall.

"Wait!" he snarled. "I don't understand! What do you want to know?"

"What happened?"

"But . . . nothing happened. I was supposed to pick something up from him. A . . . a package. But he changed his mind and didn't want to give it to me."

"You were supposed to pick it up from him?"

Salkith nodded desperately.

"What was in the package?"

"I don't know. I'm just a courier!"

"So what did you do?"

"I left. I wasn't about to argue with him. I reported it and came here. That's all I know."

Cutter frowned. "What were you supposed to do with the package?"

"I was supposed to meet someone at a tavern in Khyber's Gate. The . . . the Goblin's Revenge, it was called."

"Khyber's Gate?" said Cutter in surprise. "But that's Daask territory."

"That's all I know! I swear."

"Last question. Did you see a girl there? With red hair?"

Salkith frowned. "Nobody else was there. We were alone."

"Are you sure?"

"Of course I am! Now let me out of here!"

Cutter gathered his knives, then leaned over and picked up the vial of dreamlily the nurse had been holding. The bottle held at least twenty doses.

Cutter poured it all down Salkith's throat, clamping the halfling's mouth shut so he was forced to swallow.

That should keep him out of commission for a while, he

thought, closing the door on the halfling's incoherent cries.

Cutter sighed. Another dead end. He was no closer to finding Rowen. He sheathed his knives. What was he supposed to do now?

Dajin was nowhere to be seen. Cutter yanked open the door that led to the corridor.

Two men stood there. Cutter reached for his knives but someone gripped his arms from behind. He kicked out, feeling his boot connect with a hard stomach. One of his attackers staggered back, struggling to regain his breath.

Cutter was just about to kick out again when the other man lifted a glass vial filled with white fluid. He splashed it into Cutter's face.

The scent of the liquid hit him and seemed to crawl down his throat of its own accord. He felt it course through his body, a trail of warmth and heaviness.

Couldn't swallow.

Couldn't breathe.

His veins felt like they were filled with sluggish fluid. His whole body felt heavy. He sagged, his eyelids drooping.

The last thing he saw was the boot of the man he had just kicked coming at his face.

* * * * * * *

Cutter yawned and stoked the fire, sitting close to the low flames in an attempt to feed some warmth into his body. Dawn was approaching, a single line of pink and orange that stretched across the wide horizon. The solitary cry of an eagle echoed over the steppe. He looked up, but the bird was invisible against the night-touched sky.

A slight wind shivered the short grass of the steppe, but it was warm, carrying the scent of flowers and rain. Finally, thought Cutter. The first hint of spring.

The camp began to stir as the morning slowly brightened. Elves crept from their low, stretched-out tents and called greetings to each other. Wood was piled atop banked fires, hands held before the flames. The wind might promise spring, but the early mornings still belonged to winter.

He heard movement behind him, the scuffing of soft leather soles on the dry scrub. A moment later, Thalian knelt next to him.

"The Ancestors bless your day," the Keeper said formally.

"And yours," replied Cutter.

Thalian didn't say anything else. Cutter glanced sideways at him, studying his angular face. The young elf was a Keeper of the Past, the priesthood of the Valenar elves that maintained the memory of the great elf heroes of Xen'drik. They had known each other for three years now, so Cutter could tell when something was bothering the elf.

"What is it?" he asked.

"The messenger who arrived yesterday . . ." began Thalian.

"Yes?"

"King Vadallia has called our clan to serve him in Taer Valaestas."

"And?"

"And, slaves are . . . frowned upon by the King."

Cutter frowned and turned to the fire. The events of three years ago ran through his head. It was as if he were seeing them in the flames, replayed in the fire like they were replayed every night in his dreams.

He had been sleeping when it happened—or more accurately, passed out. He awoke to the horrendous rending of splintering wood as the ship he traveled on hit a reef off the southeast coast of Valenar. He was flung from his bed into the cabin wall. All around him was pitch darkness. He hadn't bothered to activate the everbright globe when he started drinking that afternoon. He could hear the screams of the passengers, the shouts of the captain and his crew as they tried to do something to save the foundering vessel. But it was too late. He crawled on hands and knees to where he thought the hatch should be, and yanked it open. Icy cold water lapped at his hands and knees. A few seconds later, it was up to his wrists.

He staggered up to the deck and saw the captain and his first mate lower the tiny fishing boat strapped to the side of the ship and make their escape. Everyone else was forced to leap into the sea and fight for their lives against the fierce breakers that tried to pound them against lethally sharp rocks.

Out of thirty, only seventeen survived, dragging themselves to the shore and gasping for air, crying out thanks to the Sovereign Host and the Silver Flame.

They should have saved their prayers. All they'd done was exchange one danger for another. Malleas and his war clan had skirted the coastline as the ship sailed north. The Valenar captured the weakened group, the chief's pet wizard binding them with a spell that he said was infinitely more powerful than cold steel.

Cutter hadn't believed him. That first night, he tried to escape.

As soon as he stepped beyond the boundaries of the camp, his whole body exploded with pain. Burning fire surged through this limbs, every vein a tiny river that carried red-hot lava to every part of his being. Each step he took increased the intensity of the pain, sent slivers of splintered glass stabbing into his brain until he had no idea who he was or where he was going. All he knew was that he had to keep moving, had to escape.

He managed to walk a full mile before he collapsed. Scouts carried him back to the camp, where Thalian watched over him, tending his body as Cutter spent the next week hovering between life and death.

Only six of the original captives were left, the others dead from accidents or killed by Malleas for displeasing him.

"Did you hear me?" asked Thalian, adding wood to the fire.

"I heard you. What does he plan on doing with us? I assume releasing us isn't on the agenda."

"I . . . don't think so, no." Thalian leaned closer to Cutter. "Maybe I can help. Find out how to break the spell—"

"Forget it. The only way we get free is if Malleas lets us go."

Cutter stood and stretched his limbs. He glanced at the largest tent, set in the center of the camp.

He looked to Thalian and smiled coldly. "Or if he's dead." Cutter strode toward the tent. "Malleas!" he shouted. "Face me, you coward!"

Cutter was aware of the whole camp turning to look at him in amazement. He didn't care. What did he have to lose? He was dead if he did nothing. He might as well go out fighting.

It was what he did best.

He stopped before the entrance to the tent. A moment later, two hands slipped between the flaps and parted the hide to both sides.

Malleas ducked through the opening. He yawned and looked around the camp, checking to make sure everything was proceeding normally. Acting like he didn't have a care in the world. Only when he had satisfied himself that all was well did he turn his gaze to Cutter.

"What did you say, little man?"

"I said you are a coward. Your ancestors have abandoned you, Malleas. You shame them with your actions."

Malleas stepped forward. He was the same height as Cutter, but Cutter was broader than the chief, the labor of the past years sculpting his body.

"What do you know of my ancestors?" Malleas said softly. He rested his hands on twin Khutai blades strapped to his waist. "My ancestor came to this continent with four companions at his side. They raided a human village and defeated their best fighters. The rest they took as slaves." He took another step forward until he was no more than an arm's length from Cutter. "So do not presume to tell me I shame my ancestors. I *praise* them."

"So do I. Every morning when I take a piss."

That did it. Malleas's eyes went dead. He moved forward until his face was inches from Cutter's. "You will choke on those words, outlander. I raise prayers to the ghosts of my ancestors every night and they whisper sweet compliments in my ears." His voice rose in volume. "I please them with my actions. The pyres I burn lift their names to the sky in honor! Every death, every wound inflicted is a salute to their names, and never is it enough! So do not tell me I shame my ancestors!" Malleas stopped, seemingly aware that he was losing control. He straightened, glanced about at those watching, then turned to Cutter with a smirk. "Now run along and do your job, *Cutter.* Chop the wood I will use to burn your worthless carcass. I will inhale the smoke of your soul. I will own your death."

Cutter waited a moment, trying to calm his erratic heartbeat. He was dead. He knew that. He reminded himself that the only choice left was to decide how he would go. He wondered what his brother would think of him now. Would he be proud? Disappointed?

"You will own no part of me, *vadis nia.*" In the months

he'd spent among the Valenar, Cutter had picked up a lot of their speech—especially insults, which they often hurled at the prisoners. *Vadis nia* was about the worst thing one could call a Valenar—*disgracer of the blood.*

That got the reaction Cutter was looking for. Malleas roared and pulled his blades out, but his anger stripped his attack of any precision. Cutter stepped into his reach and blocked the frenzied swipes with his forearms, the dull smack of skin on skin louder than the elf's snarls.

Cutter waited until he saw Malleas forcibly calm himself, saw the light of calculation enter his eyes, and in that instant of transition, Cutter lashed out and connected with Malleas's face. His first punch broke the elf's nose. Then he grabbed hold of the warlord's wrist and rammed the hilt of the blade into his head. Blood flowed from the scalp wound and dripped into his eye, forcing the elf to blink rapidly to clear his vision.

Cutter managed to get one more hit in, a blow to the stomach, before he leaped back. But before he could dodge out of Malleas's reach, the elf brought one of the blades down in a wild slash that left a deep gouge in his arm.

The two circled each other warily. The whole camp gathered around to watch the confrontation. Cutter tried his best to ignore them. He was under no illusion that he would survive this day. Even if he won the fight, he would be executed by the clan. Honor would keep them from interfering in the fight, but it wouldn't stop them from cutting his head off and dragging it behind the horse of the new clan leader.

But that gave him the edge. It meant he had nothing left to lose.

So he ran straight for Malleas. The move surprised the elf, if only because it was suicidally stupid.

Just before he charged within reach, Cutter dropped and

barreled into the elf's legs. They both tumbled to the ground in a confusion of flailing limbs.

Cutter felt a searing pain along his back as one of the blades cut through his clothing. They tussled for position and Cutter grabbed the first thing he could lay his hands on—Malleas's kneecap. He twisted it as hard as he could. It popped and the elf screamed in pain, thrashing beneath him.

Something smashed into the side of Cutter's head—the pommel of one of the blades, held awkwardly in Malleas's hand. Cutter grunted and snapped his head forward, again and again, smashing his forehead into Malleas's face. All the while he could feel the elf reaching over his shoulder and stabbing into his back with the free blade. The thrusts were weakening, however, and Cutter loosened his grip so he could grab hold of the elf's neck.

But it was a ruse. As soon as he tried to shift his hold, Malleas grunted and pushed up with his leg, lifting Cutter to his feet. The human stumbled back a few steps, trying to keep his balance, but his heel caught on a clump of scraggly grass and he fell onto his backside.

Malleas was on him in an instant. He collided with Cutter knees-first, forcing Cutter flat onto his back, and brought his knives in on either side for killing blows. Cutter punched the elf in the throat. When Malleas swayed backward, Cutter pulled his legs out from under the elf and kicked him as hard as he could in the chest, sending the elf staggering back into the fire. His trousers caught in the flames, and Cutter used the distraction to push himself to his feet.

He felt blood trickling freely down his back from the numerous wounds. He knew he wouldn't last much longer. He staggered forward and picked up a piece of wood from the fire. Flames licked at his hand and he felt his skin blistering. Cutter ignored the pain. He brought the log up in a swinging arc that caught the elf beneath the chin. Cutter heard the crack as Malleas's jaw broke. His head snapped up. Teeth and blood burst from his mouth and fell sizzling into the fire. Cutter dropped the brand and grabbed hold of Malleas's wrists. He still held the curved knives, now covered in Cutter's blood. He looked into Malleas's eyes. The white of the right eye had filled with blood. His face was a ruined pulp of meat. He heard a wet, nasal gurgle as the elf tried to breathe.

Cutter gasped for breath. "You . . . named me Cutter. You . . . you thought it an insult."

Malleas struggled in his grasp.

Cutter tightened his grip. "It is not. I accept the name."

With that, Cutter lifted Malleas's arms and forced the elf to cut his own throat, the razor-sharp blades slicing deep into the soft skin of his neck.

Malleas gurgled as he tried to speak, the action causing bubbles to burst from the wound. Then he twitched and fell backward into the fire, sending up an explosion of sparks and smoke.

Cutter staggered away from the flames, then fell to his knees. He was aware that he was holding Malleas's blades. When had he grabbed them?

He lifted his head to face the death he knew was coming. The elves hadn't moved. They stood watching Malleas's body as his clothes caught fire and the flames consumed him.

Then one stepped forward. Vael. He was—had been—Malleas's second in command. He stood before Cutter, looking down at him.

Cutter tried to smile. "Do what you will. I die free."

"You will not die this day, Cutter. You have fought fairly and honorably against an armed opponent. Your ancestors would be proud."

Oh, really? You hear that, brother? Cutter's thoughts dripped with sarcasm.

"Many here were not . . . comfortable with Malleas's leadership of the clan. We—I—planned on challenging him when we reached Taer Valaestas, with the High King as witness."

And now I've done your dirty work for you. Cutter laughed inwardly.

Vael seemed to sense what he was thinking. "Travel with us, Cutter. As a free man." Vael glanced around, then dropped to his knees so he was level with Cutter. He leaned forward and placed his forehead against Cutter's, his hand over his heart. "You are a fighter of skill and honor. I invite you to join our clan. Will you accept?"

Cutter hesitated. "Release the others—the slaves."

"Done. Slavery has no place in my clan."

Cutter raised his hand and placed it over Vael's heart.

"Are we one?" asked the elf.

"We are," said Cutter, and then his eyes rolled up into his head and he collapsed.

Cutter opened his eyes to darkness.

Is it still night, then? His head swam.

He should get back to sleep. They were moving in the morning, heading west to Taer Valaestas. It would be a long ride, and he needed his rest. His head throbbed. His mouth was parched. He smacked his lips, trying to find some moisture, but it was a pointless exercise. Had he been drinking last night? Couldn't remember. Regardless, he needed water.

He tried to get up but found that he couldn't move. His hands and legs were tied to a chair. What was this? Betrayal?

Cutter blinked his dry eyes, trying to focus on something, anything, in the dim light. Vague shapes began to materialize—crates, barrels of ale, a few chairs, a broken table.

It took him only a moment more to realize he wasn't in Valenar. He was in the storeroom beneath Silvermist. He thought back to what had happened. Opening the door onto his attackers. That noxious fluid in his face.

Dreamlily. They had given him a concentrated dose of dreamlily. A wave of panic washed over him. How long had he been under? How much time had passed?

He strained against the ropes binding his arms, but they were too tight to give. He tested the bindings around his legs and found they were a bit looser. He braced himself and strained against the bonds. The old chair creaked, the wood slowly giving. He paused for breath then tried again. The wood creaked and splintered, groaning as if in pain. Then, with a final *crack,* the right front leg snapped and the chair collapsed beneath him. He landed on one knee, the jolt sending a wave of pain through his body.

Cutter winced and pushed himself up. He was hunched over, a leg and both arms still tied to the broken chair. He hopped over to the wall and swung his body around, slamming the chair as hard as he could into the stonework until it smashed apart. He quickly untied the rope and picked up one of the broken legs. It wasn't heavy, but it would have to do as a weapon. The bastards had taken his blades.

What did they want with him, anyway?

He could make out a faint rectangle of light outlining the door. He hurried through the darkness and put his ear to the wood.

Then he pulled away. He could hear voices on the other side, the sound of people approaching.

He looked quickly around the room. It was too late to pull out another chair and pretend he was still tied up. He had to face them.

He pushed himself up against the wall. A moment later, the door opened and the light from the hall flooded into the room. He could see the shadows of two men in the swath of light that fell across the floor.

"—couldn't believe it when I saw him. Word is, Tiel wants him bad."

Tiel? What in Khyber's name does he want?

Then it hit him. The money he was supposed to collect. Tiel thought he'd stolen it. Cutter frowned. Tough for him, then. He didn't have time for this.

The two men entered the room. They froze when they saw the pieces of broken chair, but Cutter didn't give them a chance to do anything more. He stepped forward and swung the chair leg into the back of the near one's head. The man cried out and dropped to his knees. Cutter shifted his grip and swung again, this time backhand. It slammed across the face of the other man. His head jerked to the side and Cutter brought the leg back for another hit, sending him sprawling on his face. The first man was trying to get to his feet. Cutter brought the leg down on his skull. Blood sprayed across the floor and he collapsed to the side, his head hitting the floor first.

Cutter didn't hang around. In the room beyond were a table and two chairs. On the table were an empty bottle, two glasses, and a pile of cards.

And his blades. Sitting near a small pile of coins. The bastards were playing cards for his weapons.

He picked up his knives and the money, then climbed the stairs to the club beyond.

Chapter Eight

The second day of Long Shadows

Far, the 27th day of Vult, 998

Wren and Torin hurried along the crowded streets of Callestan, dodging between drunken revelers and worse-for-wear courtesans.

"How much did this information cost you?" asked Torin.

Wren cleared his throat. "Not much," he said evasively.

"Wren, he found out where this Salkith hangs out in under two hours! That kind of service doesn't come cheap."

"No, it doesn't."

"So how much?"

Wren sighed. "Thirty galifars," he said, and winced, waiting for the explosion.

"Thirty galifars!" shouted Torin. Some of the less drunk stragglers turned to stare. Torin glanced at them and lowered his voice. "Are you mad? You have to stop throwing money about like that. We're not even getting paid for this!"

"No, but Larrien will be indebted to us, and that is much more valuable than money, my tight-fisted friend. By the way, you're bordering on clichéd behavior again."

"It's got nothing to do with me being a dwarf!"

"Oh? What does it have to do with?"

"With you being insane!"

"Oh, pish-posh, Torin. Relax."

"Don't—! Hey, isn't that him?"

"Where?"

"Over there. Coming out of the alley."

Wren looked to where Torin was pointing and saw a big man staggering into the main street. He didn't look well. "Are you sure that's him?"

"Definitely."

"Why is he stumbling around like that?" asked Wren.

"How would I know? Maybe he's been drinking to forget what happened."

"Ah," said Wren sorrowfully. "A mistake that brings many a downfall." Wren patted Torin on the shoulder. "You could tell him a few stories about that, couldn't you, Torin?"

Torin shook his head. "Are we going to follow him?"

"I think it would be a waste *not* to. I mean, since we're here and everything. Unless . . . did you have something better in mind?"

But Torin was already walking away from Wren, keeping an eye on Cutter's back as the human walked as fast as he could without falling over. Wren picked up his pace to catch up with Torin.

"He's heading for the lifts. Run ahead and catch it, a few levels up. I'll keep an eye on him from this side. If you see the Watch, alert them."

Torin nodded and slipped away into the crowds. Wren followed Cutter as he made his way along the streets to the nearest lift. It took some time, as the human wasn't moving very fast. Wren was worried that maybe the man had forgotten where it was and he'd have to tackle him on his own, without Torin's help. *Had* he been drinking? It certainly looked that way.

The reached the lifts without much incident. A couple of goblins had thought to take advantage of what they thought was a helpless drunk, but Cutter proved himself capable of taking care of himself. He slammed his fist into the throat of the first goblin. It dropped to the ground with a broken neck. The second came at Cutter with a rusty short sword. He slid inside the goblin's guard, grabbed its sword arm, and pushed it back in a direction it was not meant to go. The arm snapped and the blade sank deep into the goblin's chest.

Wren made a note to be very careful around Cutter.

When they arrived at the lift, Cutter climbed aboard and leaned wearily on the safety railing, his head resting on the backs of his hands.

Wren checked to make sure his dagger was easily accessible, then followed after. Cutter didn't look up.

The lift jerked and started to move. Cutter was definitely as big close up as Torin had said. But, Host, did he look a mess. Wren's gaze dropped to the weapons hanging from his hips. The scabbards were curiously shaped—long and curved. It took Wren a moment to realize they were Valenar blades.

Wren had barely gotten over his surprise when Cutter spoke to him.

"Why are you following me?" he said.

Wren's eyes snapped up. Cutter had turned his head to stare at him over his shoulder.

"I'm afraid you're mistaken. I am merely returning from a night's frivolity. I like to slum it, you see. Much more exciting."

Cutter didn't move. Wren did his best to keep his face nonchalant, the kind of look he frequently saw on the rich and bored.

"You're lying. Are you from Tiel?"

Wren frowned. "Where is Tiel?"

"Not where. Who. Tiel is a person."

"Oh. Then no, I'm not. I take it this Tiel is after you for some reason?"

Cutter was silent for a while. "A misunderstanding," he said.

"Ah."

The lift rose past the lower levels of the city. It stopped at a darkened street and a halfling and a dwarf staggered aboard, laughing as they passed a flask of spirits between them. Wren realized he didn't know where Cutter was getting off. If he wanted to learn anything, he'd have to take a calculated risk. Just as the gate swung closed and the lift started to move again, Wren straightened up and cleared his throat. "Go to the university often?" he asked.

Cutter tensed and pushed himself up from the rails. He glanced at the halfling and the dwarf, then locked eyes with Wren. Neither looked away.

The two drunks lurched off at the next stop. As soon as the lift was rising again, Cutter moved, yanking his blades out and stepping toward Wren faster than he thought possible for a man in his condition. At the same moment, Wren pulled out his depleted wand with one hand and his dagger with the other. Cutter froze.

"Why are you asking about the university?"

"Curiosity," replied Wren.

"Curiosity about what?"

"About why you killed the professor. I *think* it had to do with dreamlily, but I'm not sure."

"I didn't kill anyone! It was that damn warforged."

Wren frowned. "What warforged? What are you talking about?"

Cutter hesitated.

"You don't seem to understand," said Wren. "Everyone thinks you killed him. *I* think you killed him. If you have a different story, now is the time to tell it."

Still Cutter hesitated. He glanced at the towers drifting past. Then he sighed.

"When I reached the university, the professor was dead. I was looking for . . . something, and this . . . black warforged attacked me. It was like nothing I've ever seen before. It wrapped shadows around its body like a cloak. I barely got away in one piece. If it wasn't for some dwarf coming to investigate the noise, that thing would have killed me."

"Interesting. And where does Rowen fit into all this?"

Cutter's eyes narrowed. He moved to grab Wren, but the half-elf twitched the wand in the direction of Cutter's face and he stopped, taking a deep breath to calm himself. "What do you know about Rowen?" he asked in a low voice. "Where is she? Have you seen her?"

Wren hesitated, trying to decide which route to take. Lies, or truth? Which would glean him the most information?

Probably the lie.

But he couldn't do it. He wasn't sure what was going on, but the man deserved the truth.

"Cutter, Rowen is dead. I'm sorry. Whoever she stole the package from killed her."

Wren watched as Cutter tried to reject his words. It was almost as if he was fighting a battle, the words ricocheting against some kind of armor he had hastily erected around his mind.

But even the best armor had weak spots.

"You're lying," Cutter whispered.

"I wish I was." He paused, searching for words. "She was a very beautiful woman," he finally said.

"You . . . saw her?"

"I did."

Cutter shook his head. "No. I was with her earlier tonight. It's impossible."

"Death can happen in an instant, Cutter. Believe me, I speak the truth."

"No. It can't be. We . . . we fought. We can't leave it like that. She can't be gone. Not when we're fighting. That . . . that's not fair."

Wren didn't know what to say. He was dimly aware of the lift slowing to a stop, but all he could see was the pain in Cutter's eyes. The man was massive, a brute by any other name, but he was brought down by his love for a woman.

Wren heard the scrape of metal on metal. He blinked, pulling his eyes away from Cutter to see the lift surrounded by the Watch. Torin stood with them. The commander stepped aboard, sword point leveled at Cutter's heart. Wren took a step back, unsure how the man would react in his current state of mind.

He didn't do anything. He looked as if the life had simply drained out of him. He stood still while he was disarmed and then cuffed. He locked eyes with Wren just before he was pulled off the lift. He didn't say anything, but Wren felt some kind of connection there, a kinship.

The Watch led Cutter through the streets, his head hanging low.

"Pretty good, aren't I?" said Torin.

"What?" Wren glanced down at the dwarf.

"I found the Watch."

"Oh. Yes. Well done. I think that's it for tonight, Torin. Go home to your wife."

Wren stepped onto the street and walked away.

"I can never please you, you know that?" Torin called behind him.

Wren returned to his apartments overlooking Skysedge Park. He stood on the balcony and stared over the gentle hills as the morning mist slunk down the banks and slowly filled the hollows and depressions.

It was over. For all intents and purposes, the case was solved. No judge would look beyond the facts as they were presented. Two lovers, one a courtesan, conspired to steal something from one of her clients. The man then killed the client in a fit of jealousy, and the courtesan was killed as revenge for the theft.

No one would investigate to find out who had killed her. These kinds of crimes were not important enough for the Watch to waste their time. Cheap courtesans in the lower levels died all the time. Just another death among a thousand others. No one cared.

But something wasn't right. This whole thing, far from being an open and shut case, was a confused muddle of lies and mistaken assumptions, and Wren was as much to blame for that as anyone. He sighed, recognizing the feeling that was building inside his chest, that tight knot of impatience that told him things weren't right. It wouldn't go away. Not until he'd checked every last lead.

Wren turned from the balcony and stepped back inside. He grabbed the satchel that contained all his equipment, slung it over his shoulder, and headed out the door.

Lucky for him, he didn't need much sleep.

Kayla let him back into the university. Larrien had placed her in charge of coordinating the Watch and fending off chroniclers from the *Inquisitive* and the *Chronicle*. She had dark rings beneath her eyes and yawned repeatedly as she reluctantly led the way to the professor's rooms.

"What did the cleric find out?"

"Nothing."

"Nothing?" Wren looked at Kayla in surprise. "He must have picked up something."

"He didn't. He seemed quite upset about it. He said there was absolutely nothing there. Said that whatever killed him must have been blessed."

"Or cursed," muttered Wren. "And the Watch? Did they find anything?"

"They didn't look. They just took the body away and said they'd be back tomorrow."

They arrived at the apartment. Wren paused before opening the door. "No point in both of us being kept from our beds. I just want to take a second look, then I'll be off."

Kayla stifled a yawn. "I'll wait. Have to lock up once you're gone."

Wren nodded and pushed open the door. "Won't be long."

The room felt different since the body had been removed. Less . . . heavy. No real sense remained that a tragedy had occurred earlier that night. It just felt—what was the word he was looking for? It felt vacant. Unlived in.

He opened his satchel and rummaged around inside. He took out a pair of Cannith goggles and pulled them over his head. He fitted them over his eyes and blinked a few times to get used to the smoky orange tinge of the lenses. He closed his eyes and concentrated, activating the magic of the goggles.

When he opened his eyes again, his vision changed drastically.

Everything was clearer, much sharper, as if he had been half-blind his whole life and then presented with his first pair of glasses. Everywhere he looked, his vision seemed to focus and then zoom in on whatever his eyes settled on, revealing tiny details that hadn't been apparent before.

Just there, for example. He saw the faint outlines of footprints in the carpet, one pair deeper than the others. A warforged, perhaps? The carpet had bounced back but not enough to hide the prints from the goggles. To the right, he spied a deep indentation then a short trail across the fibers, as if someone had landed heavily and slid along the floor on his back.

He walked to the bedroom and traveled slowly back and forth across the floor, peering straight down at his feet.

Here we go, Wren thought. He got down on his hands and knees and lowered his face to the floor, cocking his head to the side as he tried to peer at his discovery from every angle. He pulled out a wooden vial and a pair of tongs from his satchel and carefully picked up a tiny item, holding it close to the goggles.

A shaving of black metal. The kind one would find if, say, a fight had taken place and a heavy blade was scraped across the body of a dark warforged.

Wren dropped the shavings into the vial and placed it into his bag. He stood up and stared at the hole in the wall. It was vaguely man-shaped, but when he stepped forward he could see faint pinpricks of blood on the wall studs inside the hole. He reckoned that if he had a look at Cutter's back, he would see the same pattern there.

Wren put the goggles away and stood in the dark, lost in thought. He left the room and walked Kayla back to her apartment in Shava House, the tiny boarding house for the community of staff that lived on campus.

Some time later, Wren climbed the steps of Daggerwatch garrison and pushed open the reinforced metal doors that led into the building. He walked through and entered a square room with three doors on each wall. A huge desk sat against the far side of the room, about as high as Wren's shoulders. A tired-looking dwarf woman sat behind it.

Wren approached and beamed his smile. "Excuse me, my dear—"

"Do not, and I repeat that, do not *ever*, call me 'my dear.' Understood?" The dwarf stared at him.

Wren's smile faltered, but for only a fraction of a second. "Of course. My apologies, uh . . . ?"

"Sergeant."

"Yes. Sergeant. My apologies. I was wondering if you could lend me some assistance."

"Probably not, but ask anyway. I'm feeling generous."

"Thank you. I'm looking for a prisoner who was brought in earlier."

The dwarf held up her hand to stop him. Wren waited, but she simply held it there. Wren leaned to the side so he could see past it to her face. "Yes?"

"Yes, what?"

"Yes, *sergeant*. Sorry."

The dwarf lowered her hand and turned a huge ledger around on the desk. Wren leaned forward with interest. The dwarf ran her finger down a list of names, turned the page over, ran her finger down the next list, then slammed the book shut.

"Don't tell me," said Wren, becoming slightly annoyed. "Those are the names of prisoners brought in during the last watch."

"Correct."

"Can I check the list to see if his name is there?"

"No."

"Can I describe him to you to see if you remember him?"

She appeared to consider this for a moment. "Go on, then. And I'm only doing this because I like you."

"Uh, thank you. His name is Cutter. He's a human, over six feet tall, muscular. He has a tattoo of a dragon on his head that runs down his neck and wraps around his arms."

"Shaved head, growing into stubble?"

"Yes!"

"Haven't seen him."

Wren deflated. "Oh."

"Unless . . ."

"Yes?"

"What are you doing for dinner at the end of the week?"

Wren blinked in bemusement. "Sorry?"

"Dinner. You take me out to dinner, I'll tell you about your friend."

"Oh." He shrugged. "That's fine. Would Sannid's suit your taste?"

For the first time, he saw expression on her face. Her eyes widened. "Sannid's? I thought the waiting list was over a month long."

Wren shrugged. "I know the owner."

She studied him, eyes narrowed. "You're not going to back out, are you?"

"Perish the thought!" Wren leaned over the desk and pointed at a quill. "May I?" She nodded, so he took it and wrote his address on a piece of parchment. "My address. You can track me down if I don't turn up."

She took the piece of paper and read it. "Skysedge Park?"

Wren nodded. "We can meet at my place first. Try some of my wine. I collect the stuff, but so rarely get the chance to enjoy it."

"That . . . sounds good." She looked at the address again and seemed to remember something. "Your friend! Yes, your friend was moved to Warden Towers."

Wren frowned. "Moved? Why would he be moved?"

"I have no idea. Some woman came in and spoke to the captain. Cold bitch, she was." She shrugged. "We don't care. One less mouth to feed."

"I see. Thank you for your time. You've been a great help."

"Don't forget our date," she called after him.

The foyer of Warden Towers was laid out in the same arrangement as Daggerwatch, except that a male elf sat behind the desk.

Wren briefly considered using the same tactic, but decided against it. He knew he was charming, but even *he* had limitations.

He waited until a pair of guards finished processing a prisoner, then approached the desk.

"Excuse me."

The elf looked him up and down and sighed. "What do you want?"

"A friend of mine was brought in earlier today. I was wondering if I might see him."

"What for?"

"I'll be acting as his legal counsel," Wren said.

"I see. What's his name?"

"Cutter."

"Cutter what?"

"Just Cutter."

The elf pushed himself to his feet. "Wait here. And don't touch anything."

Wren raised his hands in the air. "Promise."

The elf disappeared through a door. When he didn't return, Wren was about to follow him inside to find out what was taking so long, then the elf emerged with a captain of the Watch. Her long black hair was tied into a braid that fell down her back. She didn't look pleased to see him.

"What do you want with Cutter?" she asked.

"I'm his counsel."

"How did you know he was here?"

"I was witness to his arrest."

"Were you, now? May I ask what you were doing associating with a known criminal?"

Wren frowned. "No, you may not. It has absolutely no relevance."

"Don't get smart with me. Unless you want to join your friend in a cell."

Wren looked over at the elf, but he was studiously reading a ledger and trying to ignore the conversation taking place before him.

"I'm sorry. I don't quite understand. Are you threatening me?"

"Are you *accusing* me of threatening you?"

"All I want to do is see my client. That is his right."

The woman walked forward until she was nose to nose with Wren. "Don't talk to me about rights, half-elf. You know, I really don't think I like the look of you. Maybe you *should* join him in the cell. Then you can talk all you like." She turned to the elf standing behind the desk. "Sergeant, if you would be so kind as to escort—"

The doors behind Wren burst open and three men stumbled in, two of them falling to the floor at the captain's feet. She stepped back as two guards came through the door behind them and hauled them up. Wren used the opportunity to slip out onto the street and run.

He thought it a wise move, given the circumstances.

• • • • • • •

Far from Warden Towers, Wren slowed down to think. Something was going on, and he didn't like it. The captain seemed too eager for Wren, a witness to Cutter's arrest, to join him in his cell. Why would she want that? Unless . . .

Unless it all linked back to the dreamlily theft? Could the Boromars want Cutter eliminated as well? It was very possible. The captain seemed like the type who would be in the pay of the halfling clan.

Wren didn't like this. Didn't like feeling responsible for another man's life—or death, as the case might be. And he *was* responsible. He was the one who tracked Cutter down. He was the one who got him arrested.

So where was he going with this? Wren thought about it a bit more, then stopped walking and stared at the cobbles beneath his feet. Damn it. Was he really considering it?

He was. He really was.

Wren lifted his eyes to the brightening sky and sighed deeply.

He was going to break Cutter out of prison.

Chapter Nine

The second day of Long Shadows

Far, the 27th day of Vult, 998

In Wren's considered opinion, taverns lacked souls. Certain buildings had them. Old historical sites, for example. Even newly built houses occupied by young families had a certain *something* you could feel as soon as you walked inside. But taverns fed off the spirits of others. They needed people to give them life. The light and the laughter soaked into the walls like water in the desert.

If one wanted to see the truth behind the pretense, one needed only to visit in the cold gray light of early morning, when rooms once filled with raucous celebration became drab, sad places. Sunlight filtered through grimy windows, but instead of adding cheer, it highlighted blemishes and scars best left hidden. Walls were revealed to be patchy and stained. The chairs were threadbare, the bar pitted and sticky. Ashes lay dead in the fire grate.

It depressed Wren to be in places like this. It reminded him of just how disheartening life could be.

And this particular tavern was a perfect example. It reeked

of desperation, of money lost and lives ruined. The rugs were littered with betting stubs, each a testament to a desperate hope for a better life, or, since he was feeling uncharitable at the moment, a testament to addiction.

Wren looked around the empty common room. "Callian!" he shouted. "Where are you?"

A muffled thump came from upstairs. Then a scratchy voice floated down. "Who's there? Go away. We're closed!"

"Come and see who's here before I rob you blind," called Wren. He glanced around the room. "Not that there's much to steal," he muttered to himself.

He walked around the tables, avoiding what looked suspiciously like a puddle of vomit, and pushed open the doors that led to the balcony. He stopped breathing through his mouth and leaned over the railing, closing his eyes and inhaling a great lungful of fresh air. He let it go, then took another one, and finally opened his eyes.

A wave of vertigo washed over him as he looked down at the Stone Trees hrazhak field far below him. The huge indoor coarse was littered with piles of stones, clumps of trees, water courses, and anything else the organizers thought would add to the excitement of the shifter game. Wren thought he could see splashes of blood spattered on some of the rocks. His gaze traveled up to the spectator stands that circled to either side of him. They were empty, but they would fill again when the next games started.

He heard footfalls on the stairs behind him. He looked over his shoulder and saw Callian appear in the doorway behind the bar. The gnome looked like an ancient raisin left out in the sun for a few decades. Wren had known him for years, and he'd always had the same deep wrinkles, the same limp in his right foot. Although . . .

"The eye patch is new," he said. "What happened?"

"Nothing," said Callian, joining Wren on the balcony. "It impresses the ladies."

"Really?"

"Yes, really. They think I'm windswept and interesting." He squinted at Wren, and must have seen the look of doubt on his face. "Just because I'm old doesn't mean I don't have needs."

Wren raised his hands in surrender. "Something I *don't* want to get into, thank you very much." He paused. "It's good to see you again, Callian."

"Of course it is. Now what do you want?"

"A favor."

"Yes, obviously. Otherwise you wouldn't be here. What *kind* of favor?"

Wren sighed and stared into the deserted stands below him. "I've got myself into a bit of a mess."

"Always knew you would. Illegal?"

"Not yet."

"Ah. Is Torin involved?"

"Not in what I'm about to do."

"Good. Keep him out of it. He's got a family to think of."

"I know."

"So . . . are you going to tell me what you need?"

He turned to face the gnome. "I need you to get the old crew together."

Callian's eyebrows raised in surprise. "Why?"

"Because I need to break someone out of Warden Towers, and this is the only way I can do it. Now, here's what I'll need . . ."

At midday, Wren was seated at a table atop a magically strengthened glass platform that floated a hundred feet above the center of the hrazhak field. Callian said it was so honored patrons could watch the game without having to mix with the common folk. Wren had to admit that it afforded stunning views of the playing field. He could see the employees—mostly ogres and bugbears—rearranging the piles of stones and huge logs in preparation for the night's games.

Wren had never been interested in the sport himself. He considered it barbaric and lacking in subtlety. It involved two teams of shifters beating each other to a pulp while trying to get hold of the opposing team's wooden idol so they could deposit it in their goal. Of course, this being Sharn, hrazhak was fast becoming one of the city's most popular sports.

He lifted his face to the warm rays of the sun, feeling the heat sinking pleasingly into his bones. It was a refreshing change after the past few days of steady rain.

He hoped he had made the right decision. Getting the old crew together could be a colossally bad move. He'd thought about contacting his one-time protégé, Soneste Otänsin, but had ultimately decided against it. It had been a while since he last saw her, but he'd heard she was working for Thuranne d'Velderan's Investigative Services. That meant she was working legitimately, and Wren was hesitant about getting her involved in something illegal. Especially since she was enjoying a small amount of fame as a result of a recent case. She even managed to get a mention in the *Inquisitive.*

It was a shame, because she was really good at what she did, and he would have liked to catch up with her again.

The sound of distant voices caused him to look across to Callian's inn poised above the grandstands. A soarsled had just left the balcony and was approaching the viewing platform, the round disc teetering slightly beneath its heavy load. Wren couldn't help smiling when he caught sight of the ragtag group it transported. At the front was Bex, half-orc and druid. Wren noted that he still wore clothing bright enough to cause blindness in the unwary. And Salka was there. Wren's smile faded. She was human, so he knew she would age quicker than he did, but she looked a *lot* older than he remembered. It seemed as though life had been tough on her since they'd parted ways. Behind her sat Callian's nephew, Dalen. Wren breathed a sigh of relief when he saw the gnome. His whole plan depended on a good illusionist to cause a realistic distraction. Without Dalen, he didn't think they'd be able to pull it off.

A new face was in the group as well, a young shifter Wren didn't recognize. She stood at the side of the sled, her bearing tall and proud. No, Wren amended. Not pride. The set of her face, the look she gave the others—was arrogance.

Wren rose from the table. The sled slowed, ready to bump against the platform. While it was still an arm's length away, Bex leaped across the gap, a huge grin on his broad face. The half-orc lifted Wren from the platform and clasped him in a painful hug.

"Wren! Good to see you! Didn't think we'd hear from you again. Heard you'd gone legitimate."

"I have," Wren said.

Bex dropped him back to his feet and went to investigate the food laid out on the table.

Wren turned his attention to Salka as she stepped onto the platform. "Salka." He leaned forward to hug her. She grasped his back tightly and held on for what seemed like a long time. "How are you?" he whispered into her ear.

"Later," was all she said, before releasing him and taking a seat.

Dalen hopped onto the platform and shook Wren's hand. The gnome couldn't speak. His tongue had been torn out decades before in the War, and he refused to let a cleric heal it. No one had the guts to ask him why. He now communicated with his magic.

The shifter held back while Callian hopped off the sled and approached Wren.

"Who's she?" asked Wren.

"That's Ravi. She's on one of the teams here. She's good."

"She looks like trouble."

"Trust me," said Callian. "She's a little rough around the edges, but she's a good person to have watching your back in a fight."

Wren was still unsure.

"You're going to need all the help you can get on this one, Wren. Let her come."

Wren sighed. "Fine."

Callian turned and gestured for her to leave the soarsled. Wren noticed she did it with an arrogant slouch as if to say, *I'm coming because I want to, not because I was given permission.*

Everyone took seats at the table and poured chilled fruit juice from the chipped glass pitchers Callian had provided. Wren sat at the head of the table and looked them over. It felt good to see them again. Except for a few extra wrinkles and lines, it was almost like the old days.

"So, half-elf," said Bex, speaking around a mouthful of food. "What's so important?"

"Yeah," said Salka. "Thought you were too good to associate with us?"

"Now, Salka. We all agreed to keep contact to a minimum after that last job went . . . sour." Wren grimaced slightly.

Bex barked a loud laugh. "That's one way to put it. Another

way is 'catastrophic failure.' Or 'suicide run.' "

Wren smiled. "Fair enough. I'm afraid this one isn't much better. I won't hold it against any of you if you don't want any part of it."

"Danger comes with the territory," said Ravi in a low voice. "Anyone who's scared should get a proper job."

The old group glanced at each other. Dalen raised his eyebrows at the shifter.

"What?" she growled. "You got a problem with me, gnome?"

Dalen smiled sweetly then lifted his hand into the air. Everyone stared at him, waiting for some kind of magical illusion.

Dalen slowly arranged three fingers in a gesture used during the War as an insult when vocalizing was not possible. Everyone burst into laughter, except for Ravi. She rose in her seat and looked ready to lunge across the table, but Callian held her back.

"Sit!" he snapped at her. "I vouched for you, Ravi. Do not embarrass me in front of my friends. I won't stand for it."

The shifter reluctantly sat down, but not before pointing a clawed finger at Dalen and mouthing, *Later*, to the grinning gnome.

"Right," said Wren. "If we've all finished posturing, I'd like to get started on this. First off, I'm going to tell you your pay."

"It's not a robbery, then?" asked Salka.

"No, it's not. And the pay is five thousand galifars each."

Silence ruled the table as everyone digested this. Even Callian looked shocked.

"Five thousand?" asked Bex. "Who's putting up the money?"

"I am," said Wren. "I'll leave it with Callian in case anything happens to me. You can collect after the job. I'm telling you this now because the job is dangerous."

"So what is it?" asked Ravi. "For five thousand, I'd kill the king himself."

"I'm sure you would. But thankfully, regicide is not part of the plan. I want to break a prisoner out of Warden Towers."

Silence greeted his statement.

"With the guards all present?" asked Bex.

"Most of them, yes."

"When do you want it done?" asked Salka.

"Tonight."

Bex burst out laughing. "Wren, you really know how to keep life interesting. Gods, but I've missed you."

Wren grinned and glanced around the table. "Everyone in?" Those gathered nodded in turn. Wren clapped his hands together. "Excellent. Callian, the plans?"

Callian hopped onto the soarsled and picked up a leather folder, which he handed to Wren. Wren untied it and pulled out a small pile of vellum. Intricate sketches covered each piece. Wren spread them out on the table and placed the cups and glasses over the edges to keep them from blowing away.

"Plans for Warden Towers," he said. The others leaned over the table to get a good look. Wren pointed to the middle section of the tower. "The cells are here, right in the center. On the bottom floor is a lobby, where everyone is brought in for processing. Here's the mess hall, then the baths and recreation area." Wren pointed to the floor above the prison level. "Above the cells are the barracks, interrogation rooms, offices, and such."

"So how do you plan on getting us in?" asked Salka.

"Through the roof." He tapped the top of the tower. "Warden Towers has a couple of hippogriffs. Not as many as Daggerwatch, but they stable them up here, with access into the tower." He paused and leaned back in his seat. "One thing I want to make clear. This is a rescue operation. There's to be no killing." He held up his hands to forestall any protests. "Think about it. We're breaking one person out of jail. He's nothing to them. If they can't find him quickly enough, they'll drop it. They won't want it known that Warden Towers is breachable. But if we *kill* one of them, they'll keep after us until we're all dead." He looked around the table. "Agreed?"

Reluctant nods from most. He stared at Ravi. "Ravi? This is the deal. Agree, or you're out. I'm not saying we don't get physical—we may have to. Just don't kill anyone."

Ravi nodded, a brief dip of her head.

"Right. I need to gather some supplies. I suggest we meet back at Callian's place at midnight.

• • • • • • •

The large skycoach slid through the night, flying as close to the rooftops as possible. Wren fingered the delicate embroidering sewn into the seats, then opened a small compartment in the door. It held a bottle of wine.

"Where did you get this coach?"

Bex grinned over his shoulder. "Best not to ask."

Wren's eyes widened and he pointed to the front. "Careful!"

Bex turned and smoothly pulled the skycoach upward. Wren peered over the side as a thin spire receded behind them. "You almost hit that one."

"Do you want to drive?" asked Bex.

"No. I'm just saying."

"And I heard you. Now keep quiet. I'm concentrating."

Wren looked down to make sure that the enchantment woven into his shiftweave clothing was attuned to its natural state of darkweave, the shadows woven through the fabric concealing them from casual observation. It was the fourth time he'd checked, but he couldn't help it. Nerves were getting the better of him.

He glanced at the others. Ravi was perched on the other side of the coach, peering down into the darkness. Wren wasn't comfortable with her, no matter what Callian said. He'd have to keep an eye on her to make sure she didn't get out of control. He'd told Bex and Salka as well. The last thing they needed was some hot-headed shifter ruining everything.

Wren glanced over his shoulder to Salka, who stared down at her hands. There hadn't been a chance for him to ask her what was wrong. He made a mental note to talk to her once this was over. Maybe he could help with whatever it was.

Warden Towers appeared out of the darkness ahead of them. Coldfire lights and torches could be glimpsed through the windows all the way up the building. Bex pulled the coach into a climb, and Wren gazed up into the cloudy sky before the half-orc leveled out again.

The tower hunched below them. The roof was a maze of chimney stacks and little huts, the use of which was completely lost on Wren. One side of the roof was covered in rubbish—scrap metal and chunks of rock. The other side held the hippogriff stable, a long, low structure that hugged the edge of the rooftop.

No guards were about. Which meant that Dalen must have started his illusions. Wren had asked him to create the image of a small army of creatures from the Cogs attacking some buildings close to Warden Towers. The hope was that most of the guards would respond to the attack, leaving the tower with a skeletal staff of guardsmen, taking some of the pressure off Wren and the others.

By the look of things, it was working.

Wren made his way to the front of the coach and pointed to the piles of rubbish. "Bring us down over there, flush with the roof. I don't want to land this thing. We'll have to leave it in the air and hope nobody sees it."

Bex nodded and lowered the coach until it hovered next to the rooftop. The group hopped off and Bex tied a makeshift mooring rope to one of the bent pieces of metal. Then they hurried across the roof to the stables.

Iron bars formed a cage around the buildings. The bars weren't simply a fence. They had been bent backward over the stable yard itself, so that no one could climb over. Double gates were set into the fence so the hippogriffs and their riders could access the tower. A massive padlock kept them locked. Wren glanced at Salka, but she shook her head.

"It'd take too long."

Wren nodded and turned to Bex. "Ready?"

The half-orc nodded. Wren turned to the padlock and concentrated. After a moment he could feel heat emanating from the metal. He added power to the infusion until he was forced to take a step back. The metal took on a faint rosy glow, a glow which slowly grew stronger until the whole lock and some of the surrounding bars turned a deep orange.

"Bex?"

"I'm here." The half-orc stepped up behind Wren and held his hands out, almost as if he were warming them from the heat. "Now," he said.

Wren cut off the infusion and Bex released the energy he had been building. Wren felt a blast of cold on the side of his face, like laying his cheek in snow. The padlock let off an explosion of steam and a loud cracking sound, like the slow breaking of ice. Wren took out a dagger and hit the padlock with the pommel. The lock fell to pieces at his feet.

"Told you it would work," he said, pushing the remains of the padlock about with his foot.

Ravi went to push open the gate, but Wren held her back. "Hold on," he said, rummaging through his satchel. He pulled out a vial and dripped a small amount of liquid onto each hinge. "Oil," he said in response to their looks. "Many a thief's career has been cut short by squeaky hinges." He gave the gates a gentle push and they swung silently inward. "Bex, after you."

Bex hurried into the stable yard. Salka followed him, then Ravi and Wren. Bex put his ear to the door, listened, then carefully lifted the latch and pulled the door open. Darkness greeted them. Wren could hear the gentle breathing of sleeping animals. Bex slipped inside and closed the door behind him. Wren had told him to make sure the hippogriffs wouldn't wake up for the rest of the night. If they needed to make a quick escape, he didn't want the Watch chasing after them.

Wren slipped out of the yard and back onto the roof, heading for the north wall. Dalen had said he would give them a sign when a sufficient number of the Watch had shown up to confront his illusion. Any time now . . .

A small light shot upward and bloomed into a slowly-growing circle of blue stars before it faded away. That was it. Wren hurried back to the others. They were waiting inside the first room, near a door that led into the main tower.

"We've got about half a bell before they realize what's going on and come back." He nodded at the door. "Anything?"

"Not sure," said Bex. "It could be a room for the grooms."

Wren took out his crossbows, modified to carry custom-made bloodspikes. He'd spent the afternoon crafting infusions for tiny vials that would render those hit immediately unconscious. He'd handed them to everyone, but Ravi hadn't been happy. He turned to the shifter.

"Remember, Ravi. No killing."

"Fine."

"Hoods up," said Wren, lifting the hood of his shiftweave cloak over his head. The cloaks were specially made to disguise their faces as well as their clothes. To an unsuspecting onlooker, they would appear as ordinary members of the Watch, their unremarkable features instantly forgettable.

Bex opened the door. It was dark beyond, but Wren was still able to see. In fact, Salka was the only one who wouldn't be able to see. All the others had varying forms of night vision.

Wren slipped through the door and looked around. A tack room. Various types of saddles, from gilded and ornamental to functional and plain, hung from the walls. Cages held small animals—food for the hippogriffs. He could hear them snuffling and nosing about in the hay. Blankets were piled on the floor to his right, and an old rusty rack held a variety of brushes to groom the steeds.

Another door lay straight ahead. Wren put his ear against the wood and heard the sounds of snoring. He tried the handle. Locked. He nodded at Salka. She stepped forward, took out her picks, and set to work. In no time, she had the door open. Wren indicated for Bex and Salka to take one side of the room while he and Ravi took the other. The plan was for them to rush in and use the spikes without waking anyone.

It didn't quite work out that way. As Wren pulled the door open, the hinges gave a high-pitched squeal of protest. He froze, glancing at the wincing face of Bex.

"Why didn't anyone remember the oil?" he whispered fiercely. "I just *told* you—"

"Whassa?" said a voice from inside.

Wren stepped in and loosed his crossbow at the man sitting up in his bed. The bloodspike hit him in the chest, sending him straight back onto the mattress. Someone cursed to his left, then tried to raise his voice in a shout. Wren looked over but Bex was already there, his huge hand clamped over the groom's mouth. He jabbed a bloodspike into his neck with his free hand. Wren turned to find Ravi raising a fist over the last groom. She brought it down in a sharp jab that knocked him unconscious. She saw Wren glaring at her, and dropped her victim to the floor.

"What? Don't want to waste the bloodspikes if I don't have to."

Wren took a spike from his satchel and jabbed it into the groom lying at her feet. "We don't want them waking up, Ravi. That's the whole point."

The shifter shrugged and stepped around the body to inspect the next door. Wren lifted the man back into his bed and tucked the blankets around him so he appeared to be sleeping. Bex and Salka did the same with the others.

The door beyond opened into a long hallway lit by coldfire lamps. At its end, they emerged into a large room. Two more corridors fed into the area and a staircase in the corner led down into the tower. Wren thought back to the plans. One of the corridors headed to an identical room on the other side of the tower. The second one, that veered diagonally to his left, was the one that interested him.

"Wait here," he said, and ran down the corridor. It led to the center of Warden Towers and opened onto a gallery that wound all the way around the inside of the building. Wren leaned against the balcony and peered over the edge into the central shaft. It dropped all the way down to the ground floor, where he could make out the bustle and lights of the central hub of the tower. He could see guards scurrying on the floors below him. They shouted back and forth to each other as they tried to figure out what was going on outside. Wren counted down three levels to the cells. Guards patrolled that level, pausing every now and then to peer over the balcony.

"What's going on?" said a voice behind him.

Wren slowly turned to a sleepy-looking guard tying on his tabard. The guard glanced up at him. "I can never get this right," he said with a sheepish grin, trying to look over his shoulder to tie the ties.

Wren glanced down the corridor. He could see Bex peering around the corner in the distance. "Uh, do you want me to . . . ?"

The guard looked up and grinned. "Thanks," he said, turning to the side. Wren tied the two pieces together. "So, what did you say was going on?"

"Oh. Some bugbears and orcs are causing trouble. The Nights of Long Shadows. You know how it is. In fact, you should probably report in. Last I heard, they were looking for reinforcements."

The guard nodded, checking that his scabbard was attached correctly. "I'd better head down."

"Good luck. Wish I could join you, but I have a shift on cell watch."

The guard hurried around the balcony to the lift. Wren watched him descend, then took a deep, shaky breath and rejoined the others.

"What was all that about?" asked Bex.

"Don't ask," said Wren.

They took the stairs down three floors to the prison level. Wren peered along the passage that led to the central shaft, but it was empty of guards. "I don't like this. There should be more guards around."

"But they're all off fighting Dalen's monsters," said Salka.

"I know, but . . ." Wren shook himself. "Never mind. Let's go."

They hurried down the corridor onto the gallery, walking

around it until they arrived at the passage that led to the cells. They moved cautiously, then turned to a recessed doorway. Wren faced the others. "There should be five of them. Pick your target and make sure he's out cold. We don't want any alarms raised. Ready?"

Everyone nodded. Wren took a deep breath, then pushed the door open and plunged into the room, a crossbow in each hand. He loosed one at the man lounging at a desk just inside the entrance. At the same time, he loosed the other at a woman who was walking into the room carrying a tray full of steaming mugs. The bloodspike caught her in the throat and she jerked against the wall, sending the tray flying from her hands. It hit the ground with a loud crash, the mugs smashing, shards spinning through the air. He turned to the other guards, but they were already slumped into a doze.

"Which one has the keys?" he asked, loading more bloodspikes.

"Got them," said Ravi.

Wren held out his hand and the shifter threw them through the air. He caught them and hurried to the door on the opposite side of the room. "Bex. With me. You two stay and guard this side."

The door led into a narrow corridor. Cells lined both sides, fronted by heavy metal doors, each with a small grill at the height of a human's head. "Bex, you take that side. He's over six feet, short hair, tattoo of a dragon down his arm."

Bex nodded and peered into the closest cell. Wren did the same on his side. The first held a shifter who was sleeping on the floor. The next held a gnome who paced back and forth in the tiny room. He moved along as swiftly until Bex called to him.

"Wren, this him?"

Wren peered through the grill and saw Cutter sitting on his bed. He was staring blankly at the wall.

"Cutter," he called. No response. "Cutter! Can you hear me?"

The man didn't even look at him. Wren inserted keys into the lock, one after another, until he found the one that fit. He pulled open the heavy door and entered the cell, kneeling in front of Cutter.

Wren pulled the shiftweave hood down so Cutter could see his face. He indicated for Bex to do the same. "Cutter? Cutter, look at me." He waved his hand in front of the man's eyes, but he didn't even blink.

"Drugged?" asked Bex, leaning over to stare at Cutter's face.

"I don't think so. I think—"

"Well, well," said a voice behind him. "If it isn't the half-elf barrister. And you managed to see your client. That's nice."

Wren turned and saw the woman guard he had talked to yesterday standing just inside the doorway. She was accompanied by four members of the Watch. "Not going to run off again, are you? We didn't finish our chat."

Chapter Ten

The third day of Long Shadows

Sar, the 28th day of Vult, 998

My name is Jana, by the way," said the guard. "Cutter and I go way back." She peered over Wren's shoulder. "Host, is he still staring at the wall? What's wrong with him?"

"His woman was murdered."

"Oh, yes. I heard about that. Stupid bitch. But you know how it is. You push the big boys, they cut your throat. That's how it works."

Wren glanced to the doorway, wondering where Salka and Ravi were. Jana caught his look and grinned. "Looking for your friends? Or should I say friend?"

Wren frowned. What was she talking about?

"You've been set up, half-elf. Betrayed."

Wren's eyes flicked to Bex. The half-orc was frowning, probably thinking the same thing he was. *Ravi.* He should have listened to his instincts about the shifter.

"Actually, it's really handy for me. See, I needed to kill Cutter here—"

Wren's attention shot back to Jana.

"Oh, yes. Didn't I mention that?"

Realization hit Wren, the pieces of the puzzle falling into place. "You work for the Boromars," he said. That was why she was so interested in him when he was asking about Cutter.

"I do. As do my friends here. And certain people aren't happy with Cutter."

"Because of the dreamlily?"

That stopped her. "Dreamlily? What are you talking about?"

"The dreamlily Cutter's woman stole." Wren paused, running through all the information in his head, trying to put it neatly together. "You're not here because of the dreamlily?"

"No. I'm here because Cutter stole money from someone he shouldn't have, and they want him dead. I have no idea what his woman did." She shrugged. "To be honest, I don't care. What I *do* care about is that you've given me a perfect setup for his death. You tried to break him out, we caught you, a fight followed while we bravely tried to stop you, then you were all killed." She smiled. "Nice and tidy. The way I like it."

Wren barely heard her. So this was about two different cases. Jana didn't want to kill Cutter because of the dreamlily. She didn't even know about it. She was after him for something else.

Wren heard a noise behind him. He glanced over his shoulder and saw that Cutter had straightened up. His eyes were red-rimmed, shadowed. Cutter looked at Wren and the half-elf fought an urge to step back. There was no humanity in his eyes—only the flat stare of an animal on the hunt. His eyes flicked to Jana.

"How did you hear about it?" he whispered.

"What?"

"I said, how did you hear about Rowen's death? Who told you?"

Jana didn't answer straight away.

"Answer me!" shouted Cutter, surging to his feet. This time, Wren did step back. He stumbled into Jana, felt her hands on his back as she tried to push him away.

Wren acted instinctively. As soon as he felt Jana's hands on his back, he grabbed a bloodspike from his belt and plunged it into her neck. Her legs gave out, dropping her to her knees. But Wren was still holding the bloodspike. It snapped in his hand, Jana's blood spouting from the hollow tube sticking out of her neck.

Cutter grabbed the sword strapped across her back. He pulled it free, knocking her off balance so she fell at his feet. Wren glanced down at her, then looked up just in time to jerk aside as the point of the sword darted through the space he had been occupying, catching the closest guard in the stomach.

Cutter pushed on the sword, propelling the impaled man backward into his comrades. Then he yanked the blade free and barreled into them, scattering them to the sides.

He swung the sword to the right, catching the closest guard in the side of the neck. One still struggled beneath the body of the first guard, but the remaining guard had his sword out and was aiming a thrust for Cutter's back. Wren drew a dagger from his belt and flicked it past Cutter's shoulder, hitting the guard in the eye. His body jerked upright, then he collapsed backward. Cutter glanced down at the body, then at Wren.

"I thought you said no killing," said Bex from behind him.

"I meant real guards. Not these bastards."

Cutter set off down the passage. "Wait," called Wren. "Cutter, wait! There are more out there. We were set up."

Cutter paused and stared at him. "Speak quickly."

"I made a mistake. I realize that. You weren't responsible for the professor's death. We came to break you out, but it looks like one of my crew betrayed us. Turned us in to your friend back there."

"What's your point?"

"My *point* is that you need us to get out of here. Let me take the lead. I have a few tricks up my sleeve."

Cutter thought about it, then shook his head. "Find your own way out. I don't need your help."

"Cutter, I know where Rowen's body is. I can take you to her."

That made him pause. He thought a few moments, then reluctantly stepped aside. Wren hurried past him to the door, pressing his ear to the wood.

Bex came up behind him. "What tricks?" he whispered.

Wren glanced over his shoulder to make sure Cutter couldn't overhear. "I don't know. I didn't want him running out there killing everyone he laid eyes on."

"Yes, he is rather . . . enthusiastic, isn't he?"

Wren couldn't hear anything through the door, so he opened it a crack. The guard room looked deserted. He pushed the door wider.

There.

Ravi was seated behind one of the desks, her back to him. He looked around, then froze.

Salka was lying on the floor at the shifter's feet.

Wren's mind went blank. He yanked open the door and plunged into the room, crossing the distance to the shifter before the others were even aware he was moving. He grabbed his dagger and pulled back on the chair. It tipped over backward and hit the floor. Ravi didn't react.

An instant later, he saw why. She was dead, a single knife wound through the neck.

Wren lowered his dagger in confusion. How . . . ?

"Wren, down!" shouted Bex.

Wren ducked and spun just in time to see Jana's sword embed itself halfway to the hilt in Salka's chest, thrown there by Cutter. Salka dropped the sword she had been swinging at Wren, a look of disbelief on her face. She stared into Wren's eyes, beseeching.

"No!" Wren shouted. He leaped up and grabbed hold of Salka, lowering her into almost the exact same position she had been in when pretending to be dead. He turned to Cutter, glaring at him through hate-blurred eyes. "What did you do?" he shouted. "What did you do?"

"Wren . . ." said a weak voice. Salka.

Wren looked down at her.

"Wren, it's fine. It's good. He saved . . . save you. I'm so sorry."

"Shh," he said, rocking the woman in his arms. "Don't talk."

"Had . . . had to. Had—had no choice, Wren."

"Stop talking, Salka." Wren turned to find Bex standing behind him. He tried to hold her up to the druid, but the blood pooling beneath them made her slip in his arms. "Bex! Save her. Fix her."

"I can't, Wren," whispered Bex. "She's too far gone."

Wren shook his head and turned to Salka. He tried to smile at her. "Don't listen to him, Salk. We'll get you fixed up. It doesn't matter what you did. It'll be like it never happened."

Salka coughed. Blood welled from her mouth. The next moment, she grabbed hold of his arm, her nails digging into his flesh. She stared deep into his eyes and spoke in a fierce whisper. "Don't judge me on this, Wren. Please. Judge me on wha—what came before."

Her eyes fluttered closed and she went limp in his arms. It

was as if a weight lifted from her body. She just . . . *emptied.*

He laid her gently down. Bex put a hand on his shoulder. "Wren, we have to go."

Wren shook his head and stood up. "Why? Why would she betray us like that? After all this time?"

Bex shrugged. "She was . . . different, Wren. Said she was having problems of some kind."

"I know," said Wren softly. "I didn't even ask her what they were."

"Things have been moving a bit fast today, Wren. No one's had a chance to catch up."

Wren grabbed hold of Bex's arm. "No one hears of this, Bex. No one has to know what happened. She died in a fight with the guards. That's it."

Bex nodded. "I understand."

Cutter had taken the keys from one of the unconscious guards and was opening a wall safe.

"What are you doing?" snapped Wren. He knew he shouldn't be angry with Cutter. He'd saved his life, after all. But . . . he *killed* Salka. Wren had known the woman for twenty years! And now she was dead.

Cutter ignored him while he rummaged around inside the safe. A moment later, he withdrew two curved knives—the weapons Wren had seen him with earlier. He thrust them into his belt and turned to Wren.

"How do we get out?"

"We have a skycoach waiting on the roof."

Cutter nodded and headed for the door. Bex followed. Wren paused, took one last look at Salka, then pushed his grief away, bundled it into a tiny box that was kept hidden away at the back of his mind.

It was an exercise that had served him well in the past.

⊙ ⊙ ⊙ ⊙ ⊙ ⊙ ⊙

They retraced their steps to the balcony overlooking the interior of Warden Towers. Wren took a quick look over the side and saw many more guards than there had been earlier. They seemed to be milling around in confusion. That probably meant Dalen's illusions had been discovered for what they were.

They ran to the staircase that spiraled up to the top floor. No sooner had Wren placed a foot on the first step than he heard a shout from up above. Then the sounds of jingling metal, the sound one usually heard when armored guards were running. He looked at Bex.

"Think they've discovered the grooms?"

"I think it more than likely. Come."

They sprinted back to the balcony.

"What's going on?" asked Cutter. "I thought you had a way out."

"We did."

"The operative word being 'did,' " said Bex.

"So we fight," said Cutter, pulling out his knives.

Wren looked at the hunger for death he saw shining in Cutter's eyes. If they let him get started, it wouldn't end until they were all dead.

"No. Cutter, if you want revenge for Rowen's death, this isn't the way to go about it. You can't take on the whole of the Watch."

"He's certainly willing to try," said Bex.

"What do you suggest?" asked Cutter.

"We walk out," Wren declared.

"What?" the two men unisoned.

"Bex and I are dressed like everyone else. You're our prisoner. With all the confusion down there, no one will notice a thing."

"I don't know, Wren," said Bex doubtfully. "Why don't we get Ravi's shiftweave?"

"No time. Those guards will be here any moment now." He turned to Cutter. "If you want your revenge, this is the only way. Do you understand me?"

Cutter hesitated, then nodded curtly, hiding his knives beneath his shirt. The trio ran around the balcony to the lift. Wren passed his hand over the sigil that summoned the lift and peered over the edge. He cursed beneath his breath. It was still on the bottom floor. He watched as the black disc shuddered in response to the sigil and slowly started to rise.

"How long?" asked Bex.

"Not sure."

"It better be quick because someone's trying to get our attention."

Wren looked up and saw that three hippogriff riders were signaling them. Wren waved back. "Did anyone check the stables to see if all the hippogriffs are there?"

"Afraid not. We heard noises and just assumed. Perhaps we should have made sure."

"Perhaps," said Wren.

The lift was halfway up now, but the riders were hurrying around the balcony toward them.

"Put your hands behind your back," Wren told Cutter.

Cutter obeyed, and Wren placed his hand on the big man's wrists, so it looked like he was keeping a tight grip on his prisoner.

The lift rose higher, but they weren't going to make it before the riders reached the group.

Bex stepped away from the balcony.

"What are you doing?" asked Wren.

"Stalling them. One of us needs to go this way to get the

skycoach, anyway. I'll catch up with you later."

Before Wren could stop him, Bex hurried forward to meet the riders. He caught up with them and they stopped to talk. The riders gestured over their shoulders at the corridor that led to the stables. Bex said something and gestured to the hallway that led to the prisons. The riders frowned at whatever he said and looked toward the hallway.

"Lift's here," said Cutter.

Wren hesitated a moment before leading Cutter onto the round platform. He passed his hand over the sigil for the bottom floor. The lift lurched, then started to descend. Wren watched Bex until the balcony cut him from sight. Then he turned his attention to Cutter.

"Hunch down a bit," he said critically. "Look cowed."

Cutter stared at him from beneath lowered brows. "I don't do cowed."

"Well, you'd better try. We'll slip along the wall, but if anyone stops us, *please* don't pull out those blades of yours and start hacking away at anything that moves. Let me talk to them first."

"Why? Are you going to bore them to sleep?"

"Very funny."

Wren watched the activity below as the lift dropped to the ground. The air was filled with nervousness and barely contained energy, the kind of feeling one gets after a battle. Even though the enemy wasn't real, adrenaline was still pumping through the guardsmen and they were looking for an outlet. It made them more alert, a potential problem.

The lift touched the floor and Wren pushed Cutter ahead of him, past desks and closed offices. They reached the middle of the room, where the huge main desk was situated, a vast circle of darkwood perched on a high rostrum. About fifteen guards stood behind this desk, taking down details from prisoners and dealing with complaints.

Wren heard the guards talking about Dalen's illusion. They seemed to be of the opinion that it was some kind of Daask prank or initiation rite.

They crossed the floor and walked through the door into the outer lobby. Wren closed it firmly behind him, then headed for the entrance to the tower.

"Hold."

Wren turned and felt his heart sink. It was the same elf who had been on duty when Jana confronted him yesterday, and Wren had forgotten to put the shiftweave hood up. Didn't the idiot ever have a day off? He lowered his head behind Cutter's back. "Yes?"

"Where are you taking him?"

"Transfer. Bit of a mix-up. He wasn't supposed to be brought here. Daggerwatch wants him."

"Well, you have to sign him out."

"Oh. Yes. Sorry. Forgot about that."

He dragged Cutter to the elf's desk and turned around, keeping his head lowered. How many people did the elf see every day? Enough that he wouldn't recognize him? Wren hoped so.

The elf pulled a book out from under his desk. Wren quickly slid the book around and signed a fake name. "Is that it?"

The elf glanced at the name. "Yes, that's fine." He held out his hands.

Wren frowned at them. "What?"

"Transfer papers."

"Trans—but I just signed for him."

"So? You know the procedure. No moving prisoners without papers."

Wren made a show of patting down his uniform. He heard a sigh at his side and Cutter leaned forward, took hold of the elf's head, and slammed it into the desk. The elf did not get up.

"Can we go now?" said Cutter.

"Uh, yes. Yes, of course. Well done."

He turned and marched Cutter to the doors leading outside. He pulled them open and stood face to face with a guard—a corporal, judging from his uniform. The corporal looked at Wren, then glanced over his shoulder at Cutter. His eyebrows shot up in surprise. He opened his mouth to say something but Cutter yanked Wren to the side and shoved the guard hard in the chest. The man stumbled, slipping on the steps and falling backward. Cutter pulled the door shut and turned to Wren.

"We need another way out."

Wren didn't say anything. What was the point? Instead, he grabbed hold of Cutter's wrists and they hurried back into the main offices of Warden Towers. He pushed Cutter to the first door they came to. It led into a short hallway with glass windows looking into offices. Wren pulled the door closed and checked the next one. The doors behind him slammed open and the watchman Cutter had pushed down the stairs ran through.

"Stop!"

Wren and Cutter ducked through the door and pulled it closed. A staircase wound up through the levels. "Did he see us?" asked Wren, running past the big man and taking the stairs two at a time.

The door slammed against the wall behind them.

"Stop!"

"That answer your question?" Cutter grunted.

They ran as fast as they could, the sounds of pursuit growing as more guards joined the chase.

"Out here." Wren pulled open a door after they had climbed a few floors. It led out onto the balcony that ran around the central shaft. Wren tried to get his bearings as they ran. He realized they were on the prison level once again. They sprinted around to the branching corridor that took them to the corner staircase. Just before they took the passage, Wren glanced around and saw the lift stopping on their level. Five guards disembarked and pointed at them.

"Khyber's ghost," muttered Wren under his breath. "Why is nothing ever easy?"

The watchmen who had followed them up the stairs appeared on the balcony behind them, shouting for reinforcements. Wren turned and followed Cutter, who was already at the spiral staircase that climbed to the roof.

They sped upwards and through the rooms, past the unconscious guards. Into the open air. Host, he hoped Bex was there. Wren took the lead and they ran across the rooftop. Wren leaned over the edge, his breath coming in ragged gasps.

The skycoach was gone.

He searched frantically in the night and saw it dropping away below them.

"Bex!" he yelled. "Bex! Up here. Bex—"

Cutter grabbed Wren by the arm and yanked him behind a brick hut. Wren heard the stable yard gate bang and peered around the corner. The watchmen fanned out into a line, weapons drawn as they swept across the rooftop.

He pulled back. "Any ideas?" he asked Cutter. "Because if you do, now's a good time to get them out. Don't be shy."

But Cutter wasn't listening. He nodded his head, indicating Wren should look over his shoulder.

"Friend of yours?" he asked.

Wren whirled around and saw Bex steering the skycoach toward them. He was level with the roof, but still some distance away. Relief flooded through him.

"Over here!" shouted a voice.

Wren looked and saw a watchman leveling a crossbow at them. He grabbed Cutter by the shirt. "Run."

"What?"

"Run!"

Without waiting to see if he was following, Wren ran for the edge of the roof, putting everything he had into building up speed. Bex stood up at the controls when he saw him coming. The half-orc's eyes widened in shock when he realized what Wren was planning. He steered the skycoach down slightly so it was below roof level.

But it was still too far away.

Oh well, thought Wren, and hit the edge of the roof, pushing off as hard as possible with his feet. Air whipped at his face and hair, soared in his ears. He saw the skycoach below him, Bex trying to guide it closer.

And then he landed on the front of the vehicle. It dipped alarmingly. He scrabbled up and grabbed hold of Bex's arm as the half-orc lunged forward to grab him. Cutter landed behind Bex, smashing into the seats and breaking their backs. Wren heard him swearing furiously.

Bex dragged Wren inside and pushed the controls forward, sending the skycoach plummeting into the mist—away from the watchmen who were leaning over the edge, staring at them with looks of amazement, annoyance, and hatred.

"That's some good timing you've got there, Bex."

"No problem," called the half-orc. "Where to?"

"Back to Callian's," said Wren.

"Consider it done," said Bex.

Wren smiled and gingerly prodded his limbs to make sure they were all still there.

Then he closed his eyes and let out a long, slow sigh of relief.

Chapter Eleven

The third day of Long Shadows

Sar, the 28th day of Vult, 998

The half-orc settled the skycoach down in the vicinity of Stone Trees. Cutter sat in the back, watching as Bex and the half-elf disembarked and stood whispering together. When they finished talking, they clasped hands and the half-orc disappeared into the night while the half-elf climbed back onboard and turned to face him.

"Let's get everything clear and out in the open," he said. "My name's Wren. I'm an Inquisitive. I was called in to investigate the death of the professor. And seeing as you were spotted standing over his body with your blades in your hands, covered in blood, you were our main suspect." He paused, then said wryly, "You can see why we made that assumption."

Cutter didn't answer.

"Do you have anything to add?" asked Wren.

"Like what?"

"Well . . . anything. Who was the warforged that killed the professor? Why is this package so important? We thought it was dreamlily at first, but it seems like a lot of trouble to go through for some drugs."

"Sounds like you know as much as I do. The only thing I wanted to do was find Rowen. I couldn't care less about who killed who."

Wren looked disappointed. "I was hoping you'd have more information."

"You said you knew where Rowen is."

Wren hesitated. "I do. But first . . ." Wren fished around in his pockets. He pulled out a piece of paper and leaned over the ruined seats to hand it to him.

"Rowen asked a friend of hers to deliver this to you."

Cutter stared at the folded piece of paper. His stomach dropped. This must have been the last thing she ever wrote to him. His hands shook as he reached forward and took it.

He thought he could smell her perfume as he opened it, but that was probably just his imagination. He fought back tears when he saw her neat, elegant handwriting.

Got dreamlily. Hidden it at the family crypt. Will meet later.

"Do you know what it means?" asked Wren. "Is it a graveyard or something?"

"I know what it means." Cutter folded the note and slipped it inside his shirt. He leaned forward, his elbows on his knees, and rubbed his hands over his face. He knew what he had to do. He wouldn't be able to rest until everyone involved in her death had been made to suffer. But he had to take care of something first.

"Take me to her."

"I'm not sure that's a good idea . . . she's . . ."

"I don't care," Cutter snapped. "She died alone, half-elf. I won't leave her there any longer. Understand?"

Wren sighed. "It's your choice. But I warn you, it's not pretty. She was . . . coerced."

Cutter's heart hardened. He would make whoever had done this suffer a thousand times what they had inflicted on her. He would keep them alive while he stripped the skin from their bodies.

"I just need to make a little detour first," said Wren. "To pick someone up."

* * *

Cutter peered over the side of the skycoach as Wren lowered them between two tenement buildings. The walls were only inches away. One twitch of the controls would send them crashing into someone's home.

"I'm sure it's one of these," Wren muttered. He stopped the car and leaned against a window, cupping his hands to either side of his face as he tried to see inside.

"What are you doing?"

"Shh. Yes, I'm sure this is the one."

He tapped lightly on the window, then looked over his shoulder at Cutter.

"In reply to your question, I'm picking up my assistant." He turned back to the window just as the curtains were yanked aside, revealing a dwarf woman in her sleeping clothes. She saw Wren and screamed. Wren let out a frightened shout of his own and grabbed the controls.

"Sorry," he called. "Wrong window."

He nudged the skycoach up to the next floor. He leaned back in his seat and counted the floors in the building. "This *must* be it."

He tapped again. After a moment the curtain moved slightly and an eye peered out. When the owner of the eye saw Wren standing there grinning, he leaned forward and pushed the window open.

"Torin, my friend," said Wren.

"What are you doing, Wren?" whispered the dwarf.

Cutter leaned forward. He recognized this dwarf from somewhere. Where was it?

Of course. Back at the university. This was the dwarf who had barged into the professor's room. The one he punched as he escaped.

"What am I doing?" said Wren. "The night is still young, and we have investigating to attend to. The game's afoot!" He leaned forward and lowered his voice. "And it's also gotten complicated." He jerked his head in the direction of Cutter.

The dwarf straightened up and peered over Wren's shoulder, stared at Cutter for a second, then turned his attention back to Wren.

"Wren," he said calmly, "is that man sitting in the back of your skycoach the same man we had arrested last night?"

"*Stolen* skycoach," Wren corrected. "And yes, it is. We broke him out of jail!"

Torin stared hard at the half-elf, then leaned back and pulled the window closed. "Good night, Wren."

"Wait!" Wren grabbed hold of the window. "Things have changed, Torin. Cutter here isn't responsible for the professor's death."

"Oh? Then who was?"

"A warforged," said Wren, in the manner of one imparting a great secret.

"Oh, really? And did he tell you that?" Torin nodded in Cutter's direction.

"Maybe," said Wren defensively.

"The man accused of killing the professor, the man I saw standing over the body covered in *blood* holding *knives*, tells you it wasn't him, but some unknown warforged? *Right.*"

"No, really. New evidence has come to light. We're going to the place his woman hid the dreamlily, to see if she left any more evidence."

"And then?"

"And then Cutter here wants to track down those responsible for her death and do nasty things to them. I'm hoping we can find out the identity of the warforged before he does so."

Torin sighed. "This is a dangerous game, Wren."

"I know," said Wren quietly. "That's why I want you watching my back."

Torin thought about it for a while. They heard a commotion down below. Cutter glanced over the side and saw the dwarf woman from the window standing in the street with a few other dwarves, pointing at them.

"Can we move this along?" Wren asked.

"Don't rush me," snapped Torin.

Cutter scowled and sat back. All he wanted to do was throw the half-elf over the side and take the skycoach himself, but he hadn't told Cutter the whereabouts of Rowen's body.

"Very well," said Torin. "I'll come. But why didn't you call me when you were planning his breakout?"

"You have a family, Torin. I don't involve you in things like that." His face darkened. "Besides, I probably saved your life."

"What do you mean?"

"I'll tell you later. Hurry. Get dressed."

"Torin?" called a sleepy voice from inside. "What are you doing?"

"Nothing," he called. "Now look what you've done. You've woken her up."

To Cutter's amazement, the half-elf actually looked panicked.

"Hurry!" he whispered. "Get your things."

Torin ducked back inside. Wren smiled weakly at Cutter.

"His wife," he explained. "Apparently, she doesn't like me."

"I wonder why?" said Cutter.

Torin popped his head out the window. "I'll meet you at the bottom."

"Can you just hop out the window? It'll be quicker all round."

The dwarf looked as though he was about to protest, then thought better of it and grabbed hold of the window frame. He pulled himself up.

"Torin, what are you doing?" called the voice from inside.

"Nothing, dear. I'll see you later."

"Is that Wren out there?"

"Hurry!" whispered Wren. But when Torin still did not move fast enough, he grabbed hold of the dwarf's arms and yanked him into the skycoach. He fell into the seat in front of Cutter and Wren grabbed hold of the controls, lifting them sharply into the air and scraping the building on the way up.

• • • • • • •

Cutter had seen a lot of dead bodies over the years. Host, he'd been the cause of a lot of them. But he'd never had to look at one he had any kind of emotional connection with. He'd always been able to separate himself from what he saw.

That wasn't possible this time.

He stood before the open doorway of the half-collapsed house. The hallway stretched before him, a long path into darkness.

"It's the last door on the right," said Wren quietly.

Cutter stepped into the house. The old floorboards creaked beneath his feet. Had she heard something similar? Had she been prepared for an attack, or was she surprised?

He passed a door that opened into a large living room. A

stone fireplace took up half the wall. He wondered who had lived here before. It was the kind of home he always wished for as a child, big and rambling, with places to hide and play. He could almost see them gathered around the fire on cold winter nights.

Cutter hoped they had been happy. He wouldn't want Rowen to die in a place surrounded by the ghosts of an unhappy past. It was a strange thought. People lived their lives in a house, never imagining what would happen after they had gone. That wasn't the way people thought. At the most, imagination might turn to events from the past. If people knew something had once happened in a particular room, their senses might reach out and trick them with a half-glimpsed ghost. But who was to say all such ghosts were from the past? Why could ghosts not be from some terrible deed committed in the future?

Cutter blinked, aware that his thoughts were running away from him, stalling him from doing what had to be done. He turned away from the room and walked slowly to the last room in the hallway, his stomach writhing like a pit of angry snakes.

He took a deep breath.

And stepped into the room.

He knew where to look straight away, as if he could sense her presence. He could see her familiar shape beneath the old sheet. Her pose brought back a memory, a languid night in summer. Cutter walking into their room to find her lying in the bed, a single white sheet the only thing covering her body.

Cutter almost smiled, the reaction triggered by the memory. He choked it back and walked slowly forward.

Some of Rowen's hair stuck out from beneath the sheet, and his eyes were drawn to the dark strands as he approached. He squatted down next to her, close enough to touch, but all he did was stare at the gentle curls lying against the pitted floorboards. Cutter reached out and gently touched them, no more than a graze of his fingertips against her hair.

He sat like this for a while, then he wrenched his gaze away and forced himself to look at her. What he had initially thought were black patterns on the sheet was actually blood that had seeped from her many wounds.

There wasn't much of the sheet left untouched.

Something strange happened to him. Even though he knew it was impossible, even though he knew nobody could survive the amount of blood loss he could see, he found himself thinking that maybe she wasn't dead. Maybe she was just hurt. Maybe, if he just waited long enough, she would wake up. He stared unblinking at her chest, searching for the tiniest hint of movement, the merest ghost of a breath. Something—anything—that would back up his futile hope.

It was some time before he realized it wouldn't happen.

He reached up and gently pulled the sheet down. A thick red line ran across the fabric where it touched her neck.

He carefully folded it over and rested it over the wound.

He was surprised to see her face was untouched. A few drops of blood on her right cheek were the only hints of what she had gone through.

He wiped them away. The look on her face was one he knew well. When they fought and went to bed angry, she slept with this look on her face, as if she were arguing in her sleep. That was what she looked like. Like she was somewhere on the other side arguing with ghosts.

He smiled at the image this conjured in his head. His Rowen.

His poor Rowen.

He emerged from the dark corridor of the broken house carrying her body. He had wrapped it in the sheet, making sure all her features were covered.

Wren and Torin straightened up when he approached. Cutter ignored them and placed Rowen carefully in the back seat. Only then did he turn to the others.

"She discovered that her ancestors once built a small mausoleum at Dragon Crypts in the City of the Dead. It's where she wanted to be laid to rest. That's where you'll find the dreamlily."

Atop the cliffs overlooking the north and east sides of Sharn, the City of the Dead lurked like a vulture waiting for its prey to die. It was a ghost town made up of empty streets and ivy-covered shrines, of crumbling mausoleums and weed-choked pathways. It was a constant reminder to those who happened to glance upward that death was always watching. Always waiting.

Cutter found it peaceful.

He remembered the first time Rowen had brought him here to show him the family crypt. He'd been puzzled at first, wondering why she was so excited about it, but after a while he realized that it gave her a sense of belonging, a sense of worth. She liked the idea that the family name had once meant enough to someone to build a resting place for future generations.

Cutter found that point a bit morbid, but he understood. It removed that tiny vestige of guilt she felt at what she did, that remnant of shame she couldn't quite shake no matter how often she said it was her choice. It proved to her that she wasn't just a courtesan. She had a name. She had a history.

Now, as before, they had to walk to get to the City of the Dead. It existed outside the manifest zone with Syrania, so that the spells that allowed the skycoaches to fly so effortlessly, that held the buildings up to their impossible heights, failed to work here. He hadn't minded the walk before. He'd been walking in the company of someone he loved.

Now he carried her body.

"I'm just saying it's a long walk," snapped Wren.

"And I'm saying you need more exercise," said Torin. "You're lazy."

"Lazy? How dare you! I'm fitter than you are."

Cutter, walking ahead of them, heard the dwarf snort. "Of *course* you are, Wren. You just keep telling yourself that and maybe you'll eventually believe it."

Cutter heard a *thwack,* like someone hitting cloth. He paused and turned. Wren was standing in front of Torin, smacking himself in the stomach.

"Come. Give me your best shot."

"Wren, I'm not hitting you."

"Why not? I want you to. I *order* it."

"No."

"Coward."

"What?"

"Scared I'll show you up? Come. Hit me. I won't feel a thing."

Torin sighed. "Fine. You ready?"

"Yes—no, wait." He leaned forward and tensed his stomach. "Right. Now."

Torin swung his arm and jabbed the half-elf in the stomach. He dropped like a sack of sand falling from a great height. The dwarf stood over him. "I didn't even hit you that hard!"

Cutter turned and resumed his march, leaving the bickering voices far behind him.

Rowen's family crypt stood on the outskirts of the city itself, nestling amidst the crags of the cliffs and overlooking the district of Dura. Cutter wasn't sure if that was because her ancestor couldn't afford a better plot, or if the city itself hadn't existed back then and he just picked the spot he wanted.

The last time they'd come, it was a clear day. They'd stood on the crumbling steps of the mausoleum, her back against his chest, his arms encircling her, and looked out over Sharn. A fierce wind buffeted them, flicked her hair against his face. The Dagger River had been visible way to the south. She'd talked idly about finding a ship and sailing away. Like it was that easy.

And why couldn't it have been? Host, if they'd just gone, simply upped and left, she'd still be alive.

They'd still be together.

Cutter stood on those same crags, the same wind slapping at his face, and gazed into the night. Sharn unfolded below him, an untidy mess of twinkling lights and inky blackness. Skycoaches drifted through the air, crisscrossing each others' paths, their lights winking out as they descended behind invisible buildings.

He watched for a moment longer, then turned and walked up the steps into the dark doorway of the crypt.

As he entered, a small everbright lantern flickered on above him and cast an orange glow over the interior. Rowen must have come back on her own and placed it there. Unless she'd brought it with her recently when she hid the dreamlily.

He looked around for signs of her recent visit. Faint footprints had disturbed the dust, leading to one of the rectangular alcoves that lined the walls. Thick cobwebs hung over these like silk sheets hanging over the beds of the dead.

He carried her to the center of the room. A crude plinth emerged from the tiles, an obtrusion of the rock itself as high as his waist. It had been carved into a rough hourglass shape and a smooth slab of stone placed atop it.

Cutter laid Rowen on the stone, then stared down at the shrouded shape. He still found it hard to believe it was her.

But it wasn't. Not anymore. She had been full of life, full of passion. This was just a vessel, something that tried to contain her spirit while she was here.

He knew that, but he couldn't quite *feel* it. Not yet.

He turned down the sheet, gently kissed her cold lips, then covered her face for the last time.

He bowed his head for a moment, then stepped back and turned away. He closed his eyes, squeezing them so tight that his head started to ache.

He breathed in. Held it. Let it go in a shuddering sigh. He breathed in again.

Fight it, he told himself.

Hide it.

Push the pain away until you need it.

You can't tame the beast. You can only chain it. And you *know*. Know that one day that chain will break and it will rise up and devour you, grown and fattened by the energy you've pumped into it in your attempt to keep the shackles strong.

But that day was far away.

Right now was what mattered.

Cutter opened his eyes and stared at the wall.

Right now was what *always* mattered.

"You can come in," he called.

Wren and Torin entered, both of them subdued. They cast sidelong glances at the plinth.

Cutter nodded to the alcove in the wall. "Her footprints lead there."

Wren nodded and hurried to the wall. He pushed aside the cobwebs and peered inside. After a moment, he turned back.

"There's nothing here."

"What?"

Cutter hurried forward and looked for himself. The hole was empty. But there were signs in the dust that something box-shaped recently lay inside.

"But . . ." he looked at Wren, confused.

"Maybe she gave up its location. They tortured her, Cutter. Not many can hold out against that."

"Wren!" said Torin urgently.

Wren and Cutter turned at the tone of his voice. He was staring at the entrance to the crypt. A young woman stood there, dressed in white robes and smiling at them.

"Hello," she said. "Are you looking for something? Maybe I can help."

Chapter Twelve

The third day of Long Shadows

Sar, the 28th day of Vult, 998

The young woman explained that her name was Gaia. She was a cleric of the Silver Flame, and she was simply *ecstatic* to have some company other than the dead bodies she was usually forced to talk to.

They were such terrible conversationalists, she said.

Wren thought she was a bit touched in the head.

She led them through the thoroughfares of Dragon Crypts, babbling all the while about how lonely it was, and how it wasn't fair that she was stuck here on her own, and something about a stupid lich over in Halden's Tomb.

Wren had to interrupt. "Sorry, did you say *lich?*"

She glanced over her shoulder. "Yes. That's what I said. He hangs about with necromancers and the like. Not a nice creature, I can tell you that."

"No," said Wren weakly. "I'm sure he's not." He exchanged a look with Torin. The dwarf raised an eyebrow as if to ask, What are we doing?

Wren gestured for him to keep quiet and follow his lead. He just hoped Cutter would do the same. The man was starting to show signs of impatience.

Gaia led them to Warden Tower, a soaring white monolith that stood on the edge of the cliffs and overlooked Clifftop. Wren counted the windows that dotted the pitted surface and reckoned the structure was twenty floors high.

"Do you live here?" he asked.

"Yes. All the Wardens do."

"And how many of you are there?"

"Oh, just me. The powers that be think one cleric is sufficient." She stopped and turned to them. "But they're all fools! Don't they know how dangerous it is here? I'm *beset!* Beset from all sides!"

Wren glanced warily to the right and left of the deserted concourse. "By what exactly?" he asked.

"By them! Necromancers, worshipers of the Keeper." She leaned forward conspiratorially. "Creatures of *evil!*" She smiled and straightened up again. "The last Warden couldn't handle it," she said matter-of-factly.

"What happened to him?" asked Torin.

Gaia pointed to the top floor. "He threw himself out of that window." She turned and pointed to the spot where Wren stood. "And he landed right there."

Wren took a step to the side.

"He made quite a mess, I can tell you."

"I can imagine," said Wren.

She hurried ahead and disappeared into the tower. A moment later she appeared at a window one floor up. "Come, then. If you want to know what happened to your box."

The three looked at each other. Cutter shrugged and started forward. The others joined him and they walked through the open door into the tower.

It was dark, but enough light filtered in from outside to reveal that they stood in a small anteroom. A door stood closed directly opposite them. Wren pushed it open and paused as a wave of warmth and golden light spilled out, catching him by surprise. The room beyond was lit by a massive fire almost as high as Torin. The flames roared in a huge, ornately carved grate, the smoke disappearing up the chimney. Wren wondered where the chimney led. He hadn't seen any smoke coming from the tower outside.

They stepped into the room.

"Up here," called Gaia.

A staircase started at the base of a dark archway and curved around the inside of the tower. They followed it all the way to the top and emerged into an untidy attic room. Windows were all around, affording a panoramic view of the City of the Dead. Gaia sat on a small stool at one of the windows, waiting for them.

Cutter looked around. "So where's the box?"

"Hmm? Oh, it's not here."

"But you said—"

"I said I know where it is. And I do." She turned to the window and pointed outside. "It's there."

The three crowded to the window and stared out. There were no lights among the crypts. The streets and tiny square buildings were shrouded in darkness.

Except for one spot.

Far away, close to the outskirts of the city, they could see twinkling lights.

"And what is that?" asked Torin.

"The Mausoleum of Gath."

"Oh. And who is Gath?"

"Gath is the lich. Haven't you been listening?"

"Are you saying the lich stole the box?" asked the dwarf, turning to face the cleric.

"Not the lich. He's not there. His priests did."

"Why?"

Gaia shrugged. "I've no idea."

"She's lying," said Wren, glancing over his shoulder.

"What?" said Torin.

"She's lying." Wren turned and stared at Gaia. "See, we inquisitives have a few tricks up our sleeves. One of them is a little infusion that tells us when we're being lied to."

"And?" whispered Gaia.

"And I activated it when I entered this room. Now, why don't you tell us where the box really is?"

"No."

"No?"

"No. It's hidden safely away. That's all you need to know. If you want it back, you have to do something for me."

"Like what?" asked Torin.

"The lich stole something from me—a chest with scrolls in it—ancient teachings. I want you to retrieve them for me. If you do, I'll give you your box."

Wren looked at the others. "What do you think?"

Torin shrugged. "Your call."

"Why is it his call?" asked Cutter. The others looked at him. "What? I mean, do we even need to get it back?"

Wren looked surprised. "But it has the dreamlily in it."

Cutter shrugged. "So?"

"Excuse me," interrupted Gaia. "What are you talking about? What dreamlily?"

"The dreamlily in the box. We're trying to return it to someone."

"Who told you it contained dreamlily?"

"What are you talking about?" snapped Cutter, his patience giving out. "We *know* it contains dreamlily."

Gaia shrugged. "Don't get angry with *me*. It's just . . . I happened to open the box and look inside. It's not dreamlily."

"Well?" prompted Wren. "What is it?"

"A Khyber dragonshard."

⊛ ⊛ ⊛ ⊛ ⊛ ⊛ ⊛

Wren, Cutter, and Torin sat on chairs around the fire on the lowest level of the tower.

"So what are we thinking?" asked Wren.

"That this has suddenly gotten a lot more complicated and a lot more dangerous," said Torin.

"Agreed. But it explains why they're so desperate to get the package back. Now that we know it's a Khyber shard, that opens up a lot of possibilities. Maybe we've walked into a fight for ownership."

Cutter leaned forward. "The guy who was supposed to pick up the package . . ."

"Salkith?"

"Right. He said he was supposed to deliver it to someone at an inn in Khyber's Gate."

Wren leaned back in his chair. "Interesting." He glanced over at Torin. "Torin, my friend, what am I thinking?"

Torin scowled. "If you're not thinking about women, then you're probably thinking we should sneak into this mausoleum and steal her precious chest of scrolls, get back the shard, then deliver it to the contact in Khyber's Gate and follow him."

Wren grinned and glanced at Cutter. "He's very good, you know. I trained him myself."

Cutter stared at Wren a moment before speaking. "I can see

why *I* need to do this. It's the only way I'll find out who was responsible for Rowen's death."

"Yes. And?"

"And I want to know why you're so interested."

Wren looked surprised. "It's part of my case. Larrien asked us to find out why the professor was killed. The shard is part of that reason. If we trace the shard to the top of the chain, we find out who ordered his death. And Rowen's. Our goals are the same, Cutter."

* * *

Gath's Mausoleum wasn't like any of the other buildings in the City of the Dead. It was a proper temple, a structure the size of a mansion that sat at one side of a huge courtyard. A doorway wide enough for five horses to walk through stood open and gaping, lit by torches mounted in metal stands.

"It goes underground, as well," whispered Gaia from their position behind a crumbling crypt. "That's where the chest is located. It's a huge hall on the very bottom floor. The chest is black, with silver clasps."

"And what about this lich you keep talking about?" asked Wren.

"He's not there. I keep an eye on his comings and goings. He left a few days ago and hasn't returned."

"Then why haven't you gone to get it?"

"I can't. He has laid warding spells against my entry."

"So what's the plan?" asked Torin.

"We have only one suit of shiftweave," said Wren, "and I happen to be wearing it. So I think only I should go in." Torin opened his mouth to protest, but Wren held up a hand before he could say anything. "This is one of those times when stealth is more beneficial than strength, Torin."

"It's not a complicated layout," said Gaia. "There are rooms above ground and a few shrines. You need to take the stairs down. You'll know you're in the right place when your breathing starts to echo."

"Big, is it?"

"No."

"Then why—"

"It's massive."

"Ah. I see." Wren stood up and muttered something under his breath. The colors of the shiftweave clothing ran into each other and darkened to a deep black. But it wasn't simply black. It was the color of night. The color of shadow. Wren pulled the hood up and lowered it over his face.

"That won't help if someone looks straight at you," said Torin.

"I know. I plan to kill one of the clerics and steal his clothing."

"What about weapons?" asked Cutter.

"What about them?"

"Well . . . do you *have* any?"

Wren gave Cutter the look he usually reserved for banking clerks and junior politicians. "Of course I do. What kind of an imbecile do you take me for?"

Cutter looked at Wren in surprise. "Then why didn't you use them when you were breaking me out of jail?"

"Didn't need to. Everything was under control."

"Stick around," muttered Torin. "It'll come."

Wren patted the shiftweave over his wands and took a deep breath. "Right," he said. "I'll be off."

"Try not to die," said Torin.

"I'll definitely do my best."

Wren slipped out from behind the crumbling crypt and

skirted around the wide concourse. He took his time, keeping to the shadows, pausing every time he had to cross open spaces to make sure no one was around.

The half-elf was partway across one of these empty spaces when he glimpsed movement in the periphery of his vision. He froze in mid stride, then slowly turned his head. A black-robed priest walked across the square, heading for the entrance to the temple.

Wren waited until the priest was about to leave the square—a square, Wren noticed, that was covered in black stains that looked suspiciously like blood—and pulled out the last of his specially made bloodspikes. He quickened his pace until he was no more than half an arm's length away. The cleric must have sensed him, because he paused and started to turn around. Wren wasn't expecting that, and almost walked straight into his back. He stopped and quickly jabbed the spike into the priest's neck. He caught the priest as he fell and dragged him away from the open space and behind a low wall. He stripped the robes from the unconscious body—an old man, as it turned out—and slipped them over his head.

Wren straightened up, wrinkling his nose as he took a deep breath. The robes had a strange smell to them—the intoxicating Kaarnathi spice, *riek,* if he wasn't mistaken.

"Naughty evil cleric," he whispered to the old man. He straightened his back, folding his arms into his sleeves in the same manner as the cleric, then stepped into the open once again.

A wide colonnade fronted the temple, the high ceiling supported by huge pillars engraved with brutal scenes of sacrifice and death. Wren walked past them, trying not to look too closely at the carvings, and entered the temple.

The first thing he noticed was the cold. It was like walking into a meat cellar. His breath clouded the air before him. Couldn't they light a fire? Was the Keeper against heat or something? No wonder he didn't have more of a following.

He stood in a circular room that had four arches leading into complete darkness. Oily torches flickered and spat in iron wall sconces.

Wren belatedly realized that he made the perfect target to anyone standing beyond the arches, so he hurried through the closest one into a darkened corridor. With nowhere else to go, he followed it as it sloped gently downward. The flagstones were slippery, so he kept close to the wall in case he needed to steady himself. On closer inspection, he realized it probably wouldn't do him much good, as the walls were coated with moss and slime.

The hall ended at a low doorway. The lintel that supported it was made of old rocks that had been jammed together. He prodded it with his finger, setting off a cascade of dust and loose stones. He didn't like the look of that.

He leaned through the opening to have a look. Stairs led down into darkness. The air was even colder here, a miasma that seemed to seep into his body like the chill of a midwinter morning.

Wren felt a sudden wave of regret. Maybe strength in numbers was the best bet after all.

He decided to go back for the others, then heard voices coming from behind him. Wren looked back and saw torchlight approaching in the distance, the faint glow glistening on the damp walls. He looked around the featureless hallway and found no options. There was nowhere for him to go.

He ducked under the lintel. The steps were concave, the passage of feet over the centuries forming smooth depressions in the stone. The walls leaned in on him, giving him no more than a hand's breadth of space to either side of his shoulders. Water trickled freely down the walls and gathered in the shallow bowls at the center of each step.

He hurried down, praying that he wouldn't meet anyone coming from the opposite direction. Not only did he not wish to encounter any of the Keeper's priests, but he also didn't think two people could fit in the confined space without one of them having to back up.

And sure as Khyber, it wasn't going to be him.

As Wren descended, he found the light slowly increasing, an orange glow that reached up the stairs so gradually that he noticed it only when he could see his feet as they tentatively felt their way on each step. He ducked down and peered ahead. A short distance away he saw an opening, and beyond that the source of the light. Wren slid along the damp wall, grimacing at how easily his back skated across the rock.

He paused at the entrance and looked around. It led into what could only be the massive room that Gaia described. The far walls were lit by flickering torches, but they were so far away he could barely see the flames. Thick pillars supported the ceiling every few feet. They extended the breadth and width of the cavernous room, hundreds of them.

He waited as long as he dared but didn't see any signs of life. He slipped inside and moved to the wall. He didn't run, even though every fiber in his body was telling him to. He walked calmly, trying to keep to the shadows as much as possible.

Gaia had said that the clerics performed their rites and worshiped in this room. As he walked, Wren could see an open, circular area in the center. An altar stood in the middle of the circle, and some kind of large cage hung above it, held by a rusting chain.

She'd said there was a room directly opposite this circle and altar. Wren saw that it could open off any of the walls, and it was difficult to see across with the pillars blocking his view.

Wren studied the chamber, then decided to walk the perimeter of the room. He turned when he reached a wall, walking opposite the entrance to the stairs. Wren picked up his pace until he could once again see the altar and cage.

He found the door a few moments later, a solid slab of stone set flush with the wall. The only hint of it was a faint black crack outlining the shape. He almost walked right past it.

Wren lifted his hands to the stone, searching for some kind of release. As soon as his palms touched the granite, he heard a faint click and the door swung open with a loud grinding noise.

The half-elf winced and looked over his shoulder. The sound echoed horribly in the huge chamber. A waft of even colder air puffed out, carrying the smell of mustiness and mold. The torches all around the room flickered as if touched by the breeze.

Wren paused, took a look around, then stepped into the room.

He saw the chest Gaia had described. It rested on a small, yellowish table to his left. It wasn't large, only about the length of his forearm. A row of small everbright globes set into the wall above the chest cast a dim light.

Something bothered him, but he couldn't figure out what it was. He shook off the feeling of disquiet and hurried to the table. No time to wait around. He muttered an infusion that checked the chest for hidden traps. The box was clean.

He reached out and tentatively touched the lid.

As his fingertips grazed the black wood, the room plunged into darkness as if someone had dropped a sack over his head.

He heard a noise behind him. It was a soft, dry sound, like the hiss of sand over stone.

It wasn't that, though. It was the sound of something laughing.

⁂

Cutter peered out from behind the crypt, watching as Wren disappeared through the door. He turned to Torin.

"I don't get it. What's with all the 'I'm going in alone' stuff? Strength lies in numbers. In having someone to watch your back. Am I wrong?"

"No."

"So . . . what? Does he have some kind of death wish? Or a hero complex?"

"Death wish, no. Hero complex—only when women are around."

They both paused, then turned slowly to face Gaia.

"What?" she said, looking between them.

"Nothing." Cutter stood. "I'm not waiting here. We've got more of a chance of getting the shard with two people searching."

"And what about me?" asked Torin.

Cutter looked down at him. "Do you think they have many dwarf clerics?"

"I have no idea."

"Neither do I. You want to head in? That's fine, but keep away from me. You draw attention to yourself, you deal with it."

Without waiting for an answer, Cutter turned and sprinted through the night, heading for the huge doorway. He pulled his blades out, holding them flush against his forearms.

He flattened his back against the wall and ducked his head around to see what lay beyond. His eyes flicked around, then he pulled back and paused. A circular room. Torches lighting it. Arches leading to darkness. Perfect place to ambush someone.

He took a few deep breaths then bent low, trying to make himself as small a target as possible, and slipped inside. He moved to the right and ducked beneath the first arch.

It opened into a short corridor. Two doors opened off either side and a spiral staircase stood at the end, leading up to the second floor of the temple. Cutter crept forward and listened at the nearest door. He couldn't hear anything, so he opened it and had a quick look inside.

Nothing. Empty of everything but cobwebs and dust.

He closed the door and slipped back to the entrance hall. Just before he entered the torch-lit room, he heard voices. He stopped, knowing he would be invisible to anyone beyond, and waited for the owners of the voices to appear.

He didn't wait long. Two dark-robed clerics walked into the room and headed beneath the archway to the left of the main doors. Cutter waited a moment to make sure no one else was coming, then followed them.

They led him down a long, sloping corridor. He hung back, able to see their position by the torch they carried. Cutter reckoned this was the passage Wren must have taken, since it headed downward.

He realized that Wren would be moving slowly, scouting the way before he moved. The priests in front of Cutter, however, were moving quite fast—quickly enough to catch up with Wren if Cutter didn't do something about them.

He hurried his steps and before long, he could see the priests' outlines as they walked in single file down the cramped tunnel. He drew closer, shifting his hold on his blades. Cutter glanced over the priests' heads and saw that the corridor soon came to an end at a low doorway. He couldn't wait any longer.Cutter sprinted the last few steps and grabbed hold of the closest one's chin. He yanked the priest's head back and drew the blade quickly across his neck. Blood sprayed everywhere. The remaining cleric let out a shocked cry. Cutter spun around and stabbed him in the heart before he could do anything else. They both collapsed to the flagstones.

Cutter wiped the knives on their robes, then stepped over the bodies and ducked beneath the lintel onto the stairs. He descended as quickly as possible and soon found himself in a massive room filled with pillars. No one was about, so he headed forward.

He saw Wren—or at least thought it was him—disappear through a distant doorway. He jogged forward, slowing briefly to study an altar with a cage hanging above it. Cutter arrived at the doorway moments later. A faint light glowed from within.

A moment later, all the torches in the huge hall flattened and flickered out as if buffeted by a giant gust of wind. Darkness sank over him like a mist.

Then Cutter heard someone laughing.

Wren reached for a wand at his belt.

"Please do not do that," requested a raspy voice. "Or I'll be forced to kill you and your accomplice."

"What accomplice?" asked Wren. "I'm here alone."

"Then who is the large human lurking around outside?"

"Ah." Wren raised his voice. "Cutter, can you come in here?"

"I can't see anything," Cutter called back.

"Forgive me," said the wispy voice. Two pinpoints of red light flared to life.

"Oh, dear," whispered Wren.

"If you are at all religious," said the voice from the same vicinity as the glowing eyes, "now would be a good time to pray."

As if those words were some kind of release, Wren's night

vision was restored. He stared into the desiccated face of a lich. Wrinkled skin stuck to his skull, no more than a thin covering of ancient gray flesh. Two narrow holes were all that remained of the nose.

Light flared outside as the torches reignited. Wren saw Cutter move away from the door, then return a moment later carrying a torch. He held it at arm's length, the sputtering flame giving off an oily black smoke. As he entered, the torchlight crawled over the lich, revealing him in all his nightmarish glory. Tall, emaciated, he wasn't much more than a walking skeleton. His clothing was ancient and tattered, the colors drained by age.

"What I would like to know," said the lich, "is what you are doing here. It has been some time since anyone was stupid enough to enter my temple."

"You . . . weren't supposed to be here," said Wren, realizing how weak that sounded.

The lich seemed to agree, because it let loose the dry laugh once again. "Forgive me. I took you for an intelligent man."

"Maybe if you didn't go around stealing things from people, we wouldn't be here," said Cutter.

Wren winced as the lich turned his attention to Cutter. He tried to gesture for the idiot to keep quiet, but Cutter couldn't—or wouldn't—see him.

"And just what am I supposed to have stolen?"

"That!" Cutter pointed at the black chest with one of his knives.

The lich looked in the direction Cutter indicated. His red eyes shrunk to tiny pinpricks. "What makes you think I stole that?"

"Because the cleric told us!" shouted Cutter. He looked at Wren. "Why are we playing this game? Just take it!"

"Cutter—"

"We don't have time—"

"Cutter!" Wren shouted. "Shut up!"

"You would do well to listen to your friend," said the lich.

"He's no friend of mine," Cutter growled.

"Regardless, you should be thankful of his presence. He is the only thing stopping me from taking your head." The lich turned to Wren. "And the only reason I am not plucking your heart from your chest is because I am amused."

Wren frowned. "Amused?"

"Look in the chest. I give you permission."

Wren hesitated, then turned and approached the box. Cutter brushed past him and flung open the lid. He peered inside.

"It's full of scrolls," he said. "Just like she said." Cutter reached inside.

"Do not touch them!" roared the lich.

Cutter froze, his hand halfway into the chest. Wren pushed him gently aside. The scrolls were ancient and yellowed. They looked like they would fall apart if he so much as breathed on them.

"Close it," said the lich.

Wren carefully put the lid back in place. His fingertips left marks on the wood. He absently wiped the dust on his shirt.

"What's happening?" said Cutter.

"We've been tricked," Wren admitted.

"Tricked? Who by?"

"By the Silver Flame wench." The lich laughed. "She used you to try to steal my phylactery. My life force. It is the only way I can be harmed."

"Gaia?" said Cutter. "She tricked us?"

"It would appear so," said Wren.

"So there never were any scrolls?"

"Doesn't seem that way."

"And now," said the lich, "I think I will kill you after all."

Wren whirled. The lich walked toward him, hands raised. A crimson glow was forming around his fingers.

Cutter stepped to the side and opened the chest. He held the torch over the scrolls. "Hold!" he ordered.

The lich froze.

Cutter leaned close to Wren. "Run when I give the signal."

Wren looked at him. "What sig—"

He didn't get a chance to finish the sentence. Cutter thrust the torch into the chest and set the scrolls on fire. The lich howled and lunged forward. Cutter upended the box, scattering the burning scrolls over the floor. Wren sprinted for the door. Cutter came after him, but not before grabbing the chest and thrusting the torch beneath the lich's clothing. The creature went up like it was soaked in oil.

"That won't kill him," said Wren as Cutter joined him. They both ran into the huge chamber.

"No, but it might delay him long enough for us to get out." Without waiting for a response, he started running as fast as he could.

Wren joined him, the screams of rage and pain echoing behind them like a strong wind at their backs.

They skirted the courtyard and reached the crypt. Torin scrambled to his feet. Gaia turned to face them.

"Did you get it?"

Cutter threw the box at her. She caught it and fumbled with the catch, almost dropping it in her eagerness. She yanked it open and looked inside.

"But . . ." she looked from Wren to Cutter. "There's nothing in here."

Wren smiled. "Sorry, my dear. You told us to get the chest, and that's what we got. We're not responsible for its contents."

"But the scrolls aren't here! If you think I'm giving you—"

Cutter strode forward and lowered his face until it was inches from Gaia's. "Don't even *think* about trying to go back on the deal," he said softly. "You wanted the chest, we got it. And we nearly got killed in the process. You said the lich wasn't there."

"He wasn't! He must have come back when I wasn't watching."

"You will give us what is ours," said Cutter.

"Or what?" said Gaia.

"Or I send Wren and Torin away and you get to see what I can do with this." Cutter held the point of his knife close to her eye.

Gaia thought about it. After a moment, she nodded. "Fine."

"Good girl," said Cutter, and sheathed his knife.

Chapter Thirteen

The third day of Long Shadows

Sar, the 28th day of Vult, 998

When Cutter first entered Wren's apartments, he had to struggle to keep the amazement from showing on his face. He'd be damned if he let the half-elf see how he felt. He probably watched everyone who came into the place just to see their reactions.

Cutter glanced over, and sure enough, Wren was watching him with a slight look of disappointment.

The thing that was so impressive about the apartment was that it seemed to be outfitted entirely from livewood. The wood had been coaxed and shaped into everything possible: chairs and desks, bookshelves and partitions. It must have taken decades to get the apartment into its current form.

"It was my father's pet project," said Wren, launching into a little speech in spite of Cutter's apparent unconcern. "He poured all of his time and a substantial amount of money into it. Wanted it ready when he retired." Wren looked up at the gracefully curved branches that formed the rafters. "Unfortunately, that meant neglecting everything else while he worked on it, his family included."

Wren glanced at Cutter. "He died two days before he was to move in. My mother always said there was a lesson there, but we could never decide if it was about the foolishness of putting off one's enjoyment to some unforeseen future, or spending all your time on pointless projects." He grinned. "I always said it was the first, she said the second."

"And he's devoted his life to making sure he doesn't repeat his father's mistakes," said Torin, heading past them into the lounge. He took a bottle of wine from the specially grown alcoves.

"Indeed. Instant gratification is the way to go. At least if I die, I'll die happy."

Wren put the small box on the dining table and sat down. He took off the lid and set it aside while Torin poured three glasses of wine and handed them round. Cutter took his crystal glass gingerly, scared he was going to break the delicate stem.

"I don't suppose you have any ale?"

"Afraid not, no."

"Didn't think so." He placed the glass gently on the table and turned his attention to the box. The Khyber dragonshard lay on a bed of white cloth—Cutter leaned closer. It looked like a towel. The shard itself was black, about the length of his hand, with purple-blue veins running through it. Such a small thing to be responsible for so much trouble.

"So," said Wren, "what do we know?"

"Nothing," said Torin. "Everything we thought we knew was based on the assumption that this was a drug deal gone bad. Everything's changed now."

"Not so," said Wren. "We simply need to adapt our theories. First, why is the professor involved? Why did he have the shard in the first place? Cutter, did Rowen say anything to you about that?"

Cutter felt his whole body lurch at the sound of her name. He took a gulp of wine.

"Nothing that I can remember," he said. "We always assumed it was drugs, seeing as it was Salkith coming to pick it up."

"Right. Salkith. Did he say anything of interest when you questioned him?"

"Only what I told you. He was supposed to drop this off at a tavern in Khyber's Gate. The Goblin's Revenge, I think he said."

"At least that's some progress."

"Not really," said Torin. "We have no idea who he was supposed to deliver to."

"And the fact that he was delivering it there in the first place is strange," said Cutter.

"How so?" Wren leaned his elbows on the table.

"It's Daask territory. If Salkith was recognized, he'd be killed straight away. There's a war going on between Boromar and Daask. We don't just traipse around each other's territories setting up meetings and drops."

"Now that *is* interesting," said Wren. "So what would make someone from Boromar set up a meeting with someone from Daask?"

"You're making assumptions," said Torin. "One, you don't know it was someone from Boromar, and two, you don't know it was someone from Daask. This could have been a private deal."

"I don't think so," said Wren. "The speed with which Rowen was tracked down implies someone with a lot of resources. No, until we know differently, let's assume this is a Boromar deal."

"That opens up more questions than answers," said Cutter.

"Boromar clan isn't just a bunch of people working for one person. It's hundreds, thousands of people with their own agendas. Most of the members of Boromar have never even laid eyes on Saidan Boromar. They do what they do and they pass money up the chain. As long as that money keeps moving, everyone is happy. To say it's a Boromar deal means it could be one of ten thousand people."

"Hmm. Point taken."

"The biggest question to me," said Torin, "is where does that warforged fit in? Does he work for Boromar? He certainly did their dirty work for them when he killed the professor and Rowen." He glanced at Cutter. "Sorry."

Cutter ignored that. "The warforged seemed a bit crazy to me. Talking all this religious stuff, you know? 'He was the darkness' kind of thing. The Boromars don't like crazy people. They're not dependable. And it was like no warforged I've ever seen. More like an animal than anything else."

"Fine. Let's leave it out of this for the meantime." Wren poured himself more wine. "So what do we do next? We have no more leads. Nothing to follow."

"I have a question," said Cutter.

"Please," said Wren, "go ahead. We're all ears. At least, Torin is, but it's not his fault the way he looks."

Cutter ignored that. "Now, understand that I've never been to a university before."

"Understood," said Wren.

"But the professor—he taught at Morgrave?"

"He did."

"The thing is—at his apartments—I didn't see any kind of course work. No books, papers, or *anything* that told me he was a teacher."

Wren and Torin exchanged glances.

"So the way I see it, he's the key. All this started with him. Why don't we check his office?"

Wren said, "Torin, did you check his office?"

"Didn't know he had one."

"And you call yourself an inquisitive?"

"Me? I've barely been at Morgrave. Why didn't you check it out? You went back there."

"I had other things on my mind."

"Hah. I'll bet you did."

"Enough. What time is it?"

Cutter glanced out the window. "Probably two hours 'til dawn."

"There's still time. We need to take a look around his office before everyone arrives for the day."

"One point," said Cutter. "Actually, two. We're wanted by the Watch. We have to keep a low profile until we can clear our names. So strolling through the crime scene of a murder I'm supposed to have committed doesn't seem such a great idea."

"Good point." Wren turned to Torin. "I'll understand if you want to sit this out. So far, your name's been kept clean."

"Please," said Torin. "I've stuck with it this far. I'm not going to bail when it starts to get interesting."

Wren grinned at Cutter. "Such loyalty. He's like the son I never had."

"I'm older than you are, idiot."

"Then you're like the father I never had."

"You had a father."

"Then the slightly aloof yet wise and knowing great uncle I never had."

Torin thought a moment, then said, "I'll accept that."

Cutter blinked, staring between the two. They were like an old married couple, bickering like that all the time.

"And what's your second point?" asked Wren, turning his attention abruptly back to Cutter.

"What? Oh. We have no idea which office is the professor's."

"Leave that to me."

"Host," groaned Torin, "do we *have* to?"

Cutter hung back and looked around nervously while Wren knocked briskly on the door of the boarding house.

There was no immediate answer, a fact that didn't surprise Cutter in the least. It was still an hour before dawn. No one in their right mind would be up.

He had to admit that it was kind of peaceful. The cold of night had faded, and he could feel a tiny hint of warmth in his bones. The sky was clear up high. Not a cloud in sight, and the stars still shining like brittle ice.

The door opened a fraction, and the point of a sword slipped through to hover a hair's breadth from Wren's groin. He looked down and raised his eyebrows in amusement.

"My dear, I did one day hope to have children. Please don't destroy that dream for me."

The door opened all the way, and Cutter saw a young dwarf woman standing in her nightdress. Her hair was a mess, flat in the front and sticking up like a bird's nest at the back. The right side of her face was marked by the wrinkles of her blankets.

"Wren? What are you doing here?"

"We need your help, Kayla."

"My help? Why not ask Larrien?"

"I don't want to wake him at this ungodly hour."

"But you'll wake me?" She looked over Wren's shoulder. "Who's that?"

"That's Cutter. He's helping us investigate the death of the professor."

"I thought that was taken care of. Didn't they arrest someone?"

"Yes, but I'm not sure he's the right man. Will you help? It's urgent."

Kayla sighed. "What do you want me to do?"

"Did the professor have an office on campus?"

"Of course he did. Oh—"

"Yes. It would have been nice if someone had told me earlier. Can you take me to it?"

"Of course. Just let me get dressed. Host, Wren, I'm so sorry. I didn't even think of it."

"That's fine. I won't say 'no harm done' because we don't really know that yet. But let's hope we can find something."

• • • ◉ • • •

The university was deserted so early in the morning. Kayla led them sleepily through the front door and across the huge plaza that would be filled with students in a few hours.

The first hallways they walked down were bare of ornamentation. The walls needed a coat of paint underneath pinned-up notices and advertisements. The deeper into the university they went, the more expensive the finishings became. Paintings of past chancellors lined newly painted walls. Busts of famous explorers stood atop marble plinths. Eventually, the walls were no longer painted but were instead lined with polished wood paneling. Pictures hung in intricately carved frames which were gilded with precious metals. Cutter looked about with interest. He had no idea there were such rich pickings in a school. He'd been through tough times—it would have been a matter of a few moments to break in here and walk away with something valuable. The security was a joke.

He was busy thinking who might possibly buy some of the paintings when Kayla stopped before a solid mahogany door.

"This is it," she said. "I should warn you. The professor was rather . . . messy."

"Not to worry. We'll figure it out. Many thanks, Kayla. I wonder—could you do one more thing for us?"

"What's that?" she asked suspiciously.

"Nothing that would get you into trouble, never fear. Do you happen to know how good the recordkeeping is here?"

"Everything is cataloged, if that's what you mean."

"And you have a collection of dragonshards, is that correct?"

"We do. Quite a substantial collection."

"I thought so. Could you do me a favor and check to see if any are missing from your collection?"

"Why would any of them be missing?"

"It's just a hunch I have. Please?"

Kayla sighed. "Fine," she said. "I'll see what I can find out. Please don't wander off. Especially you," she said, glancing at Cutter before hurrying away.

Wren grinned at him. "You have that look about you," he said, before heading into the office.

Cutter followed and felt his heart sink as he looked around. The room was an explosion of parchment. It lay everywhere, on every available surface, jammed between books, stuffed beneath books, piled on chairs, piled on the floor.

"Host, when she said he was messy, she wasn't jesting," said Torin.

Cutter stared around the room. Yellowing paper was even stuffed between the top of the bookshelves and the ceiling. "How are we going to get through all this?"

"Not by complaining about it, that's for certain," said

Wren. "Torin, you take that side. Cutter—"

"I'll take the desk, thanks." Cutter walked around the antique desk and lowered himself into the padded seat. He let out a groan and rubbed his back.

"Fine," said Wren. "You take the desk. I'll take this wall."

"What are we looking for?" asked Cutter.

"Anything that strikes you as odd or out of place. Correspondence, threats, anything."

"You think we're going to find a signed letter from the killer asking the professor to steal the dragonshard?"

"One can always hope," said Wren.

"Maybe while we're at it, we should keep an eye out for a receipt for the shard with the killer's address on it."

"Yes," snapped Wren. "That would be very helpful. Get started, please."

"This is a waste of time," said Cutter. But he tried the drawers to the desk anyway, and found them locked. He pulled out a small knife and jammed the point between the lock and the desktop. He gave it a sharp push, and the drawer jerked open with the sound of cracking wood.

The others were looking at him. "What?"

"That desk looks like it's a hundred years old," said Torin. "Don't you have any appreciation for the finer things in life?"

"Afraid not." He pulled the drawer out and dumped its contents onto the desktop. He rifled through them. Some reminder notes, a diary—he opened it but it was just birthdays and anniversaries—some old boiled sweets that had been long forgotten. Nothing interesting.

He did the same with the next drawer, then the next, until his chair was surrounded by piles of useless papers. But he didn't find anything of interest. Torin and Wren were methodically going through the bookshelves, checking each piece of paper carefully before moving on to the next. The task would take all day at this rate.

Cutter got down on his hands and knees and checked inside the empty drawer compartments. He knocked on the wood, searching for hiding places. Desks this old were usually riddled with them.

He couldn't reach in far enough so he moved around the back of the desk. He knocked on the wood, but it was too thick to hear anything. If there was a hidden compartment, he wouldn't be able to tell.

He stood up and glanced at the others. They were busy with their own searches. He turned to the desk and kicked the wooden paneling with the heel of his boot.

The sound of breaking wood pierced the room like the crack of thunder. Torin and Wren both jumped.

"What are you doing, man?" exclaimed Wren. "That desk is worth more than you are."

Cutter paused in examining the hole he had inflicted in the panel. "Desks this old usually have hidden compartments. Believe me, I know. You'd be amazed how many people who say they're broke hide their money in a desk and think it's protected."

He kicked the desk again. This time the whole panel caved in. He pulled the broken wood out to reveal an empty space.

"You see? There's room to hide a few valuables. You could fit a painting in it if you wanted."

Torin peered inside. "Pity there's nothing there for us."

"I haven't finished yet."

He proceeded to tear the desk apart, something he found immensely satisfying. Even after the other two told him to give it up, he kept at it, sure that if a professor was going to hide anything, he would hide it in his desk.

He found what he was looking for on the underside of the desktop, after prying it away from the frame with the knife.

It was a small notebook, and it was hidden in a tiny drawer that opened from within the beveled patterns that ran around the edge of the desktop.

He held up the book. "Is this what we're looking for?"

He had to admit that he got a certain amount of satisfaction from the looks on their faces. They weren't so clever now.

He tossed the book to Wren. He opened it and paged through it, frowning.

"What is it?" asked Torin.

"It appears to be a record—" he paged some more, then flipped back to the beginning— "a record of someone's movements. For a whole week. From the time they left their house to the time they returned at night. Everything the person did."

"Which person?"

"Someone called Xavien." He looked up. "Sound familiar?"

Cutter shook his head. Torin did the same.

"Why would a professor be following someone?" Cutter asked.

"Indeed. That's the question, my destructive friend."

Torin looked around at the mess. "We've found what we're looking for. Let's get out of here before someone finds us."

They opened the door and stepped out. Kayla was hurrying down the corridor toward them. "You were right," she said, stopping before them. "There's a Khyber shard listed in the manifest that isn't where it should be."

Wren glanced at the others. "Now we know why they approached the professor." He turned to Kayla. "Does the name Xavien mean anything to you?"

"Of course. He's a city councilor. Donates a lot of money to the university. He even has a wing named after him."

"Is that so?"

"Why do you ask?"

"Hmm? Oh, no reason. My dear, thank you ever so much. You've been a great help to us." He gestured over his shoulder. "I wouldn't go in there, if I were you. It's a bit of a mess."

They headed down the corridor. Kayla ignored them and opened the door.

"Hey!" she called angrily. "What have you done?"

"Uh, I think you have woodworm," said Wren over his shoulder. He lowered his voice. "We should run now."

Chapter FOURTEEN

The third day of Long Shadows

Sar, the 28th day of Vult, 998

By the time they left the university, dawn had broken over the city. It was strange for Cutter to see the sky at daybreak, instead of noticing the odd beam of light that managed to shoulder its way down to the lower levels through gaps in the huge towers.

"I'm not happy about this," said Wren.

Cutter turned from his perusal of the sky. "Not happy about what?"

"Politics. You think the people *you* hang out with are bad? Well, they're nothing compared to politicians. A bunch of useless, self-serving sycophants who are good for absolutely nothing."

"As always," said Torin, "your faith in our government institutions leaves me amazed."

"Oh, come now," snapped Wren. "All they do is swan around trying to look busy so no one will notice they don't actually do anything. And believe me, they'd kill to protect those positions."

"Wren, that's the stupidest generalization I've ever heard from you. And that's quite something, let me tell you."

"Think what you want. But just wait, Torin. When all this is over, you'll see I'm right. Dirty politics and corrupt officials."

"So what's the plan?" asked Torin.

Wren opened the diary. "It says here that Xavien works at Sun Tower in Upper Central. He's there first thing in the morning to last thing at night."

"He sounds conscientious," Torin pointed out.

"Doesn't he just? Pity he seems to be involved in our little problem, isn't it?"

"We don't know that for sure."

"Come now, Torin. Your natural suspicion seems to be wearing tiresomely thin these days."

"I'm just saying that the professor could have been following him for other reasons. We have to keep an open mind. Cutter, what's your opinion?"

"Mine? Go in assuming the worst. That way, things can only get better."

"You see?" said Wren to Torin. *"That's* the mind of an inquisitive."

"Wonderful. Maybe the two of *you* should be partners then."

"Don't be absurd." Wren snapped the diary shut. "Whatever we decide to do, I can't be seen there. The Highest Towers district is only a casual stroll from my apartments. I'd be recognized in an instant."

"You being the world famous inquisitive that you are," said Torin sarcastically.

"Exactly."

"I may have a plan," said Cutter.

"You?" said Wren, in much the same tone of voice Cutter imagined he would use to point out a fly in his soup.

"Yes, *me*. A moment ago you were saying I had the mind of an inquisitive."

"Yes, but I didn't mean it." He sighed. "Go on then. What is it?"

"I pretend to be Salkith. If he's involved, Xavien will come running like a headless chicken wondering what I'm doing at his place of business. If he's not involved, then he won't be bothered."

Wren frowned. "But what if he knew Salkith?"

"Then I'll improvise. But I don't think he would know him. Salkith is just a courier. He's an independent contractor. People hire him *because* they don't know him. That way, they can keep their distance if anything goes wrong. If I go in there pretending to be him, I can try to draw information out of Xavien."

"It might work," said Torin.

"And it might not," said Wren.

"But we don't have any other options right now." Cutter held out his hand. "And I'll need the shard."

Wren looked at him in amazement. "What?"

"The shard. Give it to me. I need it to prove who I am."

"But what if you lose it?"

"I won't." Cutter sighed. "It doesn't belong to you, half-elf. If anyone has a right to hold onto it, it's me."

Wren thought for a while, then sighed and pulled out the silk-wrapped shard from his inside pocket. He reluctantly handed it over and opened his mouth to say something.

"Yes, yes, I know," said Cutter. "Be careful with it." He tucked it into his pocket. "Stop worrying so much. I've got it taken care of."

"Oh, that's good. For a moment, I was actually concerned."

• • • • • • •

Sun Tower was one of many civic buildings in the district of Highest Towers. All the city laws were passed within, political lives were built up and ruined by the merest whisper, and a simple glance at the wrong person during a weekly city council meeting could end a career.

At least, that was how Wren put it before Cutter left them at a restaurant across the street.

When the council wasn't in session, tourists could buy tickets to tour the council hall and see the famous view from the top of Sun Tower, one of the tallest buildings in Sharn. It was the quickest way Cutter could think of to get to the top of the building where Xavien had his offices, so he handed over his last few coins with a wince and took the lift to the top floor.

Cutter had to admit, it was almost worth the money.

Even before he arrived at the top floor, Cutter could see bright golden light spilling down the lift shaft above him. As the lift rose higher and bumped gently to a stop, the grandeur of the Council Hall was revealed in all its glory. The room was massive. Ornate pillars were spaced evenly along the highly polished marble floor. They supported the high ceiling, where a painstakingly detailed mural of the continent of Khorvaire had been painted. He noted that it was kept up to date, with the latest lightning rail lines painted in.

Golden light from the early morning sun bathed the whole room in a syrupy radiance. Long black shadows fell across the floor where the pillars cut into this light. The central pillar formed a shadow that pointed directly at Cutter, the rest forming a fanlike pattern as they angled to either side.

Cutter left the lift, his footsteps echoing in the vast chamber. A few people walked briskly through the hall, carrying files and piles of papers and trying to look as if they were doing important work. Cutter stopped at this last thought and shook his head. He was starting to think like Wren.

A huge wooden table lay in the center of the room, directly beneath the painting on the ceiling. As he passed, Cutter noted that the table was inlaid with a detailed mosaic of Breland, the decoration even more detailed than the painting above.

Cutter squinted against the light as he approached the huge windows that overlooked the city. The towers and neighborhoods receded into the far distance, glinting in the morning sun. Everything looked so clean by the light of a new day.

But soon it will tarnish, thought Cutter. Clouds would appear, shadows bringing dampness and dirt. For now at least, for a brief, tiny moment, it seemed like anything was possible, the hope of a new day borne on that golden light.

He stared through the window for some time, until the increasing sounds of the business day getting underway brought him back to the job at hand.

He turned around and stopped a young, flustered looking woman. "Do you work here?"

"What?"

"I asked if you worked here."

She held up the huge pile of files she had cradled against her chest. "What do you think?"

Cutter shrugged. "I'm looking for a man called Xavien. Do you know him?"

"*Lord* Xavien. And yes, I know him." She made to move on.

Cutter stepped in front of her. "Could you go and fetch him for me?"

"I *beg* your pardon? Do I look like someone who runs around fetching people?"

Cutter stepped back and looked her up and down. "Actually, you look like a woman trying too hard to look younger than she actually is."

The woman's face flushed red and she opened her mouth to say something clever and witty to put him in his place. Cutter held up his hand to stop her.

"Just go to Lord Xavien and tell him Salkith is here. Believe me, if you don't, the absolute best that will happen to you is that you lose your job."

She stared at him. Cutter could see her trying to decide how to react, wondering if she should call security. Cutter gazed back impassively until she turned and stormed back the way she had come.

Cutter turned back to take in the view once again. He found it calming.

Some time passed before Cutter heard footsteps approaching behind him. He tensed, but carried on looking through the window.

"Are you looking for me?"

Cutter turned slowly, a bored look on his face. The man who stood before him was in his fifties, corpse thin with gray hair swept back from a high forehead. He held his hands behind his erect back as he waited for a response. He was trying his best to look officious, but Cutter could see the old man's arms tensing as he clenched and unclenched his hidden hands.

"That depends," said Cutter. "Who are you?"

They stared at each other, Cutter deciding then and there that this guy didn't know what Salkith looked like. They wouldn't be playing this game otherwise.

"Are you Xavien?" he asked.

The man hesitated, then nodded. "I am."

Cutter nodded. "You know who I am, then."

"I would hear you say it."

Cutter sighed. "I'm Salkith."

Instantly, the man's demeanor changed. He leaned forward

angrily. "Then what in Khyber's name are you doing here?" he snapped. "How do you even know of me?"

Cutter waited until the man finished. "You done? I hope so, because you take that tone with me again and I walk."

"Good! Please. Walk."

"I don't think you want me to do that."

"On the contrary. I've had a difficult time of late, and the last thing I want is someone of your caliber hanging around causing trouble."

"I see." Cutter made a show of glancing around, looking bored. Then he took the silk-wrapped bundle from his pocket. "You won't be needing this, then?"

"What is it?" Xavien reached out and took the bundle, unwrapping it to see what was inside.

When he saw the shard, he actually dropped it. Cutter couldn't believe his eyes. Xavien yanked his hands out from under it as if it burned him. Cutter caught it before it hit the floor.

"Are you insane? Do you know how much trouble it was to find this?"

Xavien gripped him by the shoulder and moved him closer to the windows. He made sure no one was nearby before he spoke. "Where did you get it? I was told it was lost."

Cutter shrugged. "I don't like to leave a job undone. I went back to the university after the Watch left. He'd hidden it in his office."

Cutter could see Xavien running everything through his mind. The old man looked out at the rising sun. "There's still time," he said to himself.

Cutter kept quiet, hoping Xavien would say something else that would tell him what was going on.

No such luck. Xavien turned his attention back to Cutter.

"You were supposed to deliver this to someone."

"At the Goblin's Revenge. Yes. But I doubt they'll still be waiting for me."

"No, of course not. You'll have to take it directly to him. He doesn't have much time."

Damn. Was Salkith supposed to know where this person lived? But then, why arrange the drop at the tavern?

"Where am I meant to take it?" he said, chancing a risk.

"Quiet. I'm thinking." Xavien pursed his lips and stared at Cutter for what seemed like an age. He moistened his thin lips. "You understand I'm going to trust you with something that is dangerous to know."

Cutter didn't say anything.

"If word gets out, or if anything goes wrong, we'll know it was you. We have resources you wouldn't believe. You will never escape. You will be hunted down and killed."

"I don't like threats, Xavien."

"I understand that. I'm just telling you how it is. There's a lot at stake here. I need you to finish what you started. And just so you know I appreciate your . . . enthusiasm to finish the job, I'll triple your fee. But only if you deliver the shard."

"Who to?"

"A priest."

"A priest? What would a priest want with this?"

"Because he is a priest of the Shadow. Please do not ask any more questions, because I won't answer them. You will find him at the Temple of the Six in Khyber's Gate. He is an elf called Anriel. Are these instructions clear?"

"You want me to go down to Khyber's Gate during Long Shadows? I think I'll need more than triple."

"How much, then?"

"Ten times the original amount."

Xavien didn't even blink. "Done. Now hurry. He must have the shard before the changing of the next Watch. Tell him the rest of the plan is back on track. He will understand."

Xavien turned his back on Cutter and walked away, disappearing through a distant door. Cutter watched him go, then headed across the floor to the lift.

"Khyber's Gate?" said Torin. "Why there?"

"I've told you what he told me. You know as much as I do."

"A priest of the Shadow," said Wren. "Can it be a coincidence that this is happening now? During Long Shadows?"

"No way," said Torin. "The Shadow's priests have more power now than at any other time during the year. I'd say that whatever they're doing could only be accomplished during these three days."

"That makes sense," said Cutter. "Remember what he said about there still being time, and that it had to be done today."

"And today is the last day of Long Shadows." Wren sat back in his chair. "I don't like this. Not one bit."

"Neither do I, but if I stand any chance of finding out who did this to Rowen, I have to follow it through."

"And don't forget clearing your name of murder," said Wren. "I realize that's not quite as important as revenge, but it's high on the list of priorities."

Torin shook his head. "Are we seriously suggesting we let him take the Khyber dragonshard straight to the people who wanted it in the first place? That professor died because he didn't want it falling into their hands."

Wren frowned. "He's right, Cutter. It's too dangerous. We

have no idea what they want it for. Taking it to them is a stupid thing to do."

"What makes you think you have any say in the matter?"

"Excuse me?"

"I'm the one holding the dragonshard, and short of killing me and stripping it from my corpse, there's no way you're going to stop me from going to Khyber's Gate and finding out why Rowen died."

Wren stared at him. "You know, you're a very hard man to like."

"Just as well I don't care then, isn't it?"

"Yes. Just as well." Wren stood and moved around the table. "Torin, I seem to have left my money at home. Pay the bill, will you? We travel to Khyber's Gate."

Chapter Fifteen

The third day of Long Shadows

Sar, the 28th day of Vult, 998

The way Cutter looked at life, the rich people landed at the top of the pile—the bankers, the businessmen, the politicians (the crooked ones, at least), and the higher echelons of the criminal world.

Directly underneath were the people who kept them in those positions—the badly-paid workers, the people who borrowed their money and had to pay interest, the people who voted them into power, and the people who supported crime in any number of ways.

At the bottom were the people who did everything else. The ones who cleaned up the messes everyone else made, and the ones who took an active role in the criminal lifestyle, working directly for the crime bosses at the top.

It was the same with the city. At the very top of the pack was Skyway, a part of the city that floated above Central and Menthis Plateau. Then there was the Upper City, where all the aforementioned bankers and politicians lived. Middle City housed the workers, the people who scraped and saved just to get by. Then there was the Lower City where Cutter lived. He considered it pretty much the bottom of the barrel, but the one thing Sharn had taught him was that someone was always worse off than yourself.

Below Lower City were the Depths. The Depths held the sewers of the city—huge, algae-covered aqueducts that once carried water but now shipped the city's effluence to Khyber knew where. Beneath these sewers were ancient ruins and moldering buildings—all that remained of Sharn's earlier ages.

And underneath that, underneath everything, were the Cogs.

The Cogs stretched underground the whole length and breadth of Sharn. Lakes of fire dotted the landscape of the Cogs. Channels of sluggish lava carved through the bedrock, powering the industrial heart of the city. The Cogs were home to the city's foundries and forges, the slaughterhouses and tanneries. The stench of sulfur was ever present, and oily black smoke lurked around chimneys that were no more than uneven holes cut in ceilings, too small to handle the belching smoke. The walls were stained black, the slightest touch leaving hands covered in grime.

A short visit to the Cogs meant hacking up filth and soot from your lungs for a week.

This was where Khyber's Gate lay. Khyber's Gate was the only housing district in the Cogs, and its crumbling tenements were home to nearly all the goblins and bugbears who worked there.

"So what's the plan?" asked Wren. They walked nervously through the all-but-deserted streets.

"Identify Anriel and find out what he knows."

"What if he doesn't tell you?" asked Torin, looking around

and fingering one of the many knives he had armed himself with after learning where they were going.

"He'll tell me."

Wren stepped around something messy in the street. "I understand you need the shard to get inside the temple," he said, pausing briefly to check the sole of his shoe, "but Cutter, you can't let the shard get out of your sight. Do you understand that? Whatever they have planned for it, it can't be good."

"I'm not stupid," said Cutter. "Host, you're like an old woman, you know?"

Torin looked around uneasily. "Where is everyone? This place is like a ghost town."

"Last night was the final night of Long Shadows," said Wren. "I'll bet everyone had a bit of a party."

"Oh. So those weren't dead bodies we passed a while back? They were just drunk?"

"Mmm . . . no. I think those *were* dead bodies. Those goblins are just passed out, though." Wren pointed at three goblins and a bugbear lying on the pavement outside a tavern.

"I have to say I'm a bit confused as to how one gains entry into the headquarters of one of the most powerful criminal gangs in the city," said Torin.

"I've been thinking about that," said Cutter.

"And?"

"And I haven't come up with anything. I'll play it by ear."

"I'll lay odds you end up using your fists."

"If that's what it takes."

"There are more elegant ways of achieving one's goals, Cutter," said Wren.

"Like what?"

"Like using an invisibility potion."

Cutter stopped in his tracks. "Are you serious?"

"Absolutely. I picked it up from my apartments before we went to the college. The thing is, the effects won't last very long."

"But it'll get me inside?"

"Yes. And another one will get you out."

"Then that's all I need."

They stopped at a side road that traveled to their left and seemed to end against a sheer rock face. Except it wasn't a rock face. Cutter could see flickering light through small openings scattered all the way up to the stalactites of the distant roof. Two guttering torches framed an almost invisible doorway carved from the rock. That was it. The infamous Temple of the Six.

"Doesn't look like much," said Cutter.

"Maybe so," said Wren, "but it has warrens that extend for miles below ground. As far as I know, it was built by some of the original inhabitants of this city, long before any of us showed up."

"I'd better get moving," said Cutter.

Wren handed him two small vials.

Cutter pocketed one and opened the other. "All of it?"

"Every drop," said Wren.

Cutter emptied the contents down his throat. It tasted like the medicine his mother used to give him. He grimaced and smacked his lips, dropping the vial to the ground. He looked at his hands as they slowly faded from sight.

Cutter moved to the side, watching Wren and Torin to see if they could detect the movement. But their eyes remained fixed on the spot where he had been when he took the potion. He turned onto the road without a word and headed for the temple. He could hear his footsteps and his breathing. He should have asked Wren about that. Could other people hear him? Or were his sounds masked as well? He decided to play it safe and assume others could hear him. That way, there'd be no surprises.

The doors were closed, but as he pushed on them they slid smoothly inward. He quickly stepped to the side, in case someone was standing there. Nobody appeared, so he slipped through the door and into a long corridor. The walls were roughly carved from the rock, all angles and hard lines. Coldfire torches lit the way.

He pulled the doors closed and set off down the hall. At the bottom of the corridor was an anteroom with three passageways leading deeper into the temple.

Four priests of the Keeper stood at the far right passage. They were dressed in rags, their faces dirty and drawn. Cutter froze, but they hadn't heard him. They were too busy looking at a parchment of some kind. Cutter slipped around the wall and took the corridor closest to the entrance.

It led to a staircase that wound up through the rock. He took the stairs and reached another long corridor, this one lit by real torches. The greasy flames guttered and spat oil onto the walls. Black smoke marks smeared the rock above the sconces.

It occurred to Cutter that he had no idea how to find Anriel. He knew that Daask had allowed the shrines to the Shadow and the Keeper to be rebuilt, but those shrines could be anywhere. And he had no idea how long the invisibility would last.

He moved cautiously down the corridor, pressing himself hard against the wall every time someone approached. It was happening more and more frequently. Goblins and bugbears and orcs roamed the corridors, shouting greetings or cursing each other as they passed.

He realized he must be in the Daask headquarters. None of the creatures he passed looked like priests. In fact, the last priests he saw were those back in the anteroom.

He'd taken the wrong corridor.

Cutter retraced his steps as fast as he could. The priests were gone from the anteroom, and he took one of the corridors to the right. It led to a staircase that cut sharply down through the rock.

At the bottom was a square room with a single door. No chance of getting lost this time. Cutter eased the door open and listened. He heard distant chanting. A good sign. Chanting usually meant priests. They liked the sounds of their own voices.

He slipped into the corridor and followed it as it cut a jagged and uneven path through the rock. Cutter reckoned that whoever carved the path simply turned in another direction every time they hit a seam of hard rock, coming back to the original direction whenever they could.

The path eventually spat him out into another hallway. This one was paved with heavy flagstones, the walls more smoothly cut. Doors were spaced evenly along the corridor, and between these doors, coldfire torches cast small blooms of blue light up the walls and onto the ceiling. Cutter heard the chanting clearly now. It came from his right.

So. What was his next move? He'd stumbled in blindly, not knowing how he would find Anriel, but now that he was here, he needed a plan. He couldn't just wander around hoping to bump into him. That could take forever.

He tried one of the doors, and was surprised when it opened into an untidy room. Someone's sleeping quarters, by the look of it. Cutter entered and closed the door behind him. A desk stood against the far wall, cluttered with old books and loose pieces of parchment. He picked up a book and checked the spine. It was called *Giving Birth to the Light*. He flicked through the pages, reading a passage here and there, and realized the book was a treatise on how the Shadow spawned Aureon, and not the other way around, as was the generally accepted belief.

Finally. A bit of luck. At least he knew he was in the correct temple.

He opened the door to step into the corridor. A goblin walked past the room. It had almost passed the doorway when Cutter pulled it open. Cutter saw the goblin slow and start to turn. The human quickly pushed the door closed but didn't engage the latch. He took a few steps back. A moment later, the door opened and the goblin poked its head into the room. It took a quick look around, saw nothing out of the ordinary, and went back about its business. Cutter waited a few seconds before slipping into the hallway. The goblin was walking down the corridor, heading to the stairs.

Cutter turned and walked toward the chanting. A corridor branched to the left. He peered around the corner and saw a short hall that ended at a pair of double doors. Two priests stood guard. Cutter pulled back. The main corridor continued past the short passage and disappeared through an entrance with an iron gate barring the way. He could carry on that way, but the chanting priests were the first signs of life he'd seen down here. Would Anriel not be in there with the others? Should he wait for them to finish and try to pick him from the crowd?

He was still deciding when the chanting stopped. Cutter looked up in alarm as he heard the double doors open. He backed away, retracing his steps down the corridor.

He had just passed the room where he had found the book when a priest strode into the corridor and stopped. He was dressed in the black robes of the Shadow. His face was ancient and wrinkled, his skin so white as to be almost translucent.

The priest lifted his nose into the air, turning this way and that like an animal catching a scent.

Then he turned and looked in Cutter's direction, his face cracking with a hideous smile that revealed a mouth full of diseased gums.

"I s-e-e you," said the priest in a sing-song voice.

The two priests who stood guard at the door walked up to stand behind the newcomer. He pointed in Cutter's direction. "He stands, watching us. Bring his body to me."

In a single fluid movement, the priests whipped aside their robes and grabbed hold of crossbows, loosing bolts at Cutter. He dropped into a crouch and the bolts sailed above his head to clatter against the wall, raising sparks as they skittered against the stone.

Cutter turned and ran. The old priest shouted after him. "There's nowhere you can hide! I can smell the magic."

Cutter sprinted back to the square room, then leaped up the stairs two at a time. He heard the distant sounds of pursuit. He had an idea, but he had to hurry.

The goblin who had looked into the room was halfway up the stairs. Cutter slowed when he heard the scuff of the creature's footsteps and made sure his own passage went unheard. He slipped the second vial of invisibility potion from his pocket and uncorked it. He rounded the next turn and saw the goblin's back.

He had to judge his moment just right. Cutter approached the goblin. The ripe odor of sweat emanated from it. Cutter reached out with one hand, aiming for its scrawny neck.

The goblin whirled around and flung an elbow into Cutter's face. He staggered into the wall, almost dropping the vial. The goblin's eyes were wide as it looked frantically around the confined space for its attacker.

"Who's there?" it demanded.

Cutter grimaced, tasting blood. He pushed himself up and jabbed the goblin in the throat. The creature dropped to its knees, its mouth wide open as it gasped for breath. Cutter leaned in, wincing at the stench of the goblin's breath, and emptied the contents of the vial into its mouth. He snapped the goblin's mouth shut, holding its jaws tight so it had no choice but to swallow the mixture.

The creature was trying to gasp for breath, making the task more difficult, but the liquid soon trickled down. The goblin faded away before Cutter's eyes. He rammed the goblin's head against the wall until it went limp in his arms.

Not much time. He dragged the goblin down the stairs, pausing every now and then to listen for the priests. He heard them, but they had not started to climb the stairs yet. They were being cautious in the face of an unknown enemy.

He arrived in the small room at the same time they did. Cutter hauled the goblin round in front of him as the old priest looked wildly around.

"He's in here! I can smell him!"

The two priests spread out, leveling their crossbows. Cutter grimaced and moved directly in front of the nearest.

He heard the *clack* of the crossbows releasing, then felt the goblin jerk back against him as a bolt slammed into the creature's chest.

Cutter dropped the goblin to the floor. All he could see was half a crossbow bolt hovering in the air close to the ground. He backed carefully away as the priests approached and nudged the body with their feet.

"Bring it," said the older priest. "I want to see who it is when the potion wears off."

The priests felt around until they found the goblin's arms and dragged him out of the room. Cutter waited until they were gone and then breathed a small sigh of relief. He'd lost his way out, but he was still alive. Now all he needed was to wait for his own potion to wear off. Then nobody would be able to sense him. He hoped the old priest could only sense a generalized aura of magic and that the invisible goblin would fool him into thinking he had the intruder.

But in the meantime . . .

Cutter hurried back to the sleeping quarters. He needed something that would enable him to wander around the temple when the potion wore off—something that wouldn't draw attention to himself. He found a small trunk at the bottom of the bed and rummaged through it, pulling out a priest's black robe. Cutter pulled it over his head, trying hard not to notice the stale smell of unwashed laundry, then he sat on the bed and waited.

He didn't have to wait long. A few moments later, he saw his hands appear in his lap. He pulled up the sleeves of the robe and saw his arms were back where they should be.

Finally. He could get moving. He pulled the hood up over his head and hurried into the corridor, heading past the chamber where he'd heard the chanting. No guards stood outside.

He pulled open the gate and found another set of stairs leading down. He took them two at a time and emerged into another corridor identical to the one on the floor above.

Cutter paused. He was getting nowhere blundering around like this. If he expected to find Anriel any time soon, he needed to take a risk.

He walked down the passage and knocked on each door he came to. No one answered until the sixth door.

A young woman yanked it open and stared at him.

"What do you want?"

"I've been sent to find Anriel. Do you know where he is?"

The woman snorted. "Probably where he always is. In the dungeons." As she said this, she gave a jerk of her head to indicate a door down the hall.

Cutter folded his hands into his sleeves and nodded his thanks. The woman slammed the door in his face.

The door she had indicated led into a narrow corridor that slanted steadily downward. Torches guttered every now and then, not really adding light, but at least giving something to judge the distance by. The temperature dropped as he descended. He eventually had to clench his jaw to stop his teeth from chattering.

The passage led him into a guard room. Three tables were pushed up against the walls, and pegs hammered into the stone held rusted rings of keys. A door with an iron grate about eye level led out of the room. He looked through the grate and saw a wide flagstoned corridor with cells to either side. Two drains had been set into the floor near the walls. Water trickled sluggishly through the mold that coated them.

At the end of the corridor directly opposite Cutter was another room. Dim light filtered through the grate and fell in bars across the floor. Cutter took a steadying breath and pulled open the door. It groaned and shrieked in protest, sticking on an uneven flagstone. He braced his back and yanked it open all the way. He stepped through and paused.

"Anriel," he called.

Cutter heard the faint scuff of boots on cobbles, and before he could do anything, two points of cold steel touched the back of his neck. The owners of the blades must have been waiting on either side of the door. He froze, then slowly raised his hands in the air. "I'm here to see Anriel. I have something for him."

"Who are you?" asked a low voice. Cutter thought it sounded like an orc.

"My name is Salkith."

"He says his name is Salkith," shouted the orc.

Cutter heard something drop, then the door at the end of the corridor flew open and a tall elf appeared, hurrying toward him.

The elf pushed his lanky blond hair behind his ears. "You're Salkith?" he asked in a hopeful voice.

"I just said I was."

"But what—" He stopped suddenly and glanced over Cutter's shoulder. "Wait in the room," he commanded something behind Cutter.

An orc and a bugbear appeared from behind Cutter and headed for the room Anriel had been in. Cutter stretched his neck, rolling it from side to side. He thought he could feel blood trickling down his back. Anriel waited until they were out of earshot.

"My apologies. They don't get out much."

"Understood. With what I'm carrying, it's good to be careful."

Anriel's face lit up, his eyes dancing with excitement. "You have it, then? Truly?"

"I have it. And a message. Xavien said you're to go ahead as planned."

"Excellent. When you didn't turn up, I feared the worst."

"Problems. But they're taken care of now."

"May I . . . may I see it?"

Cutter hesitated, but he could never get Anriel to trust him without handing over the shard. Wren could complain all he wanted. He wasn't here.

He took out the pouch and handed it to Anriel. The elf unwrapped it with shaking fingers and pulled the dragonshard out, holding it up to the light as he stared intently at the blue veins.

"To think that this little shard is going to change the world."

Change the world? What did he mean by that?

"Xavien said he wants me to deliver it once you're finished."

Anriel frowned. "Why would he say that? That wasn't part of the plan."

Cutter shrugged. "I'm just telling you what he said."

"Doesn't he trust me?"

"I told you. I'm just passing on what he told me."

Anriel shook his head. "No. That's not possible."

Cutter tensed. What was he supposed to do now? Just kill him and take it back? But then they'd be no closer to finding out what was going on or who was organizing all this. There had to be another way.

"Can I come with you? While you—" He nodded at the dragonshard, not saying anything that might give him away.

"Out of the question," said Anriel. "Only worshipers of the Shadow can go through those doors." The elf appeared to think for a second. "But you can come with me when I drop off the shard. I'd feel safer with backup, anyway."

Cutter thought about it. "How long will it take?"

"Everything's still set up from yesterday, so not long."

"Fine. I'll wait outside. Do you have transport?"

"A skycoach."

"Pick me up at the end of the street outside the temple."

Anriel nodded in a distracted manner and walked into the back room, fondling and stroking the dragonshard in a way Cutter found faintly obscene. Cutter stepped through the door into the guardroom and glanced back. He saw the orc standing in the door as Anriel approached. The elf looked up at the huge creature.

"Fetch me Diadus's books. Quickly."

The orc lumbered past Anriel and headed toward Cutter. He stepped aside for the orc and then followed at a slower pace.

He wondered how Wren was going to react. He knew he'd said he wouldn't hand over the shard, but this was the only way they could find out what was going on. He'd just have to make sure he got it back before the delivery. Surely Wren would see that?

He stared at the walls as he walked, watching the faint glint of water as it trickled down the stone. He had to admit one thing. That comment about the shard changing the world had put a shiver down his spine.

Chapter Sixteen

The third day of Long Shadows

Sar, the 28th day of Vult, 998

"Please tell me you're joking," said Wren.

Cutter pulled the robe over his head and threw it to the ground. "What did you expect me to do? Say no? Did you honestly think the trail would end here?"

"I don't know!" snapped the half-elf. "I was hoping it would." He turned to Torin. "Did you think it would end here?"

"Afraid not, Wren."

"Fine. Everyone here is smarter than I am." He turned to Cutter. "So what's next? I'm assuming you have some kind of plan taking place in that rather square head of yours."

"He's going to pick me up once he's finished. I'll let him take me to whoever he's giving it to, then take it back."

"Did he tell you what he was doing with the shard?"

Cutter shook his head. "But as I was leaving, he sent an orc to fetch books by someone called Diadus."

Wren looked thoughtful. "Diadus . . . Diadus. Why does that name sound familiar? Torin?"

"No idea," said the dwarf. "I've never heard it before."

"It definitely sounds familiar." He thought for a few moments longer, then abruptly shook his head. "No. Can't think why."

"How are we supposed to know where you are?" asked Torin.

"You don't. I'll get the shard back once I'm done and meet you at the university. You can give it to that dwarf woman. I shouldn't be long."

"You're very optimistic," complained Wren.

Cutter shrugged. "I can take Anriel."

"Oh, well," said Wren sarcastically. "As long as you can take him, everything's fine."

Cutter sighed. "Look, I can see you're angry because I gave away the shard—"

"Nonsense. Why should we be angry? I mean, how many people have died because of it? Only a few. Not many in the grand scheme of things."

"Don't talk to me about who has died because of this shard," said Cutter quietly. "That's *why* I gave it to him. I want the person who's behind this whole thing, not just the lackeys. And if I have to take a risk to do that, then so be it."

"Yes, but you're risking other people's lives. You're doing exactly what they've been doing."

"Then that's something I have to deal with."

Wren sighed and shook his head. "We'll meet you back at Morgrave, then. Come, Torin."

"Good luck," Torin said to Cutter.

They turned and retraced their steps back through Khyber's Gate.

Anriel walked out of the temple some time later. Cutter stood in the middle of the street and waited for the elf to approach. Cutter was shocked by the change in his appearance. His skin looked even pastier than before—almost gray. Cutter looked into his black-ringed eyes.

"Are you well?" he asked.

Anriel nodded wearily. "The binding took a lot more out of me than I thought it would."

Cutter nodded, wondering what kind of binding he was talking about. He wished he could ask him straight out, but that would blow his cover. He'd find out soon enough.

They headed along the main street and up through the tunnels and passages that led out of the Cogs and into the Depths. Anriel didn't talk, and Cutter didn't push him. The less he said, the better chance he had of pulling this off.

When they reached the Depths, they found a rickety lift that took them up to Lower-Central. It wasn't a lift like the others, but an actual mechanical contraption that whined and rattled as it rose slowly on its chains. At one point, the gears slipped and the lift dropped suddenly, screeching as it fell before the chain caught in the cogs once again.

Once off the lift, Anriel led them to an inn, then down a small alley that ran along the double-story building. He pulled open a tall gate and they stepped into an overgrown back garden. Cutter looked around. A couple of chairs stood outside the back door of the inn. Empty bottles and tiny heaps of pipe ash indicated that someone liked spending their time sitting among the long grass and weeds. Anriel headed to the back fence, where a large shape was hidden beneath a stained tarp. He pulled the cover off to reveal a decrepit skycoach.

They climbed inside and Anriel coaxed the skycoach into the air. Despite its look, the vehicle ran smoothly. He drove them to the upper districts of Menthis Plateau and guided the skycoach until they were coasting through the well-kept streets of Crystal Bridge. Cutter looked at the massive manor houses and expensive mansions that lined the quiet streets, wondering at the kind of money needed to live there.

Anriel slowed the skycoach as they coasted along the street. He kept looking at the gates of the houses as they passed, searching for the correct address.

Cutter realized the surroundings looked familiar. He frowned, wondering why that was. But then it came to him. He'd been here before.

His stomach tensed as his mind processed this realization. Even as Anriel slowed near one of the huge mansions, Cutter was telling himself that it might be a mistake, that maybe they were headed to a different house.

But Anriel turned the skycoach into the gravel driveway and coasted up to the iron-wrought gates, and Cutter realized it was no mistake.

The person Anriel was delivering the dragonshard to, the person responsible for Rowen's death, responsible for everything that had happened, was his boss, the halfling Tiel.

Cutter sat in shock while Anriel nodded at the guards. They used a glowing crystal to deactivate the security wards and the gates swung inward. Anriel guided the skycoach up the long pathway and around to the back of the house.

Cutter struggled to think, trying to understand. Why? What was going on? Had Rowen discovered something? Had she known it was Tiel? Was that why she was killed? Or had she simply been in the wrong place at the wrong time? It was too much, too quick. He hated to admit it, but he needed Wren to sort this through.

Anriel brought the skycoach down behind a line of trees.

Cutter looked over at the house. He didn't know the answers to his questions, but he knew one thing: the person responsible for Rowen's death was in that house.

Anriel stopped the coach and said, "Well, we made it—"

Cutter slammed his elbow into Anriel's throat. The elf smacked against the seat, then slid to the floor, gasping for breath as he struggled to draw air through his crushed throat. Cutter retrieved the shard from his body, then pulled out his Khutai knives and jumped out of the skycoach. He sprinted across the grass to the back door and pulled it open.

Kitchens. Cutter looked about. Deserted. The ovens were cold. He crept through the room into a dark, uncarpeted hallway. The floor was scuffed and scratched. Cutter reckoned it was the servants' quarters.

The hallway ended at a narrow flight of stairs. He climbed up, stopped at a door, pushed it open slightly, and put his eye to the crack. A large vestibule lay outside. Carpets had been scattered over the tiled floor, their colors the rich browns and reds favored by halflings from the Talenta Plains. He heard no signs of life.

He pushed the door wide and stepped through. The door was set into the wall below a wide set of stairs that curved up behind him. The front door to the house stood to his right.

He thought he heard voices, coming from upstairs.

Cutter tested the first step for loose boards that would alert people to his presence. Nothing. He tested each step in turn as he climbed, keeping his eye on the landing above. The voices grew louder—laughter, the low mumble of conversation.

He reached the top of the stairs and checked to make sure there were no guards posted. He saw none. Tiel had no reason to fear anything in his own house.

Cutter could see the room from which the voices issued.

The door was open and bright afternoon sunlight shone in a rectangle across the hall floor. Cutter crept forward and waited. He wanted to find out how many were inside. He had to make sure he got to Tiel. After that, they could do whatever they wanted to him.

"How do you plan on getting in?" asked a voice. It sounded like Bren. Was he involved? It gave Cutter pause. He respected Bren. Thought he was a man who stood up for his own principles. He'd be disappointed to find out he had anything to do with it.

"They'll let me in." Cutter recognized Tiel's voice straight away, the laconic drawl. Whereas before it had irritated him, now it sent his heart hammering against his chest, sent a surge of hatred coursing through his body. He had to fight to keep himself from bursting into the room.

"Why?"

"The Tain gala's all about power. As soon as everyone knows my father is Saidan Boromar, they'll fall over their feet for my attention."

"And you're going to tell them?"

"Of course I am. What do you think all this is about?"

Cutter laid his head against the wall. The Tain gala? What did that have to do with anything? The Tain gala was a dinner party held every month on the floating district of Skyway and hosted by the Tains, the richest family in Sharn. Only the sixty most powerful figures in the city were invited. Anyone who mattered would be there, couldn't afford *not* to be there.

A shadow fell across the rectangle of light on the floor. Cutter tensed, but it moved on. Just someone walking across the room.

"We're going to be late," said Tiel. "Where is that idiot? You're going to have to take him out, by the way. I don't trust him."

"Fine," said Bren, sounding bored.

Cutter took a deep breath. Now or never. They were going to walk out that door. He thought about waiting for them to do just that, but he had no way of knowing who would come first. No, he had to surprise them.

He held his blades in attack positions and stepped into the room.

The first thing he noticed was that the room was huge. It easily took up half the house. Skylights let in streams of sunlight. Pillars that seemed to be made of clay or mud reached up to the ceiling. Tiel had modeled them on something from the Plains.

Bren was lounging in a chair, clenching and unclenching his adamantine arm. Tiel paced back and forward in a short line. Both were an equal distance from Cutter, but he wasn't sure if he could get to Tiel before Bren reached him. He flipped one of the knives around, holding it by the blade. The shape of the knives meant they weren't ideal for throwing, but he still reckoned he could hit the halfling.

Bren stared at him. He didn't move from his chair. "Cutter," he said, by way of greeting. "Been looking for you. Where've you been?"

"Around," he said.

Tiel turned in surprise, his eyes narrowing when he saw Cutter, knives drawn.

"What in Khyber's name are you doing here? You should have just run with the money. Always knew you were an idiot."

"I didn't take your money. Someone beat me to it."

"Then what are you doing here, Cutter?" asked Bren. "Why the blades?"

Cutter glanced at Bren. "I'm hoping you didn't have anything to do with this, Bren. *Really* hoping."

Bren frowned. "What are you talking about?"

"Anriel's here," Cutter said to Tiel, ignoring Bren for the moment.

"Who?"

"Don't play dumb. You know who. He has the dragonshard you've been so eager to get your hands on."

Tiel licked his lips. "Uh . . . where is he?"

"Dead." He threw a glance at Bren. "I've saved you the effort."

Bren sat forward in the chair. "Cutter, I'm getting a feeling here. Like you're about to do something you might regret."

"Oh, I won't regret it, Bren. Believe me. I'm going to give you the benefit of the doubt, tell you what happened. Stop me if you've already heard it." He nodded at Tiel. "See, Rowen accidentally stole this precious dragonshard of his and went into hiding. She knew they would be after her."

"Wait," said Bren. He glanced between Tiel and Cutter. "Renaia came to me asking for help. Said she thought Rowen was in trouble."

Cutter stared at Bren. "Bren, what did you do?"

"I followed the procedure. I told Tiel and he said he'd take care of her."

"He took care of her, all right." He turned to Tiel. "Did you do it, or get someone else to do it?"

"I did it. It was enjoyable, actually. Quite the little fighter, our Rowen. Even up to the end she wouldn't tell me where it was. I must admit I was quite surprised when Xavien told me it had turned up again. Was that thanks to you?"

Bren stood. "What's he saying? Cutter, what about Rowen?"

"She's dead, Bren. Tiel killed her. Tortured her, actually. Trying to get her to give up where she'd hidden the shard."

"Is that true?" Bren asked Tiel.

"Yes, it's true. Who cares? She was just a courtesan. Not even worth the effort, really."

"I cared," whispered Cutter.

Tiel grinned. "Ah, shame for poor Cutter. His woman's dead." He stepped forward, scowling at him. "I did you a *favor.*"

Cutter stepped forward. Tiel held his ground.

"Cutter," warned Bren.

"What? You going to protect him after what he did? You *knew* Rowen. You drank with her."

"I know, but that has nothing to do with this. I can't let you do anything stupid."

"It's not stupid. It's the most sensible thing I've ever done."

He stepped forward again. He saw Bren glance over his shoulder. Cutter started to turn, but too late. Something exploded against the back of his head and his legs wouldn't hold him up. He fell to his knees, his surroundings swirling like he'd had too much to drink. He looked down and saw blood pooling at his knees.

"Find the shard," he heard Tiel say, then something hit him again, and he was flung forward onto the floor, his cheek cracking against the tiles.

Chapter Seventeen

The third day of Long Shadows

Sar, the 28th day of Vult, 998

Wren and Torin made their way through the crowds of students that crammed the grounds of Morgrave University. The break for the midday meal was ending, and everyone was hurrying off to classes, research projects, or whatever it was that students did.

Probably off to get drunk, thought Wren uncharitably.

"How could we lose him? We *walk* faster than that lift moved."

"Yes, Wren. It's just a pity we can't walk up the sides of buildings." Torin stepped aside as a group of young gnomes sprinted down the hall, shouting for someone's attention. "Why did you want to follow him, anyway? He said he'd meet us in the professor's office when he gets the shard."

"Because he doesn't care about the shard," said Wren. "All he cares about is finding whoever is responsible for Rowen's death. We, however, need that shard to prove what's been going on, and that we didn't kill a member of the City Watch for no reason."

"And to stop whatever they plan on doing with it," reminded Torin.

"Yes, yes. That too."

"Have you figured out why that name sounds familiar?"

"Diadus?" Wren shook his head. "No. We're still missing too many pieces of this puzzle, Torin. Why was the dragonshard delivered to Anriel? If we knew that, maybe we could move forward."

They headed through the warren of corridors that led to the professor's office. Wren entered first. He pushed open the door and looked into the face of the young watchman who had first chased them back at Warden Towers.

"Well, hello there, Master Wren. I've been looking for you."

Wren froze, wondering what to do. Torin was still behind him. He tried to move so the dwarf wouldn't be seen, but the guardsman merely smiled at him.

"Despite appearances to the contrary, I'm not just a simple member of the Watch. Please, come in—both of you. We have a few things to talk about."

"First off, let's get things straight," said the corporal as he lowered himself into the professor's chair. Wren noted that someone had tidied up the mess Cutter had made. "I'm not a member of the Watch. I'm from the Dark Lanterns. My name is Col."

Wren's eyes widened. He looked at Torin, who simply shrugged.

"The professor got word to us a while ago that he had been approached by someone who wanted to get their hands on a dragonshard from the University's museum. As one of the senior members of the faculty, he was one of only three people who could pull that off without anyone finding out. I was supposed to be there when the exchange took place so I could follow the courier back to his superiors."

"What happened?" asked Wren.

"I don't know. The meeting was moved forward by a day. I wasn't there to help out. The professor must have refused to hand over the shard and he was killed. I've been looking for it ever since. I know a Watch captain called Jana is involved. I was transferred into her command as part of my cover, but so far, all she's been bothered with is targeting this Cutter. That's why I let you get away, by the way. I could have taken you down back at the prison, but I wanted to see how things played out. Now, why don't you tell me how you are involved?"

"Why don't you prove who you are—and who you say you are?"

Col stared at Wren for a moment, then shrugged and withdrew a piece of expensive vellum from a pocket. It identified Col as a member of the King's Citadel, and requested that the bearer be supplied with all available aid in the furtherance of his investigations. The vellum was affixed with the King's seal.

"Happy?" asked Col.

"Not really. Forged documents aren't hard to come by in Sharn. Doesn't look like I have any choice, does it?"

"Not really."

So Wren told him how Larrien asked him to investigate the professor's death, about Rowen and Cutter, the courier Salkith, and how Cutter was blamed for the death of the professor.

"I knew it wasn't him," said Col. "I just didn't know how he was involved."

Wren resumed his narration, filling in the events of the previous day. Col held a hand up and stopped him when he got to the part about finding the journal hidden inside the desk.

"Wait. The professor actually had a suspect?"

"Lord Xavien. He's on the Sharn city council."

"But why didn't he tell me?"

Torin spoke up. "He was just a professor. Probably the most exciting thing that's ever happened to him was sleeping in and being late for class. Maybe he wasn't sure if he could really trust you. Just because someone says they're someone, it doesn't always mean they are. Maybe he thought you were a rival out to get the shard for yourself."

Col looked thoughtful. "It's possible, I suppose. So what happened next?"

"Cutter pretended to be the courier and went to see Xavien. Xavien said they still had time, that whatever they were planning would take place today. Cutter was to take the shard to a priest of the Shadow in Khyber's Gate. This priest did something with the shard and they—Cutter and the priest—took it to whoever is behind this whole thing."

"He took the dragonshard to the person who is responsible for all this?" asked Col incredulously.

Wren held his hands in the air. "Don't take it out on us. We told him not to, but he wanted his revenge. He said he'd get the shard back once he knew who was behind it, and bring it back here."

"But what if he doesn't get it back? What if he's dead?"

Wren shrugged. "I don't know what to tell you. There was no way he would give it to us."

"This isn't good," said Col, leaning forward and steepling his hands against his mouth. "We knew something was being planned, something big, but we had no idea what it was. That priest could have done anything with the shard."

He was silent for a while, staring at the floor. Finally, he straightened. "I can't hang around here hoping he's going to come back with the shard. I need to have a word with this Xavien."

He stood. Wren did the same.

"What are you doing?" asked Col.

"Coming with you. I've been on this case from the start. You wouldn't have Xavien's name if it wasn't for me."

"Us," said Torin.

"Sorry. Us. I can save you time by taking you directly to him."

Col thought about it. "But what if your friend comes back? With or without the shard, someone should be here in case he returns."

"Torin—" said Wren, turning to the dwarf.

Torin sighed and sat back down. "Fine. I'll wait."

Wren raised an eyebrow at Col and waited.

"Very well," said Col. "Let's go, then. Just don't get in the way."

"I do not *get in the way,*" said Wren, offended.

"I see. Just do as you're told."

"And I certainly do not *do as I'm told!*"

Col glanced at Torin. "You sure you wouldn't rather come and leave him behind to wait?"

Torin grinned and shook his head. Wren pushed past the young man—how old was he, anyway, telling him to stay out of the way? He stepped into the hall.

"Come, Col," he called over his shoulder. "Time is short."

⊛ ⊛ ⊛ ⊛ ⊛ ⊛ ⊛

"I'm sorry," said a young woman seated behind a desk, "but Lord Xavien is in a meeting at the moment. If you'd care to leave your name—"

"We don't leave names," declared Wren, still worked up at Col's patronizing manner.

Col put his hand on Wren's shoulder. "Take it easy," he said. He pulled out the piece of vellum and showed it to the secretary.

"You see this?"

The secretary nodded.

"Do you know what it is?"

"It identifies you as a member of the Citadel."

"That's correct. So if you don't want to be hauled off to Wroat to spend the next couple of years in the King's dungeons, you'll keep quiet." He pointed to a door behind the secretary. "Through there?"

She nodded, eyes wide.

"Thanks."

Col moved toward the door and pulled it open. Wren hurried after, trying to walk at his side. He didn't want anyone thinking he was below Col.

A huge window situated directly behind Xavien's desk lit the office. Afternoon sunlight streamed in, falling across the carpeted floor and partway up the opposite wall. Xavien was seated in a highbacked chair at his desk, facing a woman and a man who were holding files on their laps. They all looked up in surprise.

Xavien started to stand up. "What is the meaning—"

Col held up his hand. Xavien stopped in mid sentence, half-risen from his chair, one hand supporting himself on the edge of the desk. Wren had to admit, Col had the touch when it came to shutting people up.

Col let him stand there for a moment before asking, "Lord Xavien?"

As if his words were some kind of signal for the lord to carry on, Xavien stood up all the way. "Who do you think you are? You can't just—"

Col clicked his tongue in irritation and held up the piece of vellum once again. He first showed it to the two people with the files. They looked at it, then glanced at Xavien.

"What?" he asked. "What is it?"

Col laid the vellum down on the desk. Xavien fished a pair of spectacles out of his breast pocket and perched them on the bridge of his nose. While he did this, his guests hastily gathered their things, darting sideways looks at Col. Wren held the door open for them as they fell over themselves to get out.

He closed it again, the click of the latch loud in the silent room. Col sat in one of the recently vacated chairs. Wren took the other. He was curious to see the young man's technique. Getting information from people unwilling to give it up was something inquisitives did all the time. It would be interesting to see how Col handled it.

Col leaned forward and took back the vellum. Xavien flopped into his chair. Wren thought he looked a little pale, and . . . were those beads of sweat on his forehead? He couldn't tell. Xavien took off his glasses, carefully folded them, and placed them back into his pocket. He forced a smile onto his face.

"How can I help you? Please. Ask away. Anything for the King's Citadel. You fight a brave fight, you lot. I salute you."

Wren almost snorted. The King's Citadel were some of the most feared law enforcers in the kingdom. Part spy, part inquisitive, sometimes executioner, always feared. They pretty much had a permit to do anything they needed to get the job done. Furthermore, the Dark Lanterns were widely considered to be the most ruthless of the lot. They frequently went undercover in some of the most dangerous places on the continent, foiling attempts—real and perceived—to undermine the Crown.

Now Wren got to see how all that training paid off.

But it seemed like he would have to wait, because Col didn't say anything. He simply sat in his chair, looking very relaxed, staring at Xavien.

The councilor shifted uncomfortably. He was trying to hold Col's stare, but after a moment or so, his eyelids flickered, like he was straining to keep them open against a fierce wind.

Finally, the standoff was too much. He blinked, then looked down at the papers on his desk and rearranged the pile as if it was what he had intended to do.

Col cleared his throat, bringing Xavien's eyes up to his once again. "Why don't you tell me about it?" he said.

Xavien frowned. "Tell you about what?" he asked innocently.

Again the stare.

"If you told me what you wanted to know, maybe I could help you," protested Xavien.

"If I told you what I wanted to know, I wouldn't need you to tell me."

"What?"

The stare, then, "Tell me about the dragonshard."

Wren had to give Xavien credit. He barely reacted. Only the tiniest flicker of panic flashed behind his eyes, quickly quashed. He supposed that was what a life in politics gave you. The ability to tell bare-faced lies in the face of damning evidence.

"The . . . dragonshard? I'm sorry—what was your name again? Cole? I'm sorry, but I have no idea what you're talking about."

Trying to play it smart. Usually a mistake, in Wren's opinion.

"Now if you'll excuse me, I have work to do. This city doesn't run itself, you know."

"Oh, are you a member of the council? I only ask because tonight's the Tain gala, isn't it? Don't all the members of the council have standing invitations?"

"I'm . . . not a senior member," said Xavien. Wren could see this was something he wasn't happy about. "I'm what they call a shadow member. I do a lot of the leg work for my superior on the council."

"Ah, I see. So you're saying that you do all the work and your boss gets to attend one of the most sought-after dinners in Sharn."

"I *never* said that."

"You didn't have to. See, with me it's about what you *don't* say that matters. Since we've been talking, I've seen jealousy, fear, anger, irritation, cockiness, superiority, and subterfuge cross your face. And we've been sitting here—what? Two minutes? So I *know* when you're lying. It's what I'm trained for."

"How dare you—"

"And please, don't start with the whole 'I know powerful people' routine. You have *no* idea how much that irritates me. Why don't we just lay it all out? We know about Anriel. We know about the dragonshard. The man you thought was Salkith? He wasn't. He was an undercover agent. So we can tie you to the Shadow priest *and* the stolen shard, which then ties you to the deaths of the professor and the courtesan."

Xavien looked afraid, and not a little confused. "What courtesan?" he asked, his voice filled with bewilderment.

"Please don't insult me, Lord Xavien. As it stands, you're taking the blame for everything."

Xavien paused. Wren could see him running all the evidence through his mind, trying to decide how damning it actually was. Quite damning, he concluded.

"Please," Xavien said, leaning forward on his desk, "you must understand. I didn't want to get involved. I was threatened. I had no choice."

"Involved in what?"

"It was Tiel. A halfling. He's in the Boromar clan. He thinks he's some kind of unrecognized heir of Saidan Boromar."

"I know who Tiel is." Col turned to Wren. "We weren't sure if he was involved or not. He's very good at keeping himself clean. All we knew was that Jana did some work for him. That was why I got myself attached to her squad." He looked back to Xavien. "So what is he up to?"

"I don't know. All I did was put him in touch with Anriel. My department is in charge of keeping track of worshipers of the Dark Six, to make sure they don't try anything dangerous. He threatened me. I had no choice! Surely you can see that?"

Wren certainly couldn't. Something wasn't making sense. If Xavien was lying, he was very good at it, the best he'd ever seen, but something didn't feel right. He decided to take a risk.

"And did you also put him in touch with Diadus?" he asked.

Xavien's response was astounding. As soon as Wren uttered the name, his eyes fixed on Wren's and his face broke into a snarl of rage. He yanked open the desk drawer and pulled out a small crossbow. Wren stared in astonishment, too surprised to move.

Good thing he wasn't the target. Xavien swung the crossbow at Col, but he was already on his feet and diving across the desk. He grabbed hold of Xavien's wrist and they went over backward onto the floor. Wren got to his feet and hurried around the desk. Xavien was struggling with Col, trying to free the hand holding the crossbow.

"To Khyber with you!" shouted Xavien. "You'll ruin everything!"

Wren stood on Xavien's wrist and put his weight on it until the councilor cried out in pain and released his grip on the crossbow. Wren kicked it out of reach. As soon as he did this, Col punched Xavien hard in the stomach, incapacitating him. He looked around.

"Get me some rope, something to tie him up with."

Wren looked around "Where am I going to get rope?"

"I don't know! Just find anything!"

Wren's glance fell on the curtains. They were made from thick velvet. He yanked one down and cut it into long strips with his knife. Col took them and tied the councilor to his chair. The man was still wheezing in pain from the punch, struggling to take in breath.

Col stood back once his work was finished. Wren glanced at him. "What was that all about?"

Col shrugged. "Guess he doesn't want us to know about Diadus."

At the sound of the name, Xavien's head snapped up. "You'll never get anything out of me."

"We'll see," said Col mildly. He sighed. "Why can your lot never make it easy?" He opened up a pouch that was slung over his shoulder and took out a tiny bloodspike.

"What's that?" Wren asked.

"It's a type of clerical magic," said Col. "Took our people ages to adapt it this way."

"What does it do?"

Col held up the small glass vial. "Whoever is injected with this is forced to tell the truth."

"Oh." Wren thought for a moment. "That's handy."

"Extremely. And top secret. So I'm afraid I may have to kill you once this is all done."

Wren waited for him to laugh or follow the comment with a joke, but he didn't. Instead, he turned to Xavien.

"Last chance," he said. "These things are still a bit unreliable. I know of a few people who still can't tell lies, years after they were injected."

Xavien glared at Col, but said nothing.

Col shrugged. "Your choice," he said, and jabbed it into the councilor's neck.

"How long does it take to work?" asked Wren.

"Lord Xavien," said Col, "are you currently involved in any criminal activities?"

"Yes."

"How many?"

"Five projects that are currently active, four more that will soon begin."

Col raised his eyebrows at Wren. "Projects. I like that." He turned back to Xavien. "Tell me about Diadus."

"He's an artificer. Cannith. But he was excoriated when the family found out he was experimenting with creating warforged."

"That's it!" exclaimed Wren. "I knew I'd heard that name before. Remember that warforged mass murderer a few years ago? Just after the war? After he was caught, there were rumors going about that it was this Diadus who created him."

"What happened to him?"

"He disappeared. No one knew where he went."

"Looks like we're about to find out. Xavien, where is Diadus now?"

"In Fallen. Where the Glass Tower fell."

"And what is his involvement?"

Xavien hesitated. Wren could see the man trying to hold back the words.

"Xavien," said Col. "I order you to tell me what Diadus is doing."

"He helped Anriel trap the Shadow elemental inside the dragonshard."

Wren and Col exchanged glances.

"Why?" asked Col. "What is the purpose of this dragonshard?"

"Tiel plans to release the elemental at the Tain gala dinner. The elemental has been ordered to kill Saidan Boromar and then wipe out all the members of the city council."

"But that's absurd!" snapped Wren. "For what purpose?"

"Tiel got tired of waiting for his father to acknowledge him. He plans on taking over all of Boromar's business."

"And the council?"

"They will be replaced by politicians who are sympathetic to Tiel."

"And grateful," said Col grimly.

"Correct."

"Are you one of those?"

Xavien smiled. "Most definitely. You are looking at the next mayor of Sharn."

Wren turned and walked to the window. "But this is insane. King Boranel will never stand for it. There will be investigations. Arrests."

"Why do you think Tiel used Anriel?" Col asked.

Wren turned. "Explain."

"Anriel is a member of Daask. He has lodgings in Daask's headquarters, for Khyber's sake. Tiel has planted enough evidence to let the blame fall on Anriel and the heads of the Daask clan."

"Clever," said Col. "In one swoop, he becomes head of one of the biggest criminal organizations in the land, plants a city council that will never speak out against him, and gets rid of the Boromar clan's closest rivals."

"We have to warn the council."

"No point," said Xavien. "Once the elemental is released, it won't stop 'til it's tracked down each and every one of them."

"Then we have to stop Tiel from releasing it."

"Good luck. Only Diadus knows where that will happen."

Wren was heading for the door, Col close behind.

"Hey!" Xavien struggled in his chair, straining against the bonds. "What about me?"

"Don't worry," called Col over his shoulder. "I'll send some watchmen up to take you into custody."

Col closed the door, but they could still hear Xavien's screams of outrage.

Chapter Eighteen

The third day of Long Shadows

Sar, the 28th day of Vult, 998

Waves of pain pulsed through Cutter's head. Every time a wave crested, it felt as though his brain was pushing against his skull, trying to escapc through his eye sockets. Then it would slowly subside and he would hope it was finished, hope that the pain had ended, until a few moments later, it started all over again.

As he struggled through the black depths of unconsciousness, he became aware of another pain, this one in the muscles just below his armpits. This one was constant, a drawn-out stretching feeling that wouldn't go away no matter how much he tried to ignore it.

He wondered briefly if he had been drinking last night. That would account for the headache. But what about the arms?

Freezing cold water hit him in the face. He drew in a huge gulp of air, gasping at the shock of the temperature. His eyes snapped open. He shook the water from his face as his blurry vision slowly focused on the floor below him.

He looked up. His arms were pulled high above him, tied

together by a rope that was thrown over a thick wooden beam, one of many that supported the roof. He scanned down the rope and saw that it was tied around one of the strange pillars. His feet dangled about five feet off the ground.

"Glad to see you're finally awake," said a voice.

He looked up and wasn't at all surprised to see Jana standing before him with an empty bucket in her hand. She had a bandage tied around her neck.

"Host, don't you ever go away?" said Cutter. "Like I told you five years ago, I'm not interested."

The bucket flew through the air. He managed to turn aside just in time to avoid it hitting him full in the face. Instead, it cracked into the side of his head. Blood trickled over his ear.

He turned and glared at her.

"That look might scare some of the people you hang out with, Blackbird, but not me. I've seen a lot worse."

"I know. When you look in the mirror every morning."

It was childish. He knew that, but he couldn't help it. The words were out of his mouth before he could even think about stopping them.

Jana shook her head and smiled ruefully. "You're really something, you know that? Here you are, not far from death, and you can still crack a joke. It's good. It shows character."

Cutter glanced up at the knots around his wrist. They looked pretty tight.

"Don't bother. You'll never get out of it. Face it, Blackbird. You're a dead man breathing. No one's going to come to your rescue. No one's going to save you." Jana walked forward and pulled out a cutthroat razor. She flicked the blade out and turned it this way and that, studying it. "Found this in Tiel's bath chamber. I learn a lot about people from what they keep in the bath chamber. It looks old. I think the handle is bone of some kind. What are you laughing at?"

She looked up and saw Cutter laughing painfully.

"You," he said. "Going through people's bath chambers like some kind of pervert."

Jana slashed out with the razor, never once breaking eye contact with Cutter. He felt a sharp slice of pain along his stomach, then warmth seeping through his clothes. He stared into her dark eyes, not moving, not giving her the satisfaction of seeing the pain.

"There's nothing you can do to me that wasn't done in Valenar."

She smiled. "We'll just have to see about that, won't we?"

"I have no fight with you, Jana. I want Tiel. That's all."

"Oh, but that's not good for me. Tiel pays me very well. He was most upset that he missed you the other night at the Hanging Garden, by the way. That's what I was doing there—meeting him about you. Although I didn't know it then. Would have saved everyone a lot of bother if you'd stayed." She took a step forward. Cutter tensed, thinking to kick her with his feet, but she was careful to stay out of range. "I'll make a deal with you—for old time's sake. Tell me where the money is and I'll kill you quick."

"There never was any money. A couple of hobgoblins got to it before me."

She stared thoughtfully at him. "Pity," she said, and darted in to punch him in the stomach. He didn't have time to tense his muscles, and Jana knew how to hit hard, jabbing in and backing out quickly. He jerked on the rope, swaying back and forth as he gasped for breath. As he did so, he caught a glimpse of something out of the corner of his eye. The knot that tied the rope to the pillar shifted as he rocked. He wasn't sure if the whole rope was moving around the pillar or if the knot was weakening, but it gave him an idea.

Cutter tensed his shoulder and arm muscles, putting his weight against the rope and pulling himself up. Not much, not so that Jana would notice. At the same time, he grabbed hold of the rope with his bound hands and focused on pulling it down.

"That's just for starters," said Jana. "I'm going to keep you alive for a long time, Cutter."

Cutter sucked in great gulps of air. "Why? What did I do?"

"What did you do? You ruined everything, that's what you did. Why do you think you were arrested in the first place? For taking some stupid bribes? There isn't one person in the Sharn Watch who doesn't take bribes. It's practically written into your contract. That's why the pay is so bad. They know we're going to get some money on the side."

"Then what?"

"You were asking questions about Leto's death. Questions quite a few of us didn't want answered."

Cutter stared at Jana in surprise. Leto had been his superior when he joined the Watch. It was his job to show Cutter the ropes, make sure he didn't get himself killed in his first week. Cutter hadn't liked him much. Leto showed him all the stuff they didn't teach you anywhere else, the least of which was that taking bribes was not a bad thing. But then one night, he was found floating in the Dagger River, and Cutter had done some digging. Nothing drastic. He didn't actually care that Leto was dead—Khyber, he'd probably *deserved* what he got.

Cutter was arrested and kicked out of the Watch not long after.

He struggled to think back, but he couldn't recall uncovering anything that implicated anyone. "But I didn't even dig that deep. I just thought it was someone with a grudge."

"Oh, it was. Me. But we couldn't take the chance you would find anything."

"Why are you telling me this? It was five years ago. I don't *care*, Jana."

Jana's eyebrows shot up in surprise. "You don't care that I was responsible for getting you kicked off the Watch? If not for that, you wouldn't have been taken by the Valenar. You were a *slave*, Cutter."

"But if you hadn't done it, I wouldn't have met Rowen," he said. "Everything happens for a reason, Jana. What happened back then . . . it brought me to a place in my life where I was happy."

Jana stared at him incredulously. "You getting *philosophical* on me, Blackbird? Didn't ever see you as much of a thinker."

"I wasn't. But three years on the Valenar plains, you learn to look inside a bit."

She searched his face, curiosity plain on her features. "I'm kind of sad to kill you now, Blackbird. You've actually become interesting."

Cutter made one last attempt. "Then cut me down. All I want is to get the person who took Rowen from me. All I want is Tiel."

For a moment he thought she was actually going to cut him down. Then she broke into a grin, and Cutter felt his hopes drip away like the blood from his wound.

"No, I don't think so. Nice try, though."

Cutter glanced surreptitiously at the knot. Was it his imagination, or had it unraveled a fraction?

"You always were pathetic," he said, turning his attention to Jana and looking as contemptuous as possible.

Jana looked at him in amazement. "Ex*cuse* me?"

"Why don't you just admit it? All that stuff about Leto. It's all rubbish. You did all this because I turned you down. You wanted me and I said no. You couldn't handle that."

Jana burst out laughing. "That's some ego you have there, Blackbird."

"And do you know *why* I turned you down? Because you were sad. Here was this old woman—and you practically are an old woman Jana, no matter how much dye you put in your hair—here was this old woman getting drunk and making a pass at the new recruit. It was embarrassing, Jana."

"Shut up, Blackbird."

"You were so desperate. And you know what? After you left, I actually felt sorry for you. I don't even think it was about sex. You were just so lonely you didn't want to wake up alone."

"I said shut up!"

Jana lunged forward and punched him in the stomach again. He didn't try to kick her. Instead, he went with the punch, subtly moving his legs like a child on a swing to get rocking back and forth. She hit him again. His breath exploded from his lungs, but again, he used the force of the punch to build up his swing.

He glanced at the knot. It was definitely unraveling, loosening in quick jerks every time his movement carried him backward. He pointed his feet forward in an attempt to get some more power, but Jana saw him and stepped back a pace.

She looked up at him and shook her head. "Nice try, Blackbird. But you're not going to get me close enough to try anything."

Cutter felt the rope jerk as he moved to the zenith of the swing. He looked at the knot and saw it parting. He pulled himself up and thrust his feet forward, swinging with as much energy as he could. The knot gave way and he sailed through the air, carried by his forward momentum. Jana's eyes opened wide and she tried to dive out of the way, but she was too late. His feet caught her full in the face and she flew backward, blood spraying from her nose.

Cutter landed heavily on his back. He struggled for breath and tried to pull his wrists apart, but that knot was still tight.

He pushed himself to his knees, then to his feet, and staggered over to Jana. She sat against the wall and shook her head dazedly, one hand trying to stop the blood flowing from her nose.

She looked up as Cutter approached. "You bastard!" she screamed, trying to stand up.

Cutter pushed her down again and wrapped the trailing rope around her neck, pulling it tight. Jana fought and struggled, squirming round in his grasp so that she was eventually facing away from him. He pulled the rope tighter, hearing her struggling for breath.

Then his hands flew apart, pulling against nothing. Jana whirled around and slashed at him with the razor. He raised his arm to block the swipe and felt it slice his skin to the bone. He lashed out with his other hand, punching her in the jaw. The razor flew through the air and skittered across the floor.

Cutter dropped the loose end of the severed rope and ran after the razor. He grabbed the bone handle and tried to maneuver it to cut the rope around his wrists. He glanced over his shoulder—

And saw the boot coming straight for his head. He jerked back, but the tip of her foot caught him on the forehead, sending him spinning to the floor. Cutter held on to the razor and tried to saw the rope beneath his body. Jana kicked him in the ribs. He cried out in pain and curled up, turning his back to her as he managed to saw through the last of the cord. He pulled his wrists apart and turned, catching her foot as it came in for another kick. Cutter twisted it hard, intending to break the ankle, but Jana saw what he was doing and leaped into the air, spinning in the direction of his twist. She fell to the floor and Cutter pushed himself to his feet, tossing aside the last of the rope.

He dropped the razor hastily into his pocket and grabbed his blades from the table, turning to face Jana. She was standing again, favoring her injured ankle. She grinned through bloodstained teeth and slowly drew the sword at her side. Cutter noted it was double-edged, so he held the Khutai knives along his forearms, ready to use them to parry her swings.

She ran at him, letting loose with a furious blur of overhead and side swings. Cutter raised his forearms to block, using the blades along his arms as armor to catch the edge of the sword. Sparks flew as they ranged back and forward across the floor, both of them evenly matched. Cutter never quite reached inside her guard to land a blow.

He didn't have the reach of her sword either, so she had the advantage. But she was pressing the attack so violently that she would tire soon. All Cutter had to do was wait.

That was, if he could stay alive that long.

Jana adapted her attack, not just battering at his arms, but twisting the sword as she drew back, trying to catch his skin under the guard of the blades. She succeeded a few times, his grip on his knives slipping with sweat and enabling her to inflict numerous slashes and cuts. His arms were soon slick with blood.

But she was starting to tire. Her attacks became risky, opening herself to retaliation. Cutter held off from taking advantage straight away, suspecting some kind of trick.

He was right to wait. She was tiring, yes, but she still had enough left in her for one last feint. She lowered her guard, her arms dropping in what seemed like exhaustion. Cutter darted in and took a swipe, but he didn't commit himself to the lunge. He pulled up short, narrowly avoiding her sword as she brought it into the air exactly where his chest would have been if he'd followed through.

She was expecting resistance. When there wasn't any, it threw her off balance. She staggered forward and Cutter stepped past her guard and thrust the Khutai blade into her stomach. He pushed up, the curve of the blade forcing it up behind her rib cage and into her heart.

They both froze, staring into each other's eyes. She grabbed hold of his arm, her fingers digging into his skin and drawing blood.

She sagged against him, her knees buckling beneath her. Cutter pulled the blade out and stepped away from the pulse of blood as she collapsed onto the tiles at his feet.

Cutter staggered backward and fell against the wall, staring at her body. He sat for a while, struggling to calm his rapidly beating heart.

After his breathing had slowed to a less furious rate, he looked at his arms, then at his shirt and trousers. Everything was covered in blood and sweat. If he planned on getting to Skyway to track down Tiel, he needed to clean himself up.

He pushed himself painfully to his feet and limped out of the room. He paused in the hallway to make sure he was alone, but he couldn't hear any other signs of life. Obviously, Tiel trusted Jana to take care of the job.

He headed down the stairs and out the front door. The huge fountain splashed and gurgled to itself, a monument to bad taste and too much money. Cutter slipped over the side and into the water and scrubbed himself all over, trying to get his clothes as clean as possible. He stood up and looked at himself. It wasn't ideal, but it would do for the moment. As soon as he was away from the house, he would stop and get bandaged up. Maybe he could find some clean clothing along the way.

❂ ❂ ❂ ❂ ❂ ❂ ❂

Torin slumped in the professor's desk chair and tried to read the same sentence he had been trying to read. He was bored. He'd been sitting for ages, and still no sign of Cutter. Torin heard the sounds of the college outside the door: footsteps in the hallway, conversations passed between co-workers, the opening and closing of doors.

Liena would be preparing supper right about then, he mused, his stomach rumbling. It was Torin's favorite—a slowly cooked stew. His stomach rumbled just thinking about it.

He always gave Wren a hard time about his wife, but she didn't really hate him. Torin thought she was actually jealous of his relationship with Wren. She knew he would drop everything for Wren, would probably give his life to save the half-elf. But it was no more than he would do for Liena. He didn't have a large group of friends, but when he cared for someone, it was a lifelong commitment.

Wren was like a wayward nephew. He wasn't kidding when he had suggested he was like Wren's uncle. It was how he really felt. Wren needed someone like himself to ground him, otherwise he'd be chasing a tangent at every opportunity. He had a great mind, but like other great minds, it had a tendency to fragment sometimes, to spill over into triviality.

Torin's stomach grumbled again. Why did he have to wait, anyway? Why not wait somewhere he could get something to eat? It wouldn't take long. He didn't think Cutter would come back here, anyway. That man was on his own mission.

He hopped off the chair and opened the door, heading into the hallway. He almost collided with Kayla, the dwarf hurrying down the corridor with her arms full of files.

"Torin? What are you doing here?"

"Kayla. Sorry." He reached out and adjusted the pile she was holding so it wouldn't topple over. "What? Oh, waiting for Cutter. He's supposed to be bringing the dragonshard back here."

"What? You found it?"

"We did, yes."

Kayla nodded and looked over Torin's shoulder into the room. "Where's Master Wren?"

"He's gone off with Col to speak to Xavien."

"Xavien? The city councilor?"

Torin nodded. "It looks like he's part of this whole thing."

Kayla frowned. "Really? Larrien won't be happy about that. And who is this Col?"

"Sorry. I forgot you don't know about that. He's a member of the Dark Lanterns. He's been working the case as well."

"Sounds like you made a lot of progress since destroying the desk."

Torin shifted uncomfortably. "Sorry about that. Cutter. Not big on subtlety."

Kayla sighed. "It's fine. As long as it gets this case sorted out. Where were you going?"

"To find some food. I've been waiting here for ages, but I don't think he's going to show."

"You think something's happened to him?"

"I have no idea. But he was supposed to be here over an hour ago."

Kayla nodded. "I see. But what if he comes back and you've disappeared? Tell you what. You stay here and I'll bring you some food."

Torin grinned. "Thanks. And my stomach thanks you, too."

He turned back into the office. As he stepped over the threshold, he felt a sharp pain in his lower back, near his kidneys.

Thinking he'd been stung by something, he reached around to feel for a bite, but the sting blossomed into a shooting pain. He touched the spot. It felt wet. And warm. Then another blossom of hot pain. He looked at his hand. It was covered in blood.

He frowned in confusion and turned around. Kayla stood before him holding a bloody dagger. He looked at it, then at her, not understanding. His legs suddenly felt weak. He reached out to Kayla to steady himself. She grabbed him by the shoulder. He thought she was going to hold him up, but then stabbed the knife into his stomach.

He fell to his knees, his hands going to the wound, trying to stanch the blood. Everything felt like it was fading away, like he was falling asleep.

But he wasn't. He was dying.

He fell forward onto the carpet. He couldn't believe it. This was it.

Goodbye, Liena.

Just before he closed his eyes, he realized that his last words, his legacy to the world, were, *And my stomach thanks you, too.*

Wren would probably find that amusing.

Chapter Nineteen

The third day of Long Shadows

Sar, the 28th day of Vult, 998

The district of Fallen was one of the most decrepit slums in Sharn. It was once called Godsgate, one of the city's first temple districts, but as the population increased and the towers grew higher, the religious quarter moved upward as well, so they could be closer to their gods. Over the next few hundred years, the district slowly decayed and festered, but somehow managed to cling to a semblance of life, like a barnacle on a rock.

Until the day the Glass Tower fell from the sky, raining shards of death on everyone below.

Chunks as big as houses and razor pieces the size of pins showered over the area. Hundreds of people died. Some said it was punishment for the arrogance of the priests, for leaving their original homes of worship. But, as those hit by the disaster rightly asked, why not take it out on the priests who actually deserted the district in the first place?

It was a fair point, so the disaster was declared a terrible accident.

The council refused to rebuild. Although they didn't say it out loud, they were all thinking the same thing. The accident had actually done the city a favor.

And so the district of Fallen fell even lower.

There were still plenty of areas of Fallen, far away from the ruins of the Glass Tower, where people remained to try to eke out some kind of a life. They ran businesses out of half-ruined towers, patched up and repaired with scavenged supplies. There was a weekly market, supplying residents with rather desultory pickings.

But everyone avoided the area where the Glass Tower had fallen. The place was thought to be cursed. Rumors of restless spirits abounded, and over the years, sightings of a more substantial kind gained fame. A race of crazed, feral creatures claimed the area as their home. No one knew if they were survivors of the original disaster or whether they simply arrived and chose to call the deserted streets their home. Some said they had shambled up from the very depths of Khyber itself. Over the years, the people of Fallen came to give them a name, one that suited their animalistic ways. They became known as the ravers.

Col circled the darkened skycoach around the ruins of the Glass Tower. Wren had never been to this section of Fallen before. He didn't think anyone came here, so pervasive were the rumors of ghosts and the like. It was the perfect place for a criminal to hide out. In fact, he wondered if the ravers were real. Maybe they were simply rumors started by those using the area as a hideout. What better way to keep people out?

Wren stared over the side of the coach. It was like some strange magical forest. Huge chunks of glass stood embedded in the ground like colossal tree trunks. Some stood upright, but others slanted this way and that, like spears planted in the ground to repel a cavalry charge. As the skycoach moved slowly around the area of destruction, the small amount of light that trickled down winked and flashed on the faceted shards, revealing lethal edges and razor-sharp planes that promised a painful death to anyone caught inside.

And that was where they were going. Inside.

"Very bad idea," repeated Wren. "Very bad idea."

Col looked over his shoulder and frowned at him. "What's wrong with you? You've come this far."

"Sharp edges," said Wren nervously. He peered over the side again and quickly yanked his head back as the skycoach drifted past a tall shard. The glass barely missed his head. "Watch what you're doing! That one nearly sliced my face clean off!"

"You're acting like a child," said Col.

Wren vigorously rubbed his face. "You're right. You're right. Sorry. Got a fear of sharp things."

"What, like swords and knives?"

"No, they're fine. Sharper than that. Razors, all this glass." He gestured vaguely around. "It could take your finger clean off and you wouldn't know it."

"Yes, you would. As soon as the air hits the wound, you'd know. You'd feel a gentle throbbing at first, then you'd look down and see a bloody stump where you recently had a finger—"

"Yes, thank you. If you'd just shut up now, I'd greatly appreciate it."

Col shook his head in exasperation. "I'm taking us over the fall zone. Keep your eyes open for any light."

"Fine."

Col pulled the skycoach up a few feet and headed straight over the forest of glass. Towers still stood within the area, some having escaped unscathed, others half collapsed, little more than decayed remains. Wren peered into the darkness, wishing that Xavien had been more specific with his directions.

They covered the area in a grid pattern, but it seemed hopeless. Wren couldn't see any signs of life. He turned to Col to tell him it was a waste of time—

—and caught a glimpse of light out of the corner of his eye.

"Stop," he ordered.

Col stopped the skycoach in midair. "What?" he asked.

"I saw something. A light."

Col looked around. "Where about? I can't see anything."

Wren stared hard but he couldn't see anything. "I'm sure I saw it. Just a flash. Like when you see a torch through a gap in a shutter."

Col slowly moved the skycoach backward. A moment later, Wren saw it.

"There," he said, pointing. The skycoach stopped moving and Col looked to where Wren was pointing.

"Looks like an old tower."

"It's been built up, though. The top half is wooden."

Orange light speared through wooden slats. Col studied the tower. "There's no way in from the top. It doesn't look like there are any windows up there."

"So we go in from the bottom," said Wren. "Quietly."

Col nodded and turned the skycoach around. He settled it in a gentle landing outside the tower, in a space that had been cleared of debris.

"I wonder if he's been hiding here all this time," mused Wren as he dropped to the ground.

"Possibly. No one's going to come looking for him here."

Col checked his weapons, then drew his long sword. "You ready?" he asked.

Wren checked the wands in his belt. "Ready."

Col nodded and they walked around the tower until they found the door. Col stood to the side and motioned Wren to do the same. He reached around and flicked the latch, giving the door a gentle push.

It swung inward on silent hinges. They waited, but nothing happened. Col darted a quick look around the door frame.

"Clear," he whispered to Wren. He crouched down and entered the tower. Wren followed. He saw a dark room cluttered with all kinds of junk. Old chairs were stacked one on top of the other all the way to the roof. Tables had been separated from their legs and piled into a corner. Cobwebs hung from the rafters. Diadus certainly didn't spend any time down here.

Col was standing at the bottom of a spiral staircase. Wren joined him and they climbed slowly up the stone steps, keeping their eyes trained above them.

Wren leaned close to Col. "Watch out for him. He's a powerful artificer. No telling what he's got up his sleeve."

Col nodded.

The next floor was the same as the one below—empty of life but cluttered with junk. They moved up, past two more deserted floors. Then the stone and rock of the tower walls gave way to the newly constructed wooden portion. Wren tensed, as this was probably where Diadus lived. They climbed a few more steps, then Wren heard a dull clomp. Col paused to look down. The stairs had been replaced with the wooden variety.

Col indicated for them to tread more carefully. Wren hoped it wasn't too late. Maybe Diadus hadn't heard Col's footstep.

The stairs stopped at a sturdy door. Col studied it carefully, then motioned for Wren to retreat a few steps so they could talk.

"It's solid," he said. "If it's locked, there's no way we can break it down. I can pick the lock, but he may hear me."

Wren smiled and pulled an amethyst wand from his belt. "No problem," he said. "Just stand behind me, please. Thank you."

Wren pointed the wand and released a wave of blue electricity that hit the door, crackling and smoking. All went silent for half a breath, then the whole door exploded inward with an implosion of air, disappearing from sight. Wren cut off the flow of energy and Col rushed passed him, sword raised, plunging into the room. Wren followed, waving away the smoke so he could see.

The door had smashed a desk and punched through the back wall of the tower. Smoke drifted out of the hole, and after a moment, Wren saw Col standing over something.

"Couldn't you have used something with less of a bang?" he asked.

Wren joined him and looked down. "Oh."

"Yes, 'oh.' "

"Is he dead?"

Col crouched down beside Diadus and felt for a pulse. Blood seeped from a wound in his head. Wren didn't think the door had hit him, for the simple fact that his body was still in one piece. Shrapnel from the desk had probably hit him.

"He's alive," said Col.

Wren breathed a sigh of relief.

"We just have to wait for him to wake up."

Wren straightened and looked around the room. A single lantern on a table provided a small amount of light. An unmade bed was pushed against the wall. Next to it was a large table piled high with books. On the opposite wall, shelves held an assortment of jars and vials. He walked over to them and started sorting through the bottles, taking down jars and gingerly sniffing the contents.

One of the jars knocked his head back and made his eyes stream with tears. "Here," he gasped, handing the jar to Col. "Wave this under his nose—don't sniff it!"

Col froze, the jar halfway to his nose, then carefully lowered it. "What is it?"

"Smelling salts, I think."

"You think?"

"Well . . . no, no I'm sure. It's smelling salts."

Col moved it toward Diadus, then paused and glanced back at Wren, who tried to look confident.

"What are you waiting for, man? Do it."

Col shook his head and waved it under Diadus's nose. The man jerked his head away, then opened his eyes and tried to focus on Col. He saw Wren standing over Col's shoulder and sat up, scrabbling back against the wall. "Who are you?" he asked in a frightened voice.

"Just a couple of concerned citizens," said Col.

Diadus frowned. "Concerned cit—? What?"

Wren leaned over. "I remember you, Diadus."

At the mention of his name, Diadus let out a cry of fear and scrambled to his feet. He tried to push past Col, but the man was skinny to the point of sickliness. Wren reckoned a strong breeze could knock him over, so a shove from Col nearly sent him flying through the air. He fell onto his backside, then scrabbled quickly beneath a table, whimpering in fear.

"Why did you say that?" demanded Col, rounding on Wren.

"Say what?"

"You called him by his name!"

"Oh, excuse me, Master *Professional Interrogator.* What was I supposed to call him?"

"Nothing. Not until we assessed the situation."

Wren glanced across at Diadus. "I think the situation's assessed," he said. "And in my humble opinion—and understand, I'm not a professional like you obviously are—I think we've got a *slightly* unbalanced individual on our hands."

"That's impossible," said Col. "He's involved in all of this. He helped put the Shadow elemental inside the dragonshard."

"No. I didn't."

Col and Wren turned to Diadus, who had poked his head out from beneath the table.

"What?" said Wren.

"I said, 'No. I didn't.' "

"But Xavien said—"

"Xavien knows nothing. It doesn't matter, anyway. He'll be dead soon. Just like all the rest."

"What are you babbling about?" snapped Col.

Diadus shook his head. "Nothing," he said. "It doesn't matter now. Nothing does."

Col strode forward and grabbed hold of Diadus, dragging him out from beneath the table. He squealed and tried to slap Col's hands away.

"Let me go! You'll regret it. I promise you."

"What are you going to do?"

"Not me."

"Then who?"

Wren stepped forward. "The warforged?"

Diadus stared at him with bulging eyes.

"Yes," said Wren. "I told you I knew who you were. You created that warforged a few years ago. The one who was destroyed for killing all those people. You've done it again, haven't you? You've created another one."

Diadus smiled, a slow grin that made his thin face look like a skull. "Not another one. He was never destroyed in the first place."

"What?"

"He decided to stop killing. For the time being. He said he had grander things to plan. He brought me here." Diadus looked around the tower room. "I've been here ever since."

"For four years?"

"No choice. He wouldn't let me leave." Diadus seemed to reach a decision. He sighed. "Please put me down. I'll tell you what you need to know."

Col released his grip.

Diadus smoothed down his clothing and looked at them. "There's nothing you can do, you know. I meant what I said. It's too late."

"Too late for what?"

Diadus took a shaky breath. "Everything that's been happening. All this stuff about Tiel killing the council and pinning the blame on Daask. It's not real. It's a cover for what's really going to happen. When Tiel activates the shard—"

"If he activates the shard," said Wren. "Someone's already tracked him down to stop him."

"Then I wish him well. Because if Tiel manages to activate it . . ." Diadus shook his head sorrowfully. "I had to do it. Do you understand? I had no choice."

Wren looked at Col. The Dark Lantern looked worried.

"Had no choice about what? What did you do, Diadus?"

Wren sniffed the air. "Col," he said. "Do you smell smoke?"

Diadus looked at Wren in alarm, then sniffed the air. "You're right," he said, and hurried over to the shattered doorway.

"Where are you going?" snapped Col, stepping forward to pull him away.

He didn't make it in time. A warforged stood at the top of the stairs. Its body was so black that it was almost invisible, melding with the darkness around it. Wren could see it only because its eyes were bright white, flaring and dimming as if in time to someone's breathing.

The scene seemed to freeze for a heartbeat. Wren saw the fear in Diadus's eyes. The warforged reached out, almost hesitantly.

"I am sorry, father," it whispered.

Then the warforged ran Diadus through with a blade, pushing so hard that it lifted the skinny man off the floor.

Diadus screamed in pain and the warforged yanked the sword free. Diadus staggered back and collapsed at Wren's feet, curling up around the wound and sobbing in pain. The warforged looked at Wren, and the half-elf realized that the construct was probably standing there when he said Cutter was going to stop Tiel. The warforged's eyes flared white, but didn't dim. It turned and ran down the stairs. Col chased after the warforged.

Wren grabbed Diadus under his arms and dragged him across the floor, leaving a smeared trail of blood in his wake. He just managed to manhandle Diadus onto the bed when a terrific explosion ripped through the lower half of the tower. It was followed by the sounds of rending wood and collapsing beams.

Wren hurried to the doorway. As he reached it, Col staggered into the room, coughing and waving at the smoke that billowed up the stairs behind him.

"It had some sort of explosive. Everything's on fire down there."

"Wonderful," said Wren. He returned to Diadus, rolling the wounded man onto his back. "Diadus! Diadus, is there another way out of here?"

"He . . . he has *killed* me," the man whispered, and Wren thought he could hear outrage in his voice. "I . . . I created him, and this is how he repays me."

"Diadus, what will the shard do? You have to tell us."

Diadus looked into Wren's eyes and grinned. Blood trickled from his mouth. "Everyone must die," he whispered.

"The smoke's getting thicker," said Col from the other side of the room.

Wren looked over his shoulder and could see orange light flickering from the staircase. He could already feel the heat at his feet.

"Diadus, tell me! If Tiel activates the dragonshard, what will happen? What has the warforged done?"

"He has brought the end upon us," gasped the skinny man, grabbing Wren's wrist. He doubled over in pain, and a moment later he relaxed with a long sigh. Wren checked for a pulse. The man was dead.

"Wren," said Col, standing near the hole in the wall, "you'd better get over here. We've got a problem."

Chapter Twenty

The third day of Long Shadows

Sar, the 28th day of Vult, 998

Wren looked up. "Another one?" he said, getting up to join him.

"Afraid so. See, I have one charm to feather fall. I could float down there, bring the skycoach up, and rescue you."

"I fail to see the problem. That's a very sound plan."

Col looked over his shoulder as Wren approached. "It would be. Except for that."

He pointed toward the ground. Wren grabbed the edges of the hole and looked down.

"Ah," was all he said.

Milling around the clearing outside of the tower were about sixty feral creatures. They stood upright on two legs, but their resemblance to anything human ended there. They prowled around the skycoach, sniffing it suspiciously. As Wren and Col watched, one of the creatures leaped into the air and landed inside the vehicle, smelling the seats.

"Ravers," whispered Wren.

As they watched, another raver jumped into the skycoach. The creature inside whirled around with a snarl and slashed at the interloper's throat. Blood sprayed out and the creature toppled over backward. The other ravers fell onto the body, snarling as they ripped it apart and devoured it.

Wren stepped back. "I feel ill."

Col stayed where he was, assessing the situation. He turned to Wren. "You got any more of those wands?"

"Only one that's charged."

Col nodded. "Good. We use the same plan. I'll float down and secure the skycoach. You use the wand to cover me. Then I pick you up."

The heat of the fire was growing stronger. Wren turned and saw naked flames licking at the doorframe. Smoke was pouring through the opening and piling against the ceiling like a cloud bank. "You'd better hurry. I don't know how long this tower is going to hold."

Col nodded and removed the feather fall charm from his pocket. "Ready?"

Wren took out the wand and steadied himself at the hole. "Ready."

Col stepped off the tower and disappeared from view. Wren leaned over and saw him float gently to the ground, drawing his sword as he landed. The ravers hadn't seen him. They were all gathered around the fight over the corpse.

A huge crash behind Wren brought him whirling around. The staircase and part of the floor had collapsed. Flames flickered through gaps in what remained of the wooden flooring. The whole place was about to go down.

He turned his attention to the scene outside. His heart leaped into his throat. Col was busy fighting off five ravers. As the half-elf watched, the human decapitated one of the creatures, then brought his sword down in a diagonal slash that cleaved another from shoulder to hip. He kicked the thing in the stomach, pushing it off his blade, and parried a clumsy swipe by another, sending its hand sailing through the air. The others looked up from their gory feast and saw Col battling two of their kind. They raised their faces to the sky and shrieked with excitement, then ran toward Col, fighting and snapping at each other as they tried to get to him first. Col threw a look over his shoulder to glare at Wren.

"Sorry," muttered Wren, and pointed the wand at the closest raver. He released a charge of electricity. It arced to the ground and wreathed the creature in a spider web of blue light. It threw its head back and howled in pain, trying to pull the threads of electricity from its body. A second later, it dropped to the ground, smoke rising from its corpse.

Wren let loose with another burst from the wand. This time, the electricity jumped between the jostling ravers. The front line went down, writhing and shrieking. Wren kept the charge going, and every creature that touched those on the ground was immediately caught up in the arc. Col finished off the two he was fighting and darted around the side of the skycoach, slashing backhand at a raver who reached out to grab him. Its arm sailed through the air and slapped another one in the face. The victim looked down at the arm twitching on the ground, then leaped with a snarl onto the back of the one-armed creature.

Col reached the skycoach and laid about with his sword, stabbing and yanking at the creatures who had stayed close to it. Wren aimed and let loose with the remaining charge in the wand, shielding Col with a wall of electricity. Ravers ran straight into it.

It distracted the beasts enough for Col to reach the controls. The skycoach rose jerkily into the air and turned in Wren's direction. He dropped the wand and readied himself to jump aboard.

The skycoach was still a few floors below him when a resounding crash in the room sent him spinning around. The entire floor caved in, taking everything with it. Flames roared up through the gaping hole, licking hungrily at the rafters. Wren shielded his face from the heat and tried to balance on the ragged hole in the tower wall. Col was looking up at him as he guided the coach as close as he dared. Flames licked out of arrow slits in the stone base of the building.

As Wren watched, trying to judge the distance to the skycoach, two ravers jumped from a room somewhere in the tower and landed in the vehicle. One of them was on fire. The skycoach dropped with the unexpected weight and tipped to one side. Col struggled with the controls, fighting to right it before he crashed into the tower wall. The burning raver rolled around in the back seat, slapping its burning rags.

The other one, however, had spotted Col and was climbing over the seat toward him.

Wren sighed and took his dagger from his belt. He couldn't believe his luck. He was about to do an incredibly heroic thing and Torin wasn't even around to witness it. He'd never believe it when Wren told him.

He muttered a prayer to the nonexistent god of inquisitives and jumped from the tower.

As he fell, he saw Col look up at him, his eyes widening in shock. Wren had the smallest moment to grin at the stupefied human before he landed in the skycoach, one leg on the seat and the other jarring painfully against the floor. His breath exploded from his body and he struggled to pull himself to his feet.

He looked up and saw the raver's face not inches from his

own, mouth open to reveal serrated teeth. It lunged in to take a chunk out of Wren's neck.

Wren jerked backward and plunged the dagger up in an instinctive movement. The blade caught the raver under the chin and thrust up into its brain. The creature's mouth snapped shut on its tongue, cutting the tip clean off. One of its eyes closed. The other opened wide, the eyelid fluttering as if it had a tick. Wren wrenched the dagger out and the raver collapsed onto the side of the coach. The half-elf helped it on its way, kicking it over the edge.

The other raver still burned. The fire had spread up its legs and across one arm. Wren leaned over and stabbed whatever was in reach, hitting the upper arm that wasn't on fire. The raver screeched and whipped around to glare at Wren, then it stood up and leaped over the side. Wren grabbed the side of the skycoach and watched the creature plummet directly into a huge shard of glass. The spire punched through the raver's stomach and the creature slid down the shaft, the width at the spike's base ripping the creature apart.

Wren collapsed into the seat, gasping for breath. Col had righted the skycoach and was guiding it straight up into the air. Col looked over his shoulder, and Wren was astounded to see the man grinning.

"Now was that an escape, or was that an escape?" he shouted.

"Yes. Well, something like that, certainly," said Wren.

Col let out a whoop of delight. "Where to?" he called.

Wren struggled to pull himself up and climbed over the seats to the front. "To Skyway. All we can do now is find Cutter and hope he got the shard from Tiel."

"We're on our way."

Chapter Twenty-One

The third day of Long Shadows

Sar, the 28th day of Vult, 998

The first thing Cutter did when he left Tiel's place was find a House Jorasco healer, using some of the money he had picked up at Silvermist to pay. He wanted to be in top condition when he took on the halfling. He was confident he could take Tiel, but he wasn't sure about Bren. He still had to figure out what to do about him.

As he was leaving the healer, he stole an expensive thigh-length coat with intricate embroidering around the cuffs. It belonged to a nobleman visiting one of the other healers for a broken arm. Cutter buttoned it up over his bloody shirt, trying to look halfway respectable. Halfway—because no matter how expensive the outfit, he always looked like he was wearing someone else's clothes.

The House Lyrandar skycoach carried Cutter up into the late afternoon sky. The summer day had turned humid. Black clouds piled up on the horizon over the Dagger River. Thunderheads climbed high into the sky, lit golden on one side by the lowering sun. As the coach took him to his destination, the heavy clouds slowly moved across the sun. Golden streamers punched through the dense curtain to dance across the water below.

The storm would hit before the day was out.

A shadow fell across the coach as the driver took them beneath the massive floating district of Skyway. From this angle, it looked like a massive white cloud, the layers of magical cloud-stuff the floating island rested on obscuring everything else from view.

They glided out from under the shadow and rose above the lip of the island. From this height, it was abundantly clear to Cutter the kind of money needed to live here. Mansions ten times the size of Tiel's dotted the landscape. Their gardens were so large they could have been parks. Cutter watched as a griffon padded sedately along a wide boulevard, the rider sitting tall in his seat. He nodded at a carriage that trundled past, pulled by a pair of hippogriffs.

Skyway was separated into two halves—Brilliant to the north, and Azure to the south, with Cloudpool Park cutting through the middle. Cutter had heard people speak about the park, but he'd never expected to see it for himself.

Cloudpool Park was formed of clouds—or at least, a magical version of clouds that had been teased into the shapes of trees and bushes, statues, and animals. As the coach drifted slowly over the park, Cutter could see people walking along the pathways, tiny splashes of color amidst the whiteness. The scene appeared as if a blanket of snow had fallen over everything, so fresh it still held its lightness and color.

The hotel he had heard Tiel mention was not far from the park. The skycoach circled the hotel a few times, waiting for another coach to land on the roof and deliver its passengers. His driver followed suit and Cutter disembarked. The skycoach lifted back into the air, banked to the right, and soared away over the palatial estates.

Cutter glanced around. Expensive skycoaches and coaches with empty harnesses were parked neatly on the rooftop. Trees had been planted around the perimeter of the roof, adding color to the gray stonework.

A door opened into a small foyer, and two pairs of doors led from the room. One gave access to a lift, the other to a set of stairs. Cutter took the lift and it whisked him down to the ground floor.

He pushed the door open and stepped into a brightly lit entrance hall. Expensively dressed guests milled around, glancing surreptitiously at each others' clothes and jewelry. Skylights spilled the last of the lowering sun into the foyer. The dark clouds had drawn closer, now towering high above Skyway.

A huge desk occupied the center of the foyer. A well-dressed elf stood behind it, talking to a tall woman wearing—Cutter stared hard at her clothing as he approached—was she really wearing lizard skin? It certainly looked like she was. She turned and he saw fierce claws gathered around her neck. Maybe something from the Talenta Plains, then. He shook his head as she walked past. Some people just had too much money.

"Can I help you?" asked the elf. Cutter saw the brief flicker of confusion on his face as he tried to reconcile the expensive coat with the cuts and bruises on Cutter's neck and face.

"I was mugged," said Cutter, indicating his face.

"How absolutely dreadful!" exclaimed the elf. "Not here, surely?"

"No, no. In Menthis. Can't even have a peaceful night out at the opera nowadays."

"I know, I know. What is the world coming to?" The elf smiled. "How may I help you?"

"I'm supposed to be meeting a friend of mine. His name's Tiel. Can you tell me what room he's in?"

"A friend of Master Boromar's? How delightful. Master Boromar has taken one of our best suites. Room 412. But I think he's in the restaurant at the moment."

"Oh. That's fine, then. I'll join him there. Thank you for your help."

"Not at all. And watch out for muggers," he called jovially as Cutter turned away.

Cutter looked back to see him smiling. "Will do," he said brightly, matching the elf's tone.

He waited until the elf was occupied with another customer, then walked quickly to the stairs, running up them two at a time until he reached the fourth floor. He pulled the door open and walked onto a carpet so thick it covered the toes of his boots.

Room 412 was at the end of the corridor. Next to it, another staircase rose behind a dark wooden door carved with a bas relief of . . . Cutter squinted at it. He wasn't quite sure, but he thought it may have been something to do with the Silver Flame. He pushed at the door to the halfling's room to see if it was locked. It wasn't.

Perfect. He looked around to make sure he was alone, then took out a knife and jammed it between the door and the frame of Tiel's chamber. He moved it about a bit, then took it out and stepped into the stairwell, keeping the door open a fraction so he could see into the hall.

Bren sat opposite Tiel and stared out the window at the ominous clouds building in the distance. His shirt was sticking to his back in the humidity.

He liked storms. There was something . . . primeval about them. Something to put people in their place, remind them that they weren't as important as they thought.

This one looked like it would be big.

Bren took a sip from the brandy Tiel had insisted on ordering for him. "It's a celebration!" he'd said. "After tonight, everyone will know who Tiel Boromar is."

Bren had accepted the drink even though he wasn't in the mood for celebrating. He'd learned a lot in the past few hours that he wasn't happy with. He needed time alone to sort through everything, to figure out how he felt.

No. He knew how he felt. He glanced at Tiel from the corner of his eye as the halfling devoured a steak so rare the blood pooled on his plate.

Disgusted. That was how he felt.

And guilty. That was another one.

The fact was, he'd liked Cutter. *And* Rowen. He thought they made a good couple, reckoned they would soon leave all this stuff behind and try to make a life for themselves.

He'd found himself wondering if he wanted that, too.

"You know what to do?" asked Tiel, interrupting his reverie.

"You've told me ten times already. I know what to do."

"You understand I'm not scared," said Tiel, around a mouthful of food. He swallowed. "Because I'm not."

"I know you're not, Tiel."

"I just can't be at the Tain's house when all this happens."

"I know."

He looked like he was about to say something else when that irritating elf from the front desk nervously approached the table.

"Master Boromar?" he said, wringing his hands.

Tiel looked up. "What? Wasn't the tip I left big enough?"

"No, no. You were more than generous. It's just that . . . uh, we have a bit of a problem."

"What kind of problem?" asked Bren.

"It seems that the, ah . . . wards on your rooms have been broken. We've sent guards up. They haven't found anyone there, but we thought you would want to take a look around. Make sure nothing's been stolen."

Bren raised an eyebrow at Tiel. The halfling shook his head and tapped his pocket. "Safe and sound. But you'd better go have a look around. Make sure my clothes are still there."

Bren nodded and rose from the table.

The elf moved aside. "We're most dreadfully sorry about this. Nothing like it has ever happened before."

Tiel leaned back in his chair. "I'm most disappointed. I hope you don't expect me to pay for my stay now. If I were forced to pay, who knows who I might talk to? Break-ins are very bad publicity, you know."

"Of course, of course. You'll be well looked after, Master Boromar."

Bren shook his head as he left the restaurant and walked through the foyer. All that money and he was still trying to scrounge free room and board. Some people never changed.

Bren took the lift to their floor and headed down the corridor to Tiel's rooms. A guard stood outside the door.

"You can go now."

The guard nodded. "The wards will reactivate once you close the door."

Fat lot of good they did the first time, thought Bren, but he didn't say anything.

He stood in the doorway and looked around the room. Nothing had been disturbed. Nothing touched. He frowned. Nobody had been in this room. He could tell. Had they been scared away?

Or was it some kind of trap?

He whirled around even as this thought entered his head. Cutter stood in the doorway, his hands raised in the air, waiting for Bren to notice him.

"I was standing there for five seconds, Bren. I could have taken you."

Bren straightened. "Cutter," he said. "Good to see you alive." And he meant it.

"Yeah. I'm pretty happy about that myself."

"Jana?"

"Dead."

Bren nodded. "You want a drink?" he asked.

Cutter shook his head. "I want to talk."

"That why you broke the ward? To talk to me?"

"Actually, I was hoping Tiel would come up, but this is fine."

Bren strolled over to an armchair and sat down. Cutter followed him into the room and sat on the bed.

"Tiel doesn't like creased bed sheets, Cutter. You'd better straighten them when you're done."

Cutter shook his head. "Why are you working for him?"

"That's my business. What are you doing here, Cutter?"

"I want a favor."

"Oh? What makes you think I'd do you any favors?"

"Because you knew Rowen. And you know she didn't deserve to die."

Bren sighed. "She stole from him, Cutter. He has a lot riding on this deal."

"I couldn't care less about any deal!" snapped Cutter. "I want payback."

"Why are you telling me this?"

"Because I respect you. I don't want to go behind your back."

"You're asking for my permission."

"No. I'm doing this with or without your permission. What I'm hoping for is a bit of understanding. If you want to hunt me down after the deed is done, that's your prerogative. But make no mistake. I'm taking him down, Bren."

Bren thought about it. It went against every professional ethic he had, but he really did feel for Cutter. He was owed some personal justice. Bren leaned forward.

"How about this?" he said. "I give you one chance. Just one. I'm heading to the Tain manor soon. Have to do something for him. He'll be leaving for some club to get drunk and cause trouble. His skycoach is on the roof. You do what you need to do. But if you mess up—if you fail—that's it."

"Bren, the only way I fail is if I'm dead."

Bren shook his head. "I can't believe I'm doing this."

"Why *are* you doing it?"

Bren thought about it. "Because I liked her. Liked what she did for someone like you. Guess I thought if you could find someone like that, maybe I could as well. She was a good woman."

Cutter stood up and held out his hand. "If I survive past today, you let me buy you a drink?"

Bren shook his hand. "A drink? With what I'm letting you get away with, you should buy me a whole tavern."

Cutter nodded.

"Watch your back, Cutter. He's no pushover. He's got a few tricks up his sleeve."

"I will. See you round."

Bren stared at the empty doorway after Cutter left. After a moment, he shook himself.

"Guess I'll have that drink by myself."

Chapter Twenty-Two

The third day of Long Shadows

Sar, the 28th day of Vult, 998

Cutter leaned over the low wall and tried to calm his beating heart. The moment was here. He would finally get his revenge on the bastard who took Rowen from him.

The gardens of the Golden Tear rolled gently into the distance and merged invisibly with Cloudpool Park. Lightning stabbed out of the black clouds. A warm wind, rich with the smell of the coming storm, blew against his face, made his eyes water. He blinked and focused on the ground.

Bren was walking along the pathway. He stopped at a carriage with two hippogriffs harnessed to the front. He spoke to the driver, then climbed inside. Where was it he said he was going? Tain Manor? Cutter wondered what he was going there for.

No matter. Bren had said that Tiel would be leaving about the same time he did. That meant the halfling was probably on his way up to the rooftop. Cutter had chosen this place carefully to stage his attack. It was one of the most secluded areas in the park. All the guards were stationed at ground level. Nobody thought to place them up where the coaches were parked.

Col turned and rested his elbows against the wall. One of the trees that had been planted in a deep well of earth around the rooftop shielded him from the sight of anyone stepping out of the hotel. The rising wind soughed through the branches, rustling the leaves and causing the treetop to sway back and forth.

The door opened. Cutter tensed, ready to move, but it was a dwarf couple walking arm in arm. They climbed inside an expensive skycoach, then it rose gently into the air, turning gracefully and heading in the direction of Cloudpool Park.

Cutter forced himself to relax. Getting tense now would only tire him later, and he'd need all his energy for the fight ahead. He knew Tiel wouldn't be a pushover. He'd seen what the halfling could do when he got worked up.

The door opened again. Cutter was half expecting more guests, so his mind stalled for a moment before registering that it was Tiel he was looking at.

The halfling walked toward a two-man skycoach parked close to the door.

Cutter pushed himself away from the wall and hurried across the roof, pulling out the Khutai blades. This was it. Rowen would finally get her rest.

He approached the skycoach. Tiel leaned over the side, rummaging around for something. Cutter took a deep breath, let it out slowly, then took another.

He stopped a few feet away.

"You going somewhere?" he asked.

Tiel froze, then looked over his shoulder. He frowned in annoyance. "Khyber's ghost, don't you ever *die?*"

"Afraid not."

Tiel rummaged around some more, then straightened up,

turning to face Cutter. He held two short swords in his hands, crossed before him. "Guess I'll have to take care of you myself."

"No, see, that's not how it works. How it works is, I break your legs. Then I make you bleed."

"Then what?" sneered Tiel. "You make me say sorry for killing your woman?"

"No. Then I watch you die."

"Fascinating. But that doesn't work for me. I have things to do."

"Then you'll have to cancel your appointments. You're not going anywhere."

Tiel sighed. "Much as I enjoy all this manly posturing—and don't get me wrong, you're very good at it—can we just skip to the end?"

"Which end is that?"

"The one where I slit your throat the same way I slit Rowen's."

Tiel charged, his blades a whirling circle of steel. Cutter moved backward, surprised at the speed of his attack. The points of Tiel's swords flicked in and out, darting at Cutter like striking snakes. He moved his knives into defensive angles, blocking with the edges along his forearms. But he was pushed back by the sheer ferocity of Tiel's attack.

It seemed he had underestimated the halfling. His swordplay was as fast as any Cutter had seen.

They moved across the rooftop, Tiel on the attack, Cutter on the defensive. He needed to turn this around. This wasn't how it was meant to play out.

He let Tiel get closer, then jammed one of his blades down at an angle between the halfling's arms. It caught the two swords for only an instant, just long enough for him to lean in and hit Tiel in the cheek with the hilt of the other knife. He wanted to use the blade, but couldn't turn it around in time.

It did the job, though. It broke Tiel's attack and sent him staggering to one side. The halfling threw his arm out behind him, pointing it at Cutter to keep him at bay. Cutter kicked it aside and stabbed down with his blade. He was too far back to cause a severe wound, but the point dug into Tiel's upper arm and opened a deep gash. Tiel turned to face Cutter again, but Cutter was already pressing the attack, using the technique he preferred—coming in low with one hand and high with the other. It left him open to a strike in the stomach, but he considered himself quick enough that the low blade could double as defense.

It also had the advantage of drawing an opponent's attack to what was considered a vulnerable spot.

Which was exactly what Tiel did. He saw the opening and aimed a thrust at Cutter's midsection. Cutter let him come, then sliced upward with the low knife. He expected to take Tiel's hand off, or at the very least slice open his wrist, but he'd played into the halfling's plan. As he moved the blade upward, Tiel brought his other sword around in a sideways swing that caught Cutter in the thigh. His leather trousers absorbed the brunt of the attack. Even so, the sword sliced through and cut deep into his leg.

Cutter staggered back. Tiel had been onto him the whole time. He'd seen what Cutter planned and had been thinking two steps ahead.

Tiel grinned at him. "You didn't think I was much of a swordsman, did you? Just because you've never seen me wield one doesn't mean I'm no good."

The halfling lunged forward and released a flurry of swings. Cutter blocked them all, the clash of metal on metal loud in his ears. He acted on instinct now. He couldn't even see all the moves Tiel was making.

"See," said Tiel, stepping back. "You've made the mistake many people make when they meet me. They think I'm bad-tempered, rash, quick to anger. And that's all true. But I also know when to bide my time. I mean, do you have any idea how long it took for Rowen to die? And she *still* didn't tell me where the shard was."

Cutter screamed in anger and ran forward. Tiel's face showed an instant of surprise, then short sword slammed against knife, raining sparks around them with the ferocity of the impacts. They shuffled around the rooftop, sometimes defending, sometimes attacking. Each had scores of cuts and slashes over their arms and chest, but neither could press the attack long enough to land a fatal blow.

Sweat poured into Cutter's eyes, into his wounds. The pain screamed at him, slicing his mind with the sting, trying to distract him from the fight. The only consolation was that Tiel seemed to be suffering just as much. Sweat poured down the halfling's face, and blood from a wound above his eyebrow trickled around his eye. Cutter kept a close watch on it, hoping the blood would drip into Tiel's eye and give the instant of advantage the human so desperately needed.

Cutter felt something bump against his back and realized Tiel had maneuvered him against one of the trees along the wall. The trunk pressed into his spine, limiting his swing.

Tiel suddenly switched tactics, flipping both swords in his grip and swinging them around in a sideways arc. Cutter ducked as the blades cut into the trunk. He lunged forward and slammed into Tiel. They both tumbled over, Tiel's blades left quivering in the tree.

Cutter landed on top of Tiel, his arms trapped under the halfling's body. Tiel punched furiously at Cutter's face. Cutter jerked a hand out from under the halfling and raised his arm to ward off the blows. They kept coming, Tiel trying his hardest to incapacitate him. Cutter dropped his guard so he could land his own blows. He felt his fist connect with Tiel's nose, heard the crack of bone breaking. He thought he was gaining the advantage, then Tiel landed a fist straight into his throat. Cutter arched up, his hands instinctively moving up to prevent another punch, and Tiel smacked him in the stomach. Cutter's breath burst from his lungs and Tiel shoved him away.

Cutter landed on his back, but rolled immediately to the side. Tiel's heel slammed into the spot where his head had been. Cutter kept rolling, trying to keep out of Tiel's way while he fought to get his breath back.

Tiel gave him no respite. He ran after him, kicking out as Cutter tried to stay out of his way. Cutter couldn't move fast enough and the halfling connected with his ribs.

Cutter decided to try the trick he'd used on Jana. He grabbed hold of Tiel's foot as it came flying at his head and wrenched it to the side. To his surprise, Tiel didn't react as Jana had. He heard the ankle pop and Tiel screamed in pain. Cutter kept hold of the ankle as he tried to get to his feet, but Tiel was hopping backward, trying to pull his foot away. Cutter knew he wouldn't be able to hold onto it, so he yanked upward with all his might, watching as Tiel flew through the air and landed on the ground, groaning at the pain.

Cutter staggered to his feet and stumbled over to pick up his blades. He took a deep breath and turned around—

To find Tiel standing up, pulling off his gloves. He threw them aside and raised his hands in the air.

Cutter initially thought he was going to beg for his life.

Then he noticed that Tiel's hands had started to glow. A faint orange haze surrounded them. As he watched, tiny flames flickered over his skin.

The halfling advanced on Cutter, his hands held out before him. Cutter backed up until he bumped into another tree. He was about to dart around it when Tiel lurched forward and grabbed hold of Cutter's wrists.

Cutter screamed in pain as heat surged through his arms. He tried to pull away, but Tiel held his wrists in a tight grip. Cutter's skin blistered, smoke curling upward and attacking his nostrils with the smell of charred flesh. He could see Tiel's veins through his skin. They looked like tiny rivers of glowing lava.

He dropped the Khutai blades, sagging to his knees as the pain increased, his entire arms feeling like he had thrust them into red-hot coals. Still, the halfling didn't let go. Tiel grinned. "Didn't know I could do that, did you? I could say something about having a fiery temper, but that would be too obvious, and I do so hate being obvious."

He released Cutter's wrists and made a grab for his throat. Cutter saw him coming and dodged to the side. Tiel lunged and grabbed hold of the tree by mistake. His hands were glowing white hot. The tree trunk burst into flame, the fire crackling up to the lower branches.

Cutter pushed himself to his feet and staggered away. The halfling stared up at the tree, keeping his hands on the trunk as the foliage caught fire. The humid breeze fanned the flames. They rose higher and spread to another tree.

"See that? That's what I'm going to do to you." Tiel turned to look for him, saw him trying to get away. "Where are you going?" asked the halfling, releasing the tree and limping after him.

There was nowhere for Cutter to go. He stopped and faced Tiel. His skin was raw and bleeding, thin layers of flesh hanging from his wrists. He could see bone through the blackened skin. He couldn't move his fingers. The pain was excruciating, a pulsing, throbbing bloom of torment. He staggered, almost passing out. He managed to keep himself awake, but fell to his knees. Tiel grinned as he approached.

"That's right. That's where you belong. Cowering at my feet." The halfling held out his hands. Cutter could see the distortions of the hot haze wavering above them. He could feel the uncontrolled heat on his face. It dried his eyes out, forcing him to blink furiously and raise his arms to protect himself.

Tiel stepped closer.

Bren reached the Tain manor in only a few moments. Tiel had wanted their hotel room to be close by, just in case anything went wrong. But Bren had no idea what the halfling had in mind if things didn't go according to plan. Maybe run in and stab Saidan himself? Bren smiled at the picture this conjured in his head. For someone who had wanted his father's approval for so long, Tiel had made the leap to assassinating him and taking over the business with remarkable ease. But Bren couldn't blame him. He hadn't been with Tiel very long, but he knew that over the years, Tiel had repeatedly gone to his father to beg acknowledgement. All he wanted was to be accepted as a Boromar. Saidan had always refused.

Did that mean Tiel was delusional? That he wasn't really Saidan's son? Bren had no idea, although there was a resemblance between the two of them. Bren reckoned that Tiel simply got tired of being rejected, had decided to take matters into his own hands. Bren didn't really care. It would probably mean a pay raise for him.

That was, if Cutter failed in his plan. Bren frowned. He didn't truly know why he had given Cutter the information.

Because Tiel deserved what was coming to him? When had that ever been an issue? No. He'd given Cutter a chance. A small chance, because he knew what Tiel was capable of when he took off those gloves. But at least Cutter could die with some self-respect.

And what if he succeeded? Bren reached into his pocket and touched the dragonshard. If Cutter succeeded in killing Tiel, then what Bren was doing would be for nothing. He thought about it for a moment, then shrugged the thought away. No one would mourn the loss of Saidan Boromar. In fact, he'd probably be doing the world a favor.

The carriage came to a stop at the end of the long driveway. Bren climbed out and looked around. Immaculately groomed lawns spread out around him. A footpath, flanked on both sides by marble statues, led from the drive and up to the huge house. Bren had a close look at the statues and was amused to find out that they were statues of past members of the Tain family. Somebody certainly thought a lot of themselves.

A huge ogre stood at the front door, checking invitations as the guests arrived. A valet approached the carriage, but Bren waved him away and told his driver not leave. Bren wandered off the path and into the gardens. Guests strolled across the lawns, sipping wine from crystal glasses while they waited for the dinner to begin.

Bren sauntered around to the rear of the house. He found a secluded area where the servants came and went, walled off from the rest of the grounds. Bren took off the expensive jacket Tiel had insisted he wear, and dropped it on a stone table. He took one last look around. The black clouds overhead were limned with gold as they slowly enveloped the sun. Thunder rumbled in the distance. He took a deep breath, smelling the dampness in the air, hoping he would be finished before the storm hit—not because he didn't want to get wet, but because he wanted to watch it.

He passed through a gate into the rear courtyard. As he'd suspected, servants scurried around like headless chickens in preparation for the night's supper. No one even gave him a second look.

The back door of the house led straight into the first of four kitchens. Each kitchen had five brick ovens lining the back wall, and each oven had three sweating chefs tending to the food. They shouted and cursed each other as they tried to organize their courses, fighting over space inside the ovens. Bren smelled spiced meat and roasting vegetables. He smelled something else—a fragrance that reminded him of mulled wine in winter. He looked around and saw a chef making a red wine sauce. He watched as the chef poured wine into the pot, then some into his mouth.

Pity no one would get a chance to eat all this before things started going bad.

He left the kitchen, pushing his way through a group of men and women complaining about being forced to work in the kitchens while wearing their most formal serving clothes. They feared ruining them before the dinner started.

The chaos of the kitchens faded behind Bren, and he located the door Tiel had told him about. It opened onto a set of stairs descending into pitch darkness. He closed the door behind him and felt his way gingerly down the steps. When he reached the bottom, he knelt and fumbled around behind the bottom step. The everbright lantern was exactly where Tiel had said it would be. He picked it up and opened the shutter, the squeak of metal on metal sounding abnormally loud in his ears. White light blossomed through the darkness, revealing a narrow corridor stretching ahead of him. He started walking, then swore loudly as he stubbed his toe against something. He lowered the lantern and saw that the floor was made of old, chipped flagstones. Some of them had risen from their bedding.

The passage stretched the length of the house. Smaller corridors opened off either side, tunneling beneath other portions of the mansion.

The corridor he sought was close to the end of the main passage. It opened into a large basement room. Bren held up the lantern to look at the beams of the low ceiling. This was it. The dining hall was directly above him.

Bren lowered the light and shone it about the room. Crates and boxes lined the walls. Old trestle tables were piled into a corner. Tiel had told him to look just inside the door to his right.

He swiveled around and saw a square crate. He placed the lantern on the floor at his feet. The box wasn't big—the same length and height as his arm.

Tiel had been very specific. Don't try to open it. Just lift it up.

Bren did so, raising the crate into the air and placing it aside. The box had no bottom. Bren got down on his knees and stared at what he revealed.

It was some kind of machine, made from brass and copper and a few other metals he couldn't identify. It squatted on the floor in a way he found slightly disconcerting. A hole gaped in the front, a black circle shaped to look like a screaming mouth.

Bren stood up and listened. He heard voices above him. Tiel had told him to wait until he was sure everyone was seated before inserting the dragonshard into the machine.

He wouldn't have long to wait.

Wren stood up in his seat as Col guided the skycoach through the thickening clouds.

"Will you sit down? Khyber, you're worse than a child."

"I'm just trying to see."

"See what? Skyway's a big place. How do you think you're going to find him?"

As he uttered these words, the skycoach slipped out of the clouds and Wren saw Skyway spread below him, everything lit a strange, apocalyptic yellow color as the sun tried to filter through the heavy clouds.

The first thing he saw was smoke rising above a distant building. He peered closer and saw that something on the roof was on fire. He was too far away to see it, but he reckoned he'd found what he was looking for.

"Aim for that!" he yelled, pointing. "I'll lay odds it's Cutter."

Tiel lowered his hands to his sides. The white-hot glow faded. Cutter looked up in puzzlement.

Tiel lashed out with a fist. The blow hit Cutter in the eye, sending him sprawling to the ground.

"You didn't think I was just going to kill you, surely?"

He kicked Cutter in the ribs. A sharp pain told him that one of them snapped. He doubled over in pain—

And brought his face directly into Tiel's swinging foot. The halfling's boot caught him full on, snapping his head back and nearly breaking his neck. His cheek burst open. An eye ruptured, the white filling with blood.

The pain was worse than anything he'd experienced. He couldn't take it any more. His body shut down, trying to save him from the agony.

He dreamed of Rowen, seeing her lying in her room beneath the sheet. Only she wasn't dead. She was shaking her head in disappointment.

"You said you would avenge me. You promised."

"I *tried*."

"You failed."

Then he was standing in the crypt, laying her on the slab of stone. He turned away and he remembered his thoughts as he tried to bury the pain of her death.

Fight it, he had told himself.

Hide it.

Push the pain away until you need it.

You couldn't tame the beast. You could only chain it. And you knew. Knew that one day that chain would break and it would rise up and devour you, grown and fattened by the energy you've pumped into it in your attempt to keep the shackles strong.

But that day was far away.

Cutter's eyes opened.

That day was now.

Tiel had wrapped his hands around the human's neck. Cutter felt the heat in the halfling's fingers as they tightened around his throat, the pain flaring through his skin.

Cutter surged to his knees with a roar. Tiel kept a grip on his throat so that the halfling was pulled to his feet. The heat intensified, Tiel realizing he had to finish the job. Cutter fumbled in his pocket, ignoring the excruciating pain.

He found what he was looking for. Exactly where he had deposited it during his fight with Jana. He pulled it out and flicked it open. The blade of the razor flashed orange as it reflected the glow from Tiel's hands.

Cutter tightened his grip on the bone handle, screaming at the agony shooting down his arms, and slashed out. Tiel released one hand from Cutter's neck and grabbed hold of his wrist. Cutter screamed in pain as the heat flared into his raw skin, Tiel's fingers sinking into his flesh until he touched bone. Blood sizzled and spat as Tiel tried to force the razor into Cutter's face.

Cutter thought of Rowen and pushed everything he had into his arm, forcing it away from himself and toward Tiel. The halfling's eyes widened. Cutter grabbed hold of the halfling's arm with his free hand and slowly pried the fingers away. One by one they loosened, until Cutter held the halfling's arm out of the way.

Then he slashed out with the razor.

Blood sprayed into the air. Tiel looked confused. The heat faded from Cutter's neck, the halfling's grip weakening. Cutter staggered backward, breaking the contact.

Blood pulsed rhythmically from Tiel's neck. The halfling lifted a hand into the red spray, almost as if he were feeling for rain. He studied his hand, then looked at Cutter. His eyes went to the cutthroat razor Cutter held.

"That's my razor," he said in a gurgling voice. Dropping to his knees, the halfling locked eyes with Cutter. The blood slowed its pumping, slackening to a trickle that soaked his chest. He stood dazed for a few moments, then gravity took over and he hit the ground.

Cutter collapsed onto his back and stared up at the sky. The smoke from the fires in the trees drifted up into the storm clouds. He watched the smoke whisked about by the wind, then he heard a voice shouting something, but he couldn't make out the words. He strained his ears.

Don't . . . don't do something. *Don't . . . don't kill him.* That was it. *Don't kill him.*

He turned his head and stared into Tiel's lifeless eyes. Too late. Sorry.

He looked to the sky again and saw the underside of a sky-coach. A face peered over the side. Looked familiar. He knew that face.

Then it hit him. The half-elf. Wren.

Cutter smiled, then closed his eyes.

• • • • • • •

Bren listened to the growing hubbub above him, the sounds of laughter and talking. The clink of glasses and the rattle of cutlery. He reckoned all the guests had arrived by now.

He withdrew the shard from his pocket and lowered it into the machine. It pulled away from his fingers and sank deep inside.

After a faint click, the machine started to hum.

Chapter
Twenty-Three

The third day of Long Shadows

Sar, the 28th day of Vult, 998

Wren peered over the edge and tried to see through the smoke as Col lowered the skycoach for a landing. "I think they're both dead," he called over his shoulder.

The skycoach bumped to the ground. Wren jumped out and rushed over to Cutter. The wounds on the man's arms were grisly. He knelt to feel for a pulse, wincing as his fingers touched blistered skin. He could smell the charred flesh and fought to keep from vomiting.

He detected a faint flutter beneath his fingers. "He's alive," he said to Col, who approached with a pouch. Col fished around inside while Wren hurried over to the halfling—guessing he was responsible for Rowen's death. He checked his pockets twice, but there was no sign of the shard. Where in Khyber was it?

Wren stood and scanned the rooftop. Had the shard been lost in the fight? He turned to Col. The man leaned over Cutter, pouring something down his throat.

"Healing potion," he said in response to Wren's look.

Cutter coughed and spluttered, spraying some of the potion over Col's shirt. Col held Cutter's mouth closed, forcing him to swallow what remained. As Wren watched, the wounds on his arms began to heal, the blackened flesh sloughing away and being replaced by glistening red muscle and tissue. Skin crawled slowly over the raw flesh and closed across his arms.

Wren waited until Cutter's arms were smooth and pink, then leaned over and patted him down. The dragonshard wasn't there, either.

A shudder ran through the roof under Wren's feet. He frowned and looked at Col, but the man was just as puzzled as he. It came again, vibrating all the way through his body, this time accompanied by a deep rumbling.

Wren stood, his stomach twisting.

"Is that thunder?" asked Col.

Wren walked over to the wall. The hotel grounds were silent. Something floated on the air . . . anticipation. A buildup of tension on the breeze.

Then another shudder ran through the ground. Wren heard the sound of breaking glass, the scream of a woman. A statue in the gardens toppled and broke apart when it hit the ground. Wren gripped the wall. Col moved next to him.

"What is it?" he whispered.

"I'm not sure," said Wren, "but I don't think it's a good sign." He pointed to Cloudpool Park. The white cloudstuff that formed the park was changing color, turning from the fresh white of newly fallen snow to the oily black of tar.

"Not a good sign at all."

The ground shook again, more violently this time. Wren tightened his grip on the wall. Guests ran from the hotel, crying out in alarm, looking around for the source of the disturbance. More statues fell over. As Wren watched, one of them fell on top of a dwarf, crushing him beneath its weight.

A horrific rending sound filled the air, like the tortured screech of metal magnified a thousand times. Then . . . everything *moved.*

Wren was reminded of the time a lift he traveled in malfunctioned and dropped a few floors.

Wren turned to Col, a look of horror on his face. "Did you feel that?"

But Col wasn't listening. He stared up into the sky. "The clouds just moved," he whispered.

"What?" Wren looked up. "What do you mean?"

Col tore his attention away, stared at Wren. "The clouds. They moved higher into the air."

"That's imposs—"

It came again. His stomach lurched.

"There!" said Col. "They did it again."

"Khyber's breath," whispered Wren. "Come on." He ran to Cutter's side and slapped at his face. "Cutter. Wake up! Where's the dragonshard? Who has it?" He slapped Cutter harder, drawing a groan from him. "Cutter!" he shouted.

Col grabbed his hand. "What are you doing?"

"Don't you see? What Diadus was talking about? He said that Tiel's attack on the council was a cover, that the dragonshard would do something worse. Something the warforged had been planning for years."

Col looked around, realization dawning.

"It's bringing down Skyway, Col."

"It can't. That's . . ."

"Insane. We need to find it. We need to find the shard. Otherwise, Skyway will fall on Menthis and Central."

Wren grabbed Cutter under the arms. "Help me get him aboard."

Col grabbed Cutter's feet and they manhandled his limp body into the skycoach. Wren and Col climbed aboard, Col grabbing hold of the controls. The low rumbling had become constant, the shuddering running through the skycoach and vibrating their limbs. Col lifted the vehicle off the ground, rising straight up into the air. As soon as they left the ground, the vibrations stopped.

Wren turned his attention to Cutter, to find the human staring up at him with bleary eyes.

"Cutter, where is the dragonshard?"

"Wren?"

"Yes, it's Wren. Well done. Now, where is the shard? It's important."

Cutter struggled to sit up. Wren helped him up and pointed at the people running in panic. "Do you see that? We need to find the dragonshard, Cutter. What did Tiel do with it?"

Cutter shook his head, then stared down at his arms, gingerly touching the pink skin. He turned to look back at the rooftop.

"He's dead," said Wren. "You got your revenge."

Cutter was silent for a while. "I still miss her," he said softly.

Wren resisted the urge to shake Cutter by the neck. "Of course you do," he said. "Did you honestly think killing Tiel would make that go away?"

Cutter turned to look at him, the pain clear in his eyes. "I hoped so."

Col looked over his shoulder. "Slap him again, will you? If he doesn't tell us where the shard is, we're going to be sitting inside Menthis soon."

"What's he talking about?" Cutter asked, barely interested. "Isn't he that watchman? The one who chased us?"

"It's a long story. But what he's saying is true. Look around.

The whole of Skyway is dropping out of the sky." Wren waved a hand about.

Cutter looked around. "Doesn't look like it."

"It's going slowly, you idiot!" snapped Col. "Just tell us where the bloody shard is."

"I don't know!" Cutter snarled. "Tiel—"

"What? What is it?" asked Wren.

"Bren. Tiel's bodyguard. He said he had to go to Tain Manor. Said he had to do something for Tiel."

"Col?"

"I heard," said Col, turning the skycoach around.

• • • • • • •

Bren was in the garden retrieving his jacket when the first shudders ran through the ground. He steadied himself and looked around, thinking he should probably get away, that it had something to do with the dragonshard. Did the shudder signify Saidan's death?

The ground pitched beneath his feet, sending him to his knees.

He looked around. The guests from the Tain supper were filing out of the house into the front garden, looking around in curiosity. Bren stood up and saw that Saidan was among them.

A third, more violent rumble pulsed through the ground. Bren managed to steady himself before he was thrown off his feet. Some of the dinner guests were not so lucky. They fell to the ground, cursing and swearing. The statues lining the pathway toppled over and smashed to pieces.

Then the whole island lurched beneath him. The guests cried out in fear. The island shook again, and the thought came to Bren that Skyway was falling out of the sky.

And the timing could be no coincidence.

Bren looked back at the house. He had done this. Or rather, he had been tricked into doing this. Anger surged through him. He didn't like being manipulated. Using the dragonshard to kill Saidan Boromar was fine. But if Skyway kept falling, it would land on the districts below, crushing thousands of people. He wasn't going to have that on his conscience.

The dinner guests were panicking, running for their chariots or skycoaches. Bren fought against the push of bodies, shoving those too slow to get out of his way. He ran around the back of the house and through the kitchen, to the stairs leading to the basement. He picked up the lantern he'd left at the bottom of the steps and hurried back to the room with the strange machine.

The ground was rumbling constantly. Dust fell from the ceiling, creating a thin haze in the air that was hard to see through. Bren made his way into the room and reached inside the machine for the dragonshard. He couldn't reach. It had sunk too far inside for him to get hold.

He sighed. He'd have to resort to the direct method, then. He lifted his adamantine arm, intending to smash the machine into as many pieces as he could.

Something caught hold of his wrist.

He spun around and stared into two glowing white eyes. They darted toward him and a splitting pain exploded in his head.

Then nothing.

* * *

Col's skycoach sped across the Tain Manor grounds. Below, people were running around in confusion, fighting to get into their coaches. A Lysander barge rose straight into his path, forcing

Col to veer sharply to the side to avoid a collision. Cutter nearly fell overboard. Wren reached out to grab him and pulled him into the center of the seat, but he shook Wren's hand off, staring at something below.

"Down there," he shouted, pointing to something on the ground.

"What?" Wren leaned over to see what he pointed at.

"There. That's Bren—the one with the metal arm. He's running into the house. See?"

Wren did. "Col!" he shouted. "Bring us down."

Col pointed the skycoach toward the ground and they dropped from the sky. A group of milling elves and humans screamed and scattered out of the way. Wren leaped over the side before Col had even brought them to a stop. He landed lightly and sprinted to the door he had seen Bren enter. The tremors were getting worse. It felt like an earthquake was ripping through the island.

The door led into some kitchens, then into a narrow hallway. Wren ran down the hall and around the corner, but the rooms were deserted. He stopped, wondering where to go next.

He heard a faint click behind him. He turned and saw a narrow door, and realized the noise had been the door closing. He pulled it open and saw a faint light bobbing in the distance. A moment later, it disappeared.

Wren forced himself to slow down. He didn't have any wands left, and Bren looked like a powerful man. That adamantine arm would pack a punch, he was sure.

His vision allowed him to navigate the stairs easily in the dark. He followed the corridor, checking down each branching passage. As he moved deeper into the house, he became aware of a low humming sound, like a swarm of bees on a summer day. It came from up ahead. Wren moved as quietly as he could, following one of the small corridors and stopping outside an open door.

He took a deep breath, then peered into the room.

The first thing he saw was Bren lying sprawled on the floor.

The second was the eldritch machine sitting next to him, humming quietly as if it were alive. It was made of brass and gold, with intricate patterns raised on the surface that confused the eyes.

Wren darted into the room and headed straight for the machine.

As stupid moves go, it was definitely one of his stupidest.

The warforged slid out of the shadows, stepped over Bren's body, and positioned itself directly in front of the machine. Wren froze in his tracks, suddenly wondering why he had run ahead and not waited for Col.

He heard the quiet *schick* of metal on metal and stepped back as two long blades extended from the back of the warforged's hands. The warforged lifted its arms so the blades formed a **V** that framed its face.

"Why are you doing this?" Wren asked.

The floor shook violently. Wren staggered to the side, then caught himself against the wall and pushed himself upright. Even the warforged was knocked momentarily off balance.

"Why am I doing it? Are you asking me why I am doing this to Skyway, or why I am doing this to all the softskins?"

"Aren't both answers the same?"

"No. I'm doing this to Skyway because I've decided I want to die. And this guarantees me an eternity at the side of the Shadow. As to the softskins—" it shrugged— "I don't like you. I think you are weak, petty, hypocritical, lazy. You are a waste of space. What god cares for such a race?"

Wren shrugged. "Maybe none of them."

This gave the warforged pause. "And this does not bother you?"

"No. Why should it?"

"Because without gods you are . . . nothing. A sack of skin filled with blood."

"And why would the grace of a god change that?"

"It gives you something to look forward to. Something to strive for."

Wren frowned. "So, what you're saying is you spend your whole life striving for something that will only *begin* once you die? Is that what you think life is? A practice run? A . . ." Wren searched for words. "A *test* to see what rewards you will get in the afterlife? That's not living. That's spending your life waiting for something better to come along. Do you think Diadus intended that for you when he created you?"

The warforged took a threatening step forward. "Do not speak of him. He was one of the few of you who was actually worth something."

"Why? Because he created you? Because he created that machine you will use to kill thousands of innocent people? Innocent children? Where do they fall into your argument? Are they just as useless? Their whole lives ahead of them? Some of them might have become artists, inventors, saints. If not for you, one of them could become a great healer and save hundreds of lives."

"And some will become murderers. Some will become rapists."

Wren felt the anger building in him. "So you are to be the one to judge them? Do you think yourself a god, to take that upon yourself?"

"I do it in the name of the Shadow."

"No!" Wren shouted. "If you plan on doing this, take responsibility for your actions. Do *not* shrug your shoulders and say your god demanded it. You are doing it. *You!*"

"It is for my god," he repeated.

Wren stared at him, suddenly feeling tired. Sometimes you just had to realize there were arguments you couldn't win, that no matter how you put it, how much you argued, there was no way to get through to a person.

Wren stood there, feeling the rumbling through the soles of his feet, and realized that the warforged was probably thinking the exact same thing. Who was he to say who was right?

Wren caught a hint of movement behind the warforged. It looked like Bren was waking up. Perfect. Was he outnumbered two to one now? Maybe not. The warforged must have knocked him out in the first place.

Unless one of the earth tremors knocked him from his feet.

It didn't matter. Wren wasn't going to stand by while this idiot slaughtered thousands of innocent people.

The ground pitched beneath his boots. He staggered again, managing to stay on his feet. The warforged fell to one knee, then quickly tried to right itself.

Bren grabbed the warforged around the neck from behind, gripping it with his adamantine arm. The warforged tried to turn on the human, ready to stab him over the shoulder, but Wren stepped forward, activating an infusion beneath his breath.

He laid a hand on the warforged's chest and pushed, immediately feeling heat sinking into its metal body. The warforged lifted its head and screamed as its chest started to glow orange, the heat spreading throughout his body. It traveled into Bren's arm. Wren saw the human gritting his teeth against the pain, but he didn't let go.

The wood at the warforged's elbow and knee joints burst into flame, and still Wren kept on. He channeled all the power he could into the construct, keeping back only a tiny amount of energy.

That remaining energy he pushed into his free hand. When he felt the heat fading from his palm, he lifted it off and touched the other hand against the warforged's face.

Pure cold surged into the metal body with an explosion of steam. Wren felt the faceplate crack at the sudden change in temperature, then it exploded beneath his palm, shattering into a thousand tiny pieces. Wren staggered back with a cry of pain, his hand bleeding from the tiny metal shards that tore into his palm. Bren shielded his face and turned away.

After all the pieces had fallen, Wren turned back. The warforged was on its knees, headless, its arms hanging lifelessly. Bren lifted a booted foot and kicked the carcass hard in the back. The body toppled over, and when it smashed against the stone flooring, it shattered into fist-sized chunks of frozen metal.

Wren turned his attention to the eldritch machine. He put both hands on it and used the last of his energy to see into the depths of its workings. He saw what he was looking for. He closed his eyes and broke the pathways from the dragonshard to the rest of the machine.

There came a click as the shard was extruded slowly from the hole like an animal laying an unholy egg. Wren pulled it out the rest of the way.

The rumbling beneath his feet stopped.

Wren breathed a sigh of relief and stood. Bren stared at him.

"Is that it?" he asked.

"I think so."

"What did it do?"

"I think it was eating away Skyway's link to Syrania. So the island was doing what it would naturally do—sink with gravity. Now that it's stopped, the link will reestablish itself. We should be fine."

Wren saw Bren's look of relief.

"You didn't know?"

He shook his head. "Tiel told me it was for something else."

"Ah, Tiel. I think you'd better find yourself a new boss. He's . . . no longer with us."

Bren stared at him for a moment, then shook his head in wonderment. "Cutter?"

Wren nodded. "Cutter."

To his surprise, Bren grinned. "Good for him," he said, then headed to the door.

"Hold," said Wren.

Bren paused and looked over his shoulder "What?"

Wren hesitated, then sighed and shook his head. He didn't have the energy. "Nothing."

Bren nodded, then disappeared through the door. Wren could hear Col calling for him somewhere in the house above. He took one last look around, then bent over and picked up the defunct eldritch machine.

Epilogue

Dawn

Cutter opened his eyes and stared at the ceiling. The familiar ball of lead was still there, still sitting in his stomach like a cancerous growth devouring him from the inside.

Wren had been right. The pain didn't go away with Tiel's death. It just meant Cutter didn't have anywhere to channel it, that he had to face it.

It was one of the hardest things he had ever done.

He'd been willing to die in pursuit of his revenge. He hadn't cared if he lived or died, just as long as he avenged Rowen's death. But now that it was over, now that he had killed Tiel, something had changed. He found that he actually *wanted* to live. He wanted to remember Rowen, to make sure no one ever forgot her. But to do that, he needed to get over her death, to move on with his life.

And he couldn't do that where he was.

He looked around the room. His belongings would fit into his leather rucksack. He could go now—today—if he wanted to.

So why didn't he?

He looked out the window at the steady rain. Nothing was holding him here, nothing except the ghost of Rowen.

She would want him to go, to make something else of his life.

He sat up and rubbed his face. The leather satchel was hanging over the bedpost. He grabbed it and stuffed his clothes inside, then opened the chest and took out what little money he had left. He left the books; they weren't his.

All he had of Rowen's belongings was a simple silver necklace. It was her favorite. She said once that she intended to give it to her first daughter. That wouldn't happen now, but Cutter thought that if he ever had children, ever had a daughter, he would give it to her. Rowen would have liked that.

He paused with one hand on the door handle, taking one last look around the soulless room.

Goodbye, Rowen.

He pulled open the door and walked out, closing it quietly behind him. He didn't know where he was going, but he felt lighter, the heaviness in his stomach less pervasive.

He would simply see where the road took him.

* * *

Wren knocked on the door and waited impatiently. He glanced around, shivering in the unseasonably chill air. The rain fell in a fine mist that coated everything, seeping into the very bones. The past few days had been exhausting. The Watch Commander had wanted to arrest him and Cutter for the deaths of his men. It had taken the intervention of Col to get them off the hook, and he only managed it when he put together a file on the dead men and their association with Jana.

Unfortunately, Col had also been responsible for having the entire story swept under the carpet. Admittedly, he was acting on orders from higher up, but he'd told Wren and Cutter that they didn't want the true tale getting out. They were afraid that letting the general population learn that a mad warforged had nearly killed tens of thousands of people would lead to riots, with all the other warforged being blamed for the actions of one.

Wren hated to admit it, but they were probably right. That didn't stop it from chafing, though. He should have been invited to sup with the king after what he had done. *They*. What *they* had done. He couldn't take *all* the credit himself. Just most of it.

Although, he had received a rather intriguing dinner invitation from Savia Portellas yesterday. So maybe it wasn't such a well-kept secret.

He leaned forward and knocked on the door, harder this time.

A moment later it was opened by a bleary-eyed Kayla. She frowned at him, stifling a yawn.

Wren smiled widely. "My apologies, Kayla. Did I wake you?"

"Yes, Master Wren. It's just gone six."

"My goodness. Really? How naughty of me." He turned his head. "Torin, why didn't you tell me it was so early?"

Torin walked slowly around the side of the house, supporting his weight on a walking stick. "Sorry," he said. "I forgot you couldn't tell the time."

"How dare you!" Wren snapped. "You can't speak to me like that! Respect your betters!"

Torin squinted at him. "Oh, I will." He frowned and looked around. "When you show them to me, that is."

Kayla gasped in fear and tried to slam the door shut on Wren. The half-elf stuck his foot in the door as a dark figure appeared from nowhere and barged up to the house.

Wren opened his mouth to chastise the impudent dwarf with a suitably withering retort just as Col pushed past, yanking Kayla into the street. Wren held up a hand to stop Torin from saying anything more, and leaned down so he was level with Kayla's ear.

"You're lucky he managed to crawl out of that office, Kayla," he whispered coldly. "If he hadn't been taken to a healer in time . . ." He paused to make sure he had control of his voice. "I would have found out it was you. Understand? I would have hunted you down, Kayla. No matter where you went, it wouldn't have been far enough."

"I was just doing what Xavien told me!" she wailed. "He made me do it."

Wren straightened up. "We all have choices, Kayla. And now you have to live with yours." He nodded at Col. The Dark Lantern inclined his head and led her away into the mist.

Wren watched them go, then turned to Torin. The dwarf was staring at him with something approaching sorrow on his face.

"What are you looking at?" he snapped. "And why are you still using that walking stick? There's nothing wrong with you, you big baby."

Torin scowled at Wren. "Shouldn't you be getting your hair done or something?"

Wren frowned at Torin. "Whatever for?"

"Your date. You told me you promised to take that dwarf sergeant out for dinner. You weren't planning on pulling out I hope. She'd be very disappointed."

Wren sucked thoughtfully on his upper lip. "No," he said. "No, I'll take her. Poor thing. It will probably be the most exciting thing that's happened to her all year."

They turned from the door and walked slowly up the street.

After a few steps, Torin stumbled, his walking stick slipping on the wet cobbles.

Wren quickly put an arm out to steady his friend.

Neither said anything, and Wren kept his arm around Torin's shoulders as they walked slowly into the gray drizzle.

During the Last War, Gaven was an adventurer, searching the darkest reaches of the underworld. But an encounter with a powerful artifact forever changed him, breaking his mind and landing him in the deepest cell of the darkest prison in all the world.

THE DRACONIC PROPHECIES

BOOK I

When war looms on the horizon, some see it as more than renewed hostilities between nations. Some see the fulfillment of an ancient prophecy—one that promises both the doom and salvation of the world. And Gaven may be the key to it all.

THE STORM DRAGON

The first EBERRON® hardcover by veteran game designer and the author of *In the Claws of the Tiger*:

James Wyatt

SEPTEMBER 2007

HEIRS OF ASH

RICH WULF

The Legacy . . . an invention of unimaginable power. Rumors say it could save the world—or destroy it. The hunt is on.

Book 1
VOYAGE OF THE MOURNING DAWN

Book 2
FLIGHT OF THE DYING SUN

Book 3
RISE OF THE SEVENTH MOON
November 2007

BLADE OF THE FLAME

TIM WAGGONER

Once an assassin. Now a man of faith. One man searches for peace in a land that knows only blood.

Book 1
THIEVES OF BLOOD

Book 2
FORGE OF THE MINDSLAYERS

Book 3
SEA OF DEATH
February 2008

THE LANTERNLIGHT FILES

PARKER DEWOLF

A man on the run. A city on the watch. Magic on the loose.

Book 1
THE LEFT HAND OF DEATH

Book 2
WHEN NIGHT FALLS
March 2008

Book 3
DEATH COMES EASY
December 2008

A World of Adventure Awaits

The FORGOTTEN REALMS® world is the biggest, most detailed, most vibrant, and most beloved of the DUNGEONS & DRAGONS® campaign settings. Created by best-selling fantasy author Ed Greenwood the FORGOTTEN REALMS setting has grown in almost unimaginable ways since the first line was drawn on the now infamous "Ed's Original Maps."

Still the home of many a group of DUNGEONS & DRAGONS players, the FORGOTTEN REALMS world is brought to life in dozens of novels, including hugely popular best sellers by some of the fantasy genre's most exciting authors. FORGOTTEN REALMS novels are fast, furious, action-packed adventure stories in the grand tradition of sword and sorcery fantasy, but that doesn't mean they're all flash and no substance. There's always something to learn and explore in this richly textured world.

To find out more about the Realms go to www.wizards.com and follow the links from Books to FORGOTTEN REALMS. There you'll find a detailed reader's guide that will tell you where to start if you've never read a FORGOTTEN REALMS novel before, or where to go next if you're a long-time fan!

MARGARET WEIS
&
TRACY HICKMAN

The co-creators of the DRAGONLANCE® world return to the epic tale that introduced Krynn to a generation of fans!

THE LOST CHRONICLES

VOLUME ONE

DRAGONS OF THE DWARVEN DEPTHS

As Tanis and Flint bargain for refuge in Thorbardin, Raistlin and Caramon go to Neraka to search for one of the spellbooks of Fistandantilus. The refugees in Thorbardin are trapped when the draconian army marches, and Flint undertakes a quest to find the Hammer of Kharas to free them all, while Sturm becomes a key of a different sort.

Now Available in Paperback!

VOLUME TWO

DRAGONS OF THE HIGHLORD SKIES

Dragon Highlord Ariakas assigns the recovery of the dragon orb taken to Ice Wall to Kitiara Uth-Matar, who is rising up the ranks of both the dark forces and of Ariakas's esteem. Finding the orb proves easy, but getting it from Laurana proves more difficult. Difficult enough to attract the attention of Lord Soth.

Now Available in Hardcover!

VOLUME THREE

DRAGONS OF THE HOURGLASS MAGE

The wizard Raistlin Majere takes the black robes and travels to the capital city of the evil empire, Neraka, to serve the Queen of Darkness.

July 2008

YOU'VE PLAYED THE GAME . . .
NOW LIVE THE ADVENTURE!

MAGIC: THE GATHERING® books, based on the world's leading trading card game, explore extraordinary new worlds every year, previewing the card sets to come and adding depth and realism to the unique worlds found in each new expansion.

Travel to **Mirrodin**, an unforgiving plane crafted entirely of metal, and follow the adventures of an elf who seeks revenge for the death of her family.

Delve into **Ravnica**, a city-world where intrigue is more common than conversation and the machinations of its villains are only offset by the dedication of its heroes.

Wander **Kamigawa**, a world where the spirits make war on reality, and only a rogue's clever fingers and the inspiration of a princess can restore the world's balance.

In MAGIC: THE GATHERING novels, you'll see your favorite villains, heroes, and monsters from a multiverse of possibility come to life in exciting worlds that unfold in vivid detail.

"... reading the MAGIC novels makes the game more fun."

—Jordan Kronick, pojo.com

RAVENLOFT™
THE COVENANT

RAVENLOFT'S LORDS OF DARKNESS HAVE ALWAYS WAITED FOR THE UNWARY TO FIND THEM.

Six classic tales of horror set in the RAVENLOFT™ world have returned to print in all-new editions.

From the autocratic vampire who wrote the memoirs found in *I, Strahd* to the demon lord and his son whose story is told in *Tapestry of Dark Souls*, some of the finest horror characters created by some of the most influential authors of horror and dark fantasy have found their way to RAVENLOFT, to be trapped there forever.

LAURELL K. HAMILTON
Death of a Darklord

CHRISTIE GOLDEN
Vampire of the Mists

P.N. ELROD
I, Strahd: The Memoirs of a Vampire

ANDRIA CARDARELLE
To Sleep With Evil

ELAINE BERGSTROM
Tapestry of Dark Souls

TANYA HUFF
Scholar of Decay

October 2007